"What do you think of it?" Indy asked as Mara gazed in awe at forty feet of wall covered with woolly mammoths, deer, bears, and bisons. On the opposite side were more animal paintings, as well as several handprints, outlined in paint, and an array of strange symbols.

"It's fantastic, just fantastic," she replied in a hushed voice. "But are you sure they're really ancient?"

"No question about it," Indy answered. "Enough of these caves have been found around here. You're definitely looking at paintings from the Ice Age."

"Do you think this is a really important discovery?" Mara asked.

"That depends on what else is here. At a minimum, we've found some fascinating Paleolithic cave art that's comparable with what's already been discovered."

Mara moved closer to the wall, and pointed to a four-legged animal that seemed to have a single horn growing from its head. "Look at that one. It's a unicorn."

Indy laughed. "I wouldn't be so sure about that."

"I believe in unicorns," she said quietly. "They really did exist."

Bantam Books by Rob MacGregor
Ask your bookseller for the books you have missed.

# INDIANA JONES™
## and the
# UNICORN'S LEGACY

by
Rob MacGregor

BANTAM BOOKS
NEW YORK • TORONTO • LONDON • SYDNEY • AUCKLAND

INDIANA JONES AND THE UNICORN'S LEGACY

*A Bantam Falcon Book / September 1992*

*Grateful acknowledgment is made for permission
to reprint from the following:
Wind in the Rock by Ann Zwinger.
Copyright © 1978 by Ann H. Zwinger.
Reprinted by permission of the author.*

*FALCON and the portrayal of a boxed "f" are trademarks of Bantam
Books, a division of Bantam Doubleday Dell Publishing Group, Inc.*

ISBN 0-553-29666-3

*Published simultaneously in the United States and Canada*

*Bantam Books are published by Bantam Books, a division of Bantam
Doubleday Dell Publishing Group, Inc. Its trademark, consisting of the
words "Bantam Books" and the portrayal of a rooster, is Registered in
U.S. Patent and Trademark Office and in other countries. Marca
Registrada. Bantam Books, 666 Fifth Avenue, New York, New York
10103.*

PRINTED IN THE UNITED STATES OF AMERICA

OPM   0 9 8 7 6 5 4 3 2 1

For T.J. and Alison

*Special thanks to Dick Beaupre and
John Riglesberger for the translations.
It was Greek to me!*

Now I will believe
That there are unicorns . . .
William Shakespeare, *The Tempest* III, iii

Save me from the lion's mouth; for thou hast heard me from the horns of unicorns.
*Psalms* 22:21

# PROLOGUE

*Yorkshire, England—1786*

Jonathan Ainsworth hardly recognized his father. After five months in his damp, shadowy cell, Michael Ainsworth looked like a different man. He'd lost twenty-five pounds, and his hair was gray and motley. His shoulders were slumped.

"Father?"

Michael Ainsworth slowly raised his head as the jailer unlocked the cell. For a moment, Jonathan feared his father wouldn't know him, that he'd lost his mind. He hadn't seen him since the day after the trial had ended. Then Jonathan saw a faint smile and a glimmer of light in his father's bloodshot eyes, and he knew that, despite the conditions, Ainsworth still maintained his sanity.

The cell door slammed shut, and the noise echoed eerily along the hallway. The smile on his father's face changed to a look of concern. "Jon, you shouldn't have come here. It's not a place for a boy."

"It's all right. Don't worry about me." His father still thought of him as a child, but he was a grown man of twenty-one and the head of the house. "I wanted to visit sooner, but . . ."

"How are the young ones taking it?"

Jonathan sat down on the bench next to his father. "Mary had a hard time. She still cries for you. I think Charles has accepted it. Of course, he's a little older."

"And your mother?"

"She's doing her best." Jonathan wanted to tell his father that there was a particular reason why he and not his mother had come today, but he couldn't do it, not yet.

Michael Ainsworth coughed, a deep, wracking cough that took possession of his body and throttled it. "Is there trouble?"

Jonathan shrugged. "They can't do anything more to us than they've already done, Father."

Ainsworth grasped his son's wrist with surprising strength. His eyes flared. "What have they done? Tell me everything."

Jonathan explained they were losing the house. They couldn't make the payments any longer. They couldn't get credit. People didn't trust them. It was worse than that: People were openly hostile. But Jonathan didn't want to burden his father. He only wanted him to understand that they had to move to London where no one would know them, and that Mother wouldn't be able to visit him as often.

"Talk to Mathers. He said he was so concerned about you children. Maybe he'll help you find work."

Like Michael Ainsworth, Frederick Mathers was a

barrister. They'd been partners until a couple years before Ainsworth's arrest. In the trial, Mathers had testified to his partner's good character, but it had been a weak plea for leniency and the judge might as well have been stone deaf. "He can't do anything more for us. We have to leave, Father. It's no good for us here."

The elder Ainsworth nodded. "You're right. But now listen closely to me, Son."

Jon leaned toward his father, whose raspy voice was barely audible. He hoped this wasn't going to be a confession. Although Jon knew that his father was guilty as accused, he didn't want to hear him admit it.

"My trunk in the closet."

"The authorities went through it, Father. They went through everything we own."

Ainsworth shook his head. He explained that it had a false bottom, and told Jonathan to tear it out. He would find some money. Not much. But it would help.

"Why didn't you tell me this before? We could have used the money for your defense."

Ainsworth shook his head, and said it wouldn't have done any good. "You'll also find what looks like a staff made of twisted ivory and gilded silver. It's an alicorn. It's very beautiful, but you must destroy it. Do you understand?"

Jonathan shook his head. "What's an alicorn?"

"A unicorn's horn. It's what has caused all of my problems. All of them. And yours as well. Do you hear me?"

"How could a staff, an alicorn, do that?"

"You'll find a letter I wrote that explains everything. Read it, then break the wretched thing into as many pieces as you can and scatter them. That will break the spell."

"Yes, Father. I'll do as you say."

Ainsworth held up a finger. It shook as he spoke. "I know this probably sounds like nonsense, but please believe me. The staff is evil. Its powers are unfathomable."

"I'll do what you say, Father."

Jonathan left the cell convinced that his father had gone stark, raving mad. He'd blamed all his troubles on some old walking stick. It was horrible to see him this way. But the money would help. They needed every cent they could get. Maybe he could sell the staff, if it was really made of ivory and silver, if it even existed. But it might not be any more real than unicorns.

# 1

## DIVING INTO THE ICE AGE

*Montignac, France—1924*

Indy stepped into the frigid water that flowed into the dark cavern and mentally prepared himself for what lay ahead. He glanced along the riverbank to make sure no one was around, then waded into the cavern.

The water was colder than he'd expected, and he winced as icy fingers lapped at his groin. "Are you sure about this, Jones?" he asked himself in a whisper. "It's worth a shot," he answered. "Worth a shot." He grimaced as his bare foot stepped on a sharp stone. "I hope."

A hundred feet into the cavern, he paused in waist-deep water. In front of him, the roof sloped down to meet the river. There were easier caves to explore in the foothills of the Pyrenees. At least a dozen had been found that contained evidence of

Paleolithic inhabitants, who had painted the walls
with surprisingly detailed drawings. In fact, he and
the others had already visited a couple of them near
Le Tuc d'Audoubert. However, the group had hoped
to stumble on a new cave during their ten-day excur-
sion to southwestern France. Today, their final day of
prowling the hills near the Trois Frères region, was
their last chance before they headed back to Paris.

Indy figured it was this cavern or nothing. Even
though it was less than a mile from camp, no one had
bothered with it after they'd seen how the cave ceiling dipped into the water. Yet, the more he'd
thought about it, the more he'd become convinced
that there were caverns inside. The late Ice Age,
after all, had been cold and dry so that the water
level must have been lower. That meant there was a
good chance the cave had been inhabited like others
in the region.

He sucked in his breath, filling his lungs, then
ducked under the surface. The water was so cold
that he shot to the surface and sputtered. *C'mon,
Jones. Either you do it or you get out of the water.*

He took another deep breath and dove. When he
was a kid, he could easily hold his breath for three
minutes. If anything, his lung capacity was larger
now. So was his body, of course, but he had a plan to
avoid trouble. He'd swim for a minute and surface. If
the ceiling was still underwater, he'd turn back.
He'd have two minutes to make it back. He could do
it.

He took leisurely strokes, letting the current do
most of the work. Thirty seconds . . . forty. The
current was stronger than he'd suspected. He wondered how difficult swimming against it would be.
Maybe he'd better surface. He swam up and almost

instantly struck his head against a wall. He ran his hand over the smooth surface and noticed how quickly he was drifting downstream. Suddenly and unexpectedly, a streak of terror raced through him. He was losing more ground and running out of air. He wanted air. Now.

*No. You can make it back.* He turned upstream, losing another few yards in the process. Then he kicked hard against the current, and one foot shot through the surface and splashed. Indy's mind was as numb as his body, and it took a second for the significance to register: A splash required air. He arched his back, twisted, and shot through the surface. He drew in a deep, reviving breath.

He treaded water and continued drifting in an envelope of darkness. He reached for the ceiling, but couldn't touch it. He could be inside an immense cavern and he wouldn't know it. He worked his way across the current until he found a wall, which was worn smooth by the water.

"Hello," he shouted as he continued drifting with the current. His voice echoed as if he were in a large chamber, but a few seconds later his head struck the ceiling. "Ouch!"

He didn't know how much longer the pocket of air would last, and he had no reason to drift any further. He swam against the current, his heart pounding in his chest. He was gasping for breath and his head was above the surface. He'd never last three minutes underwater. He reached out, touched the wall, and found a handhold.

He rested and regained his wit. He was doing fine, he told himself, and slowly worked his way upstream along the wall until the ceiling touched the water again. Nothing to worry about. He'd make it out easily. He'd even come back with candles and matches and find out what was here.

It was time. He took a deep breath, dived, and swam furiously. The deeper he swam the less the current seemed to pull on him. But he knew he couldn't stop or even slow his pace. A minute passed. Then another. He kept swimming. His lungs were ready to burst, but he refused to give up. Then his stomach scraped bottom. He pushed off and his head punched through the surface and into the light. He was back.

"Jones, what are you doing?"

Indy slogged out of the cavern and squinted against the bright sunshine. Roland Walcott, the lab instructor who was officially in charge of the trip, was standing on the riverbank, his hands on his hips.

"I think I found a cavern."

"You think you did, or you did?"

"I've got to go back with candles. I couldn't see. You've got to swim underwater a ways before you can surface."

Walcott gave him an odd look. "I heard you were a bit daft. Now I believe it." He shook his head and turned away, giving neither support nor disapproval of Indy's plan to venture back into the cavern.

"Friendly guy," Indy muttered, and he walked back to the camp alone. Walcott was nearly thirty years old, a perpetual student who couldn't seem to finish his Ph.D. Indy had heard that the pompous Englishman spent most of his time drinking in the boîtes and lacked ambition. And yet, he was nosy and competitive, and thrived on one-upmanship, taking advantage of his experience. On this trip, Walcott seemed intent on doing as little as possible, which was preferable, Indy supposed, to dealing with someone who set all kinds of limitations on what he could do.

"Indy, you're all wet. Where've you been?"

"Hi, Mara. I was swimming in the river, where it goes into the hills," he said.

Mara Rogers, an American attending graduate school at the Sorbonne, was the only student among them who was not working toward a Ph.D. in archaeology or anthropology. She was an art history student, a rangy, good-looking woman with clear blue eyes, a heart-shaped face with high cheekbones and full lips, and a mane of blond hair tied in a ponytail. She was, so to speak, Walcott's special guest.

"You mean you followed it underground?"

"That's right."

"What happened?"

Indy looked around the makeshift kitchen. "Got anything left?"

"I saved some lunch for you."

"Swell. Let me change out of these clothes, then I'll tell you what happened."

A few minutes later, Indy described his feat to Mara as he ate a bowl of beef stew. When he finished his tale, he was surprised that she didn't seem to consider it particularly unusual.

"Are you going back?" she asked.

"Sure, and this time I'm going to be better prepared."

"Does Roland know what you're doing?"

He better watch what he said now, Indy thought. He didn't know exactly how close Mara was to the lab instructor. "Sure. I saw him down by the river."

"Can I come with you? I'd like to see the cave."

"Oh, I don't know. It's sort of dangerous. You'd have to have to be a pretty strong swimmer."

"They used to call me the blond mermaid when I was a kid. I'd swim every day for an hour or two in the San Juan River. There was a great swimming hole close to Bluff, Utah, where I grew up."

Indy liked Mara just fine, but he didn't want her messing up his plans. "What about Roland? He might not like it."

"I don't need his approval for everything I do. If I want to go for a swim, I'll go."

But if Walcott saw them together, he might order Indy to stay away from the cavern. He was trying to think of a way to discourage Mara from joining him without offending her when four of the other students approached.

"Hey, either of you seen Roland?" one of the men asked.

"He's off somewhere by himself," Mara answered.

Indy expected Mara to tell the others about his venture in the river, and he saw his discreet plans vanishing. Everyone would want to join him, and Walcott would nix the whole thing. But Mara didn't say a word about it.

"Well, if you see him, tell him we're going to follow the gully for a few miles."

Indy and Mara wished them luck, and watched them walk off. "Thanks for not making a big deal about the cavern."

"No reason to. We don't know if anything's even there yet."

By the time he finished his lunch, Walcott hadn't returned and Indy was resigned to taking Mara with him. He figured she'd probably change her mind once she stepped into the icy water, or they would cross paths with Walcott before they reached the cavern. In that case, Indy planned to keep going and leave Mara and Walcott to their own devices.

"Why didn't you go with Roland when he left camp?" he asked as they headed toward the river.

"I didn't feel like it. He's not my boyfriend, you know."

"I wasn't sure. You two have been together all the time."

"That's just it. I'm tired of tagging along with him everywhere, and that's what I told him before he left. I'm sorry if I hurt his feelings, but that's how I feel."

"I was sort of wondering what you saw in him."

"We've been friendly for a while, but to tell you the truth the only reason I came along was because I wanted to see the cave paintings."

When he'd heard that Walcott was bringing a woman from the art history department, Indy had thought the worst. He figured she'd make a fuss about sleeping in a tent and being required to help with the cooking and other chores. But Mara was nothing like his image of an art historian. She was willing to do whatever was required and she hadn't complained once, not even when she'd found a field mouse in her sleeping bag the first night.

"So do you really think we've got a chance of discovering a new cave?" she asked as they hiked along the riverbank.

"I know we'll find a cave. It's just a question of whether anyone lived there ten thousand years ago and left a calling card."

"It would be fantastic if we were so lucky. I'm so glad you let me come along."

Indy smiled, but didn't respond.

"Did you have any trouble getting away from Paris?" she asked.

He shrugged. "I made room for it. I wasn't going to miss this chance."

"No, I mean, that is . . . I was wondering if you had to leave a girlfriend."

Indy laughed. "Not really."

"What's that mean?"

"There's no one I had to tell I was leaving." The truth was he hadn't given anyone a chance to get close to him, not since he'd become involved with his first archaeology professor, who'd taken him to Greece. But that was nearly two years ago now, and he was starting to look at women in a new light again. He was just waiting to find the right one.

When they reached the base of a hill where the river disappeared into the narrow cavern, Indy sat down on the bank and took off his boots. He glanced at Mara, wondering if she was going to change her mind now that she was here.

But her mind wasn't what she was planning to change. "Don't look," she said, and she moved behind a clump of juniper.

Indy opened his pack and made sure the water-tight container with the candles and matches was still secure. The only other thing in the pack was his whip. He didn't like carrying the extra weight, but the others had claimed all of the rope in camp in the hope that they'd put it to use climbing down a hole and into a cave. Besides, the whip was a good-luck piece.

He heard Mara singing softly to herself, and stole

a glance over his shoulder just as she tossed her blouse on the top of the bush. He saw arms and legs through the thicket, and then her slacks landed next to her blouse. He smiled to himself as he turned away.

"You're not looking, are you?"

"Of course not."

"I'm glad I brought my swimming suit along," she said. "I thought it was silly at first. But I guess I knew I was going to get a chance to wear it."

"You could've gotten along without it."

"What do you mean by that?"

Indy laughed. "You could've worn your clothes on this swim. The water's cold."

"For a moment I thought . . . oh, never mind."

He liked Mara more all the time. He was already thinking ahead to when they were back in Paris. He could see them together sitting by the fountain at the Place Saint-Michel, walking through Luxembourg Gardens, or losing themselves in the Louvre.

"Is this going to be like the sewers?" she asked.

"What?"

"You know, les Égouts, the Paris sewers. You have been down there, haven't you?"

Indy admitted it was a part of Paris he hadn't visited.

"Oh, you've got to go. It's like an underground city."

"I'd probably need a guide," Indy said. "Maybe you can show it to me when we get back."

"Indy!" she shrieked.

He leaped to his feet and dashed over to where Mara was pressed against the juniper, her bare limbs rigid, her arms crossed over her chest. "Look!"

A black shiny snake was curled near her feet. Its body was as thick as his wrist and its tongue was flicking in and out. Indy slowly bent down and reached for a rock. The snake turned its head, impaling him with its weird, atavistic eyes. Indy froze; he couldn't pick up the rock. It was as if the snake had mesmerized him. The creature abruptly slithered toward him, over his bare foot, and away.

As Indy straightened up, Mara embraced him. "Oh, my God. You weren't even afraid of it."

His eyes were wide with terror. His heart was pounding. He watched the snake disappear between two rocks. "Not at all. It was just a snake."

"I was scared to death."

Suddenly, Indy was aware of Mara's closeness, of the shape of her body, of her face against his neck. She stepped back, self-consciously pulling up the strap of her swimming suit that had slipped off her shoulder.

"Well, shouldn't we go for our swim?" she said.

She looked great, he thought. "Are you still game for it?"

"You don't think there are any . . ."

"Snakes in the water? Naw, water's too cold. Snakes are cold-blooded. They get sluggish in the cold."

"Oh, good."

They walked down to the water hand in hand, and Indy was surprised by how easily they seemed to get along, how effortlessly they'd come together. It was as if they'd known each other for years.

Then Walcott crossed his mind again. Indy looked up, scanned the hills, searching for the Englishman. He imagined him somewhere up there staring at them, growing angry and charging down to ruin Indy's plans.

"What are you looking at?" Mara asked.

"Just the hills."

She stuck her foot in the water. "Ooh, it is cold. But I guess that means I have the advantage now."

"Why's that?"

"Don't you know that women have an extra layer of fat that protects them from the cold?"

Indy stepped into the stream. He thought of a response about how she could warm him up, but kept it to himself. "Lucky you." He reached into his pack and took out his whip. "Let's not lose each other."

He tied the end of it around her wasplike waist. "Good idea," she said. "Won't it get all stiff from the water?"

"The whip? I'll oil it after it dries. It'll be as good as new." He jammed the other end under his belt. There was nearly ten feet of whip between them, enough so they could swim without kicking each other. His only concern was that Mara might panic and fight him. In that case, they could both drown. "You sure you can hold your breath for a couple of minutes?"

"I've got excellent lung capacity." She drew in a deep breath and her swimming suit tugged tightly against the swell of her breasts.

"Yeah, I see." They waded into the opening, the stream pulling them forward as the light dimmed. "You think you can swim against this current?"

"Stay there," she said and without another word moved downstream to the end of the whip. She ducked under and disappeared from sight. A moment later, he glimpsed her lithe figure as she wriggled past, then he felt the tug of the whip as she surfaced.

"Not bad. I see why they called you a mermaid."

Beads of water glistened on her arms and legs. "Then let's get on with it."

When they reached the point where the ceiling met the water, Indy signaled Mara and they plunged into the dark waters. This time it seemed to take only seconds before Indy felt air above him and popped to the surface. The first time he'd gone further downstream than necessary, but it was also the knowledge that he'd done it once that made the underwater journey go so swiftly.

Mara bumped into him, then surfaced. "That wasn't hard at all. But where are we? I can't see a thing."

"Right now we're just drifting downstream. Here's the wall. I found a ledge."

"Where?"

He guided her arm. "Here."

"Got it."

Indy braced himself on the ledge, then reached into the pack and found the soap-dish-sized metal container with the candle and matches. There was no water inside, a good sign. The match roared in his ear as he struck it, and a pellucid light filled the cavern. He lit a candle, passed it to Mara, and lit another one.

"Look, Indy!"

"What is it?"

The ledge was narrow and the ceiling was only a few feet over their heads, but that wasn't what had attracted Mara's attention. Just a few yards away, the stream split into two branches, and the one veering to the left opened into an immense cavern whose ceiling was at least thirty feet above their heads.

"What a difference a little light can make." Indy let go of the ledge and sidestroked into the channel, holding the candle over his head.

He squinted up at the wall, searching for a sign of a cavity. Their best bet was that there were caverns untouched by the water and undiscovered by man since the Ice Age.

"Look up there," Mara said. Indy followed her gaze toward the ceiling. High on the wall was a gap a couple of yards across and half that high.

As Indy moved toward the wall, his feet touched a narrow underwater shelf, and he stood up. He pulled Mara up with him. "You cold?"

She rubbed her arms. "A little. How about you?"

"I'm numb."

She held the candle near his face and touched a finger to his mouth. "Your lips are blue." She leaned forward and kissed him gently.

"I think they're warming up already."

He extinguished his candle, put it in his pack, then reached around Mara's waist and untied the whip. "If it looks promising, I'll help you up."

"It's so steep. You think you can make up it there without falling?"

He coiled the whip and tucked it into his pack. "It'll be a snap. If I fall I'll land in the water." He found a handhold, then a foothold, and pulled himself up.

Slowly, he worked his way up the wall. Finally, when he was within a few feet of the hole, he realized he could see into a cavern without the aide of a candle. The light was faint, but steady, and it meant that sunlight was shining in through another hole.

He pulled himself over the lip of the gap and crawled inside.

"Mara!"

"What is it?"

"You've got to see this."

2

## SUBTERRANEAN TREACHERY

Walcott was ecstatic, simply ecstatic. Possibly the oldest artifact ever discovered was in his hands. The details in the features of the clay bear were incredible. He could see tufts of clay fur, sharp incisors, and even the ripple of shoulder muscles. Its only flaw was the pockmarks on the chest, but those would just attest to its age. Besides the bear, he'd found two clay bisons in the room, and who knew how many more rooms and more figurines were here.

He could thank Jones for pointing him in the right direction. As soon as he'd heard the student's tale, Walcott had realized that the hill must be honeycombed with caverns, and that there was probably a way of digging into one, if he found the right spot. He figured he'd look around and come back on his own as soon as he could. But a rabbit led him to the entrance.

He was poking his walking stick near a boulder when the rabbit darted out of the shrubbery. He pushed his walking stick into a hole, and four half-grown rabbits scrambled out. He pressed again and the stick kept going; he'd found an opening. Walcott briefly considered going back for tools and help, but this was his discovery, his alone. After half an hour of digging with his hands and the stick, he worked his way through the hole and into what immediately struck him as possibly one of the greatest archaeological discoveries of all time. After all, every major museum in the world wanted authentic relics from the Ice Age, and Walcott knew he could make a fortune.

But now he had to think clearly and make sure that his excitement didn't overpower common sense. He didn't want Jones finding a route into these chambers. He needed to hurry back to camp and tell him that he was not to enter the cave again, that he was lucky he hadn't drowned. Walcott had no idea whether or not it was possible to get here from the underground river, but he wasn't going to take any chances.

He set the bison down and moved into the next room. More exquisite figurines from the Stone Age rested on the floor. He counted two bears, a reindeer, and a bison, and there was still at least one more room leading off this one. If he played his cards right, he was going to be a wealthy man.

As soon as they got back to Paris he'd resign from the university. After that, he'd come back and scour the cave. He'd take out most of the artifacts, but he'd leave one or two intact, just so he could authenticate his discovery. He'd go around to the curators and art dealers and sell to the highest bidder. The Sorbonne might suspect he'd found the cave while he was in their employ, but they wouldn't be able to prove it.

He'd just say that he suspected there might be a cave in the area and he had come back to look for it after he resigned.

The walls were covered with paintings of animals, but Walcott didn't pay them much heed. You couldn't scrape paintings off a wall and sell them. Crass, but there you had it. Mara would no doubt be impressed. Maybe he'd still let her in on his discovery. It would definitely impress her. Then maybe she'd make up her mind about him and the offer he'd made her.

He was about to move into the next room when he heard a noise coming from it. He listened and moved toward the doorway to another room. He heard it again. A voice.

*The bloody bastard found a way up. And who is he talking to? Doesn't matter. Nobody is going to mess up my plans. I won't allow it.*

"What do you think of it?" Indy asked as Mara gazed in awe at forty feet of wall covered with woolly mammoths, deer, bears, and bisons. On the opposite side were more animal paintings, as well as several handprints, outlined in paint, and an array of strange symbols.

"It's fantastic, just fantastic," she replied in a hushed voice. "But are you sure they're really ancient?"

"No question about it," Indy answered. "Enough of these caves have been found around here. You're definitely looking at paintings from the Ice Age."

"Look at the color—red, yellow, brown, black. I want to touch them, but I better not."

"From what I understand the paint was made from natural iron minerals," Indy said.

"I wonder what they used as a binding agent?"

"Probably blood or animal fats."

"Do you think this is a really important discovery?" Mara asked.

"That depends on what else is here. At a minimum, we've found some fascinating Paleolithic cave art that's comparable with what's already been discovered."

Mara moved closer to the wall, and pointed to a four-legged animal that seemed to have a single horn growing from its head. "Look at that one. It's a unicorn."

Indy laughed. "I wouldn't be so sure about that."

"I believe in unicorns," she said quietly. "They really did exist."

"How do you know?"

Mara moved along the mural, examining the paintings. "I just believe it. You don't think this cave has already been discovered, do you?"

"I doubt it. Even if none of us had heard about it, one of the villagers we talked to in Montignac would've said something about it. They seemed to know about all the other caves."

"I suppose you're right."

"Let's see what else is here," he said.

Holes in two of the walls led to other rooms and Indy headed directly to the brightest one. A short passageway opened into a chamber with more cave paintings. The light entered through a chink in the ceiling in the far corner of the chamber, but Indy's attention was drawn to another discovery. A three-foot clay figure of a bear stood on its hind legs a few feet away, and as he looked around, he saw a couple of other figurines in the chamber.

Mara had already spotted the bear, and squatted down in front of it. "Look at this!"

"Now I'd say we've made a significant discovery," Indy said, dropping to one knee. "That is, if it's a true Stone Age relic."

"Too bad it's got all these little holes on the chest," Mara said.

Indy picked up a pointed stone that lay next to the bear. "Look, this stone has been worked. I'd say a shaman crouched here and stabbed at the clay bear."

"Why would he do that?"

"Probably to invoke the death of a real bear. It's sympathetic magic and old as these hills."

"What superstitious people they must have been."

Indy shrugged. "One man's superstitions; another man's religion." He walked across the room and examined the gap in the ceiling.

"Can we get out that way?" Mara asked. "I'm not looking forward to going back into that cold water."

The aperture looked just large enough to squeeze through, but Indy became immediately apprehensive. The dirt on the floor of the cave looked fresh. Then he saw the footprint. His first thought was one of disappointment; the figurines were probably of recent origin. "Someone's been here."

"What? When?"

"Not very long ago."

"And I'm still here."

Indy spun around and saw Walcott standing by the entrance to the next room, pointing a revolver at them.

"Roland?" Mara gasped.

"You won't have to worry about swimming upstream, my dear," Walcott said.

"How did you find the entrance?" Indy asked.

"I'm naturally lazy, Jones. I looked for an easier way in, and as luck would have it, a little rabbit showed me the way."

"Roland, put that gun down!" Mara snapped.

"Oh, Mara. It's too bad about you. I'd hoped things would work out differently."

"Get rid of it, Walcott, or I'll turn you in when we get back to Paris," Indy barked, trying to sound authoritative.

Walcott laughed. "You're such a kid, Jones. Too bad you're not going to get a chance to grow up."

"Roland, please. We haven't done anything," Mara pleaded. "You were here first. You get the credit for the discovery. Not us."

Suddenly, Indy knew what was going on. "It's not the credit that he wants. It's the artifacts."

"You got it, Jones. There are more rooms and more relics, and I'm going to collect what's mine."

"They're not yours to sell," Mara snapped. "You're not a treasure hunter. You're a scientist."

"Think again," Indy said.

Walcott waved the gun. "Enough talk. Get back into that room. I want to see how you got here."

As Indy retreated to the first chamber, he spotted his pack on the floor. His whip was inside it. But before he could do anything about it, Mara and Walcott moved into the cavern with him.

"Where's the entrance?" Walcott asked.

Mara pointed to the hole.

Walcott grabbed Mara by the back of the neck and pushed her toward the hole. He held the gun to her head as he peered through the hole. "So it goes right down to the river. Very good."

"Leave her alone, Walcott," Indy growled as he moved between his pack and the Englishman.

"If you don't want me to hurt her, you'd better do what I say." Walcott backed away from the opening, still holding Mara by the neck. "I want you to crawl feet first through that hole, Jones."

Indy knew instantly that Walcott planned to shoot him and then push his body into the river. He had to take a chance and do it fast. He held up his hands and pleaded: "Please, don't kill us. Don't kill us." He bent over and clutched his stomach. "Oh, I don't feel so good." He said it in a high-pitched, hysterical voice.

Walcott laughed, and as he did Indy grabbed his pack and flung it over his shoulder. But in his rush, he missed his target. *I'm dead*, he thought.

Walcott aimed his gun at Indy's head. "You bloody, no-good . . ." Mara threw her body across Walcott's legs, catching him behind the knees, and the gun exploded into the cave ceiling. Indy dived, tackling Walcott around the waist, and they rolled over as they fought for the gun. It fired again, then again. Indy grabbed Walcott's wrist and slammed it down, and the gun fell from the Englishman's grasp. Walcott lunged for the weapon, but Mara kicked it out of his reach.

Indy jerked the whip from his pack and lashed it at Walcott as he crawled for the revolver. The lab instructor yelled in pain as the knot at the end of the whip caught him across his cheek. He reared back, then reached for the gun, but the whip caught his arm and Indy pulled him away from the weapon. Walcott struggled, but Mara scooped up the gun and aimed it at him.

"Stop!" Mara yelled.

"The game's over, fellow," Indy said.

"Hey, can't you chaps take a little joke?" Walcott

chuckled, holding up his hands and grinning. "I was just testing you."

"Some joke, Roland," Mara said.

"We passed the test, but you failed," Indy countered.

Walcott unraveled the whip from his arm. "I hope you're not taking this seriously. Of course, the artifacts will go to the Sorbonne."

"And you're going to jail for attempted murder." Indy glanced at Mara. "Better give me the gun. I don't trust him."

As she passed it to him, Walcott suddenly dashed for the wall, dived, and disappeared through the hole. A second later, they heard a splash as he struck the water. Indy peered down into the darkness. "Walcott?" he yelled.

Water gurgled through the silence.

"I tell you one thing. I won't miss him. Not a bit," one of the students said as they all sat on the shore of the river waiting for the police to return. "Me neither," someone else said.

Indy and Mara had returned to camp and spread the word about what had happened. Oddly enough, no one had seemed overly surprised about Walcott's murderous assault. While Indy walked into Montignac to report the incident, Mara led the others to the cave, presumably to search for Walcott. When he returned with the gendarme and a few villagers, Indy found Mara and a couple of the others waiting outside the cave while the rest of them roamed about inside it, examining the rock art and the figurines.

The gendarme took charge, ordering everyone out of the cave. Now, while the villagers conducted their own search, Indy was growing tired of listening to the cynical comments of his fellow students, and decided to take a walk.

"Can I join you?" Mara asked.

"Sure."

"They're all acting so giddy, like it's a big joke," she said.

"They weren't in the cave with us." Indy gazed toward the point where the river reappeared from under the hills. He saw the gendarme in the distance moving toward them.

"Still . . ."

"I know. I'll be glad when this is all over, and we're back in Paris," Indy said as they headed toward the gendarme.

"Me, too."

He smiled at Mara. "Maybe we can get together and go down in the sewers or something."

She didn't answer for a few seconds. "I'd like to do that, but . . ."

"So you have a boyfriend?"

"No, it's not that. I like you, Indy. I really do. It's just that I'm leaving Paris next week."

"You're skipping next semester?"

"I'm not coming back to the Sorbonne. I've got a scholarship to finish my Ph.D. at the University of Rome. It's really the place to be for art history."

"I'm happy for you . . . I think. Good luck."

"I wish I'd met you earlier," she said, wistfully.

Indy shrugged. "It happens that way sometimes."

"Will you write me?" she asked.

"If you want."

She touched his arm. "I'd like that. I'll write you when I get settled."

"There's no sign of the body on the other side of

the hills where the river comes out," the gendarme said as he reached them. "Of course, that doesn't mean much. The body could be trapped underground somewhere, or it might have floated down river."

"But you do think he's dead?" Mara asked.

"He probably broke his neck in the fall."

Maybe, Indy thought. For some reason, he couldn't let go of the thought that Walcott might have somehow survived and escaped.

# 3

## THE THREE R's

*New England—May 1928*

Men in white overalls stood on long ladders trimming the lattice of ivy vines that threatened to turn a square window into a porthole. They worked under the watchful eye of a gargoyle, which stared down from the cornice of the old brick building. Below them, students crowded the sidewalks of the campus mall as they hurried between classes.

Indy paused a moment watching the work. He took in a deep breath of spring air, then moved on. A couple more weeks of classes and he'd be free, he thought, and he smiled to himself. His bags were already packed and his train ticket for Cortez, Colorado, was on his dresser.

It would be a great summer, and his thoughts were already skipping ahead to his plans to pursue the three R's—roaming, recreation, and romance.

The first two were assured, and the last was a fair possibility as things stood right now. Of course it would all be lumped under a fourth R, research, the real reason for his trip, and the reason the college was supporting it. But as research went, this summer's work in Four Corners would be a labor of joy.

Not only would he be returning to the Southwest, where he'd spent several years of his youth, but he was meeting up with Mara Rogers for the first time since he said good-bye in Paris four years ago. Their romance had been cut short before it had even blossomed, but in the last couple of years, they'd rekindled it through the mail, with their letters becoming more and more frequent.

As he reached the administration building, two coeds from one of his classes crossed his path and bumped into him. He knew the collision hadn't been accidental, but he apologized anyway. "Professor Jones, have you read that new book, *Anthropology and Modern Life,* by Franz Boas? I heard that it confutes the theory of a master race?"

Indy smiled. "I've heard of it, Millie, but to tell you the truth I've been too busy studying ancient life. Maybe one of these days, though, I'll catch up to modern times. Now if you'll excuse me, I've got a luncheon date."

"I wonder who his date is," the coed said as he walked away.

He rode the elevator to the top floor of the administration building accompanied by a professor with bushy white eyebrows and a cane. He was still in a good mood and without thinking about it started humming a popular song from the radio. The old professor frowned, then asked: "Do I detect an attempt to hum 'Makin' Woopee'?"

Indy laughed. "Well, it ain't 'Button Up Your Overcoat.' "

The elevator squeaked to a stop, and he stepped out onto the plush carpeting of the faculty club. Rich mahogany paneling and massive paintings of former presidents of the college covered the walls. Several overstuffed chairs were spread about the lobby area, most of them taken by men reading the *New York Times* and smoking pipes.

"Good afternoon. Can I help you, Professor . . ."

Indy turned to see a man with slicked-back hair who was garbed in a tuxedo. "Jones. I'm waiting for someone. He should be here any time."

"I'll put your name down for a table for two," the maître d' said, and he walked away.

Indy preferred having lunch at a coffee shop on the outskirts of the campus when he didn't eat it in his office, but he knew that Marcus Brody would appreciate the quieter, more august surroundings of the faculty club. As he looked around for a chair, he spotted a couple of his colleagues from the archaeology department seated on a couch. They were glancing toward him and exchanging comments. Swell, he thought. Now he had to go over and chat like they were good friends. But he was saved as the elevator door opened and Brody stepped out.

"There you are, Indy. Good to see you." Brody smiled and gave Indy a paternal pat on the shoulder. "Hope I haven't kept you waiting."

"Not at all, Marcus." Indy took the older man by the arm. "C'mon. There's a table waiting for us."

They'd barely been seated when a waiter arrived and took their orders, Hungarian goulash for Brody, and a bowl of minestrone for Indy. "So, I was in town, and decided to stop by and see how things were going," Brody said.

"Couldn't be better. I like the college and the town, but most of all I like the fact that I'm not as confined as I was when I was teaching Celtic archaeology."

Indy had lost his assistant professorship at the University of London because his interest in Celtic archaeology had waned. He'd wanted to explore other ancient cultures and that had been seen as a lack of commitment. Here, it was another story. Instead of specializing in a particular culture, his interest focused on the archaeology of ancient languages and symbols. It was a means of opening doors for him to the study and exploration of any culture and any time period. It was just what he wanted.

"Well, I'm glad to hear it." Brody nervously threaded and unthreaded his fingers. "I've heard good reports."

Brody had been a benign substitute father in the years since Indy had forsaken linguistics for archaeology and his real father had stopped talking with him. Brody, in fact, had guided his career, recommending him for his current position, and had also played a role in helping him land his first teaching job in London. Indy knew him well and could always tell when something was on his mind.

"Now tell me what you really want to talk about. What is it, Marcus?"

Brody pulled his fingers apart and flattened his hands against the table. "I'm just a little confused about this matter concerning your relationship with some of your female students."

Indy laughed. "There's nothing to it."

"Where there's smoke, there's usually fire, Indy."

"In this case, the fire's been on the low burner for quite awhile."

"How do you account for these rumors?" Brody persisted.

Indy shrugged. "It's just the statistics, Marcus. Some of my colleagues are a bit jealous."

"Statistics?"

Indy was only in his second year at the college and already there was a waiting list to attend his classes. But the statistic which excited the most curiosity was the male-female makeup of his classes. "Three quarters of my students are women, and ninety percent of archaeologists are men. Those statistics."

"I see," Marcus said as their lunches arrived. "That is a bit unusual," he added after the waiter had moved away.

Indy didn't bother telling Brody that he'd become the butt of a running series of jokes in the department. *Jones's career goal is to put skirts on every other archaeologist. . . . Have you heard that he's going to teach a course in how to apply makeup to skulls? . . . . He's teaching a special seminar on how to use a trowel without breaking your fingernails or getting your knees dirty. . . . I understand his lectures on fertility rites are especially popular.*

Brody pointed his fork at Indy. "Maybe it is about time you get involved with someone again. It's been quite a while since Deirdre died."

Deirdre Campbell had been the love of his life, and Indy still doubted that he'd ever meet anyone quite like her again. But he knew he had to move on, and he'd finally put her behind him.

Indy swallowed a spoonful of minestrone. "Marcus, I'm not abstaining from women. I just haven't found the right one."

Since joining the staff, he'd had casual relation-ships with a graduate student in history and a teach-ing assistant in the literature department. But both had heard the rumors about him and his students, and ended the relationship in spite of his denials. If they didn't believe him, he figured their friendship wasn't worth anything anyhow.

Brody nodded, a pensive look on his face. "Indy, there was another reason I wanted to see you today."

Now what? Indy wondered.

"This August there's going to be a month-long symposium on the archaeology of ancient Rome. The museum is one of the sponsors. You know we have the largest Roman exhibition, outside Rome, that is. Anyhow, I thought you might like to take part. I can arrange for your transportation. You'd be working for me, and I just bet you'd even meet some very inter-esting young—"

"Marcus, I appreciate the thought, but I've al-ready got plans for the summer. I am going out West, and as it happens, I am going to be seeing someone."

Brody looked disappointed, but only for a mo-ment. "I suppose I should've asked earlier. What are you going to do?"

He told him about his plans, and about Mara.

"It sounds as if you two do have a few things in common," Brody commented when Indy finished.

It was true. Both he and Mara had returned to America for new starts, and Indy's interest in the pre-Columbian rock art of the Southwest happened to be shared by Mara. Not only did she live in Santa Fe, New Mexico, but she'd grown up in Bluff, Utah, the town Indy was planning to use as his base for excursions into the surrounding canyons.

"So you're going to meet out in the desert. It's not my cup of tea for a romance, but I can just bet you're going to have quite a time."

Indy smiled slyly. "She wanted to make sure that I arrive in time for the solstice. Maybe she has some sort of fertility ritual in mind."

Indy was still thinking about his lunch with Brody as he walked down the hall toward his next class. He'd almost reached the door when he heard the department secretary calling his name. He turned and greeted the bespectacled young woman. "Professor Jones, glad I saw you. This just came for you." She handed him a telegram.

"Thanks, Amy. Are you going to sit in on my class today?"

"Nope. I've got a lunch date with a physics professor."

"What about me?"

She laughed. "You're just too slow, Indy. I couldn't wait forever."

"Yeah, maybe so. But when your physics prof starts coming on strong with relativity theory, you'll wish you were over here listening to me talk about old bones."

"Maybe so," she said, and she moved off.

Indy glanced at the telegram and headed down the hall. "You better hurry, Jones," one of his colleagues sniped from across the corridor. "They're already batting their eyes in anticipation."

Indy ignored him and stepped into the classroom just as the bell rang. He greeted the students. They were an attractive bunch, he thought as he scanned their faces. Most of the girls were dressed in calf-length skirts with white blouses and colored ribbons in their hair. The boys wore blazers and ties. And, once again, there were more females than males. He set the telegram on the podium and opened his notebook. On either side of the class were glass cabinets with neatly arranged artifacts: bone fragments, pottery shards, a couple of skulls, stone spearheads, clay figurines, and a necklace or two made of quartz crystals and turquoise. At the rear of the class was a slide projector, one of the latest additions to the classroom. That was the advantage of teaching in a private college. There was always money for frills.

Indy pulled on his black, wire-framed glasses and briefly examined his notes. He adjusted his tie, peered over the glasses at the students, and launched into his lecture without even bothering to introduce the topic. "I think you'll be surprised to know that one of the most important discoveries in the history of archaeology was made not by a prominent archaeologist, but by a little girl. We archaeologists usually don't like to admit such things, but I'll tell you about it anyhow and we'll keep it a secret between us . . . at least until the final exam."

The students laughed at the joke and groaned at the mention of the exam. "The little girl's name was Maria de Sautuola. One day in 1879, she accompanied her father, who was exploring a cave on his property in Altamira near the northern Spanish coast. While Daddy was digging in the entryway of the cave in the hopes of finding artifacts, little Maria was gallantly exploring the cave on her own. Suddenly, Maria shouted, *'Toros pintados!'* Painted bulls. Covering the walls were paintings of extinct bisons. Nothing like it had ever been seen in Europe."

Indy paused as most of the students furiously scribbled notes. "However, science is usually slow to recognize new things and this discovery was no different. No scholars of the time believed that Stone Age Man had the ability to create graceful paintings of the sort that were found at Altamira. For twenty years, the paintings were seen as a fraud."

He looked down at his notes. "The well-known artist, E. Lemus Y Olmos, wrote this about the paintings: 'By their composition, strength of lines, and proportions, they show that their author was not uneducated, and that though he was not a Raphael, he must have studied nature.' Lemus concluded that the paintings were 'simply the expression of a mediocre student of the modern school.' "

Indy smiled and shrugged. "Well, that was quite a review. It was too bad the artist wasn't around to hear it. He, or she, died ten thousand, maybe twenty thousand years before Lemus set eyes on the work."

"Professor Jones?"

"Yes, Marcella?"

"As I understand it, there's no way to really calculate the age of cave paintings. So how can you be so certain of their antiquity?"

"Fair question. First of all, the number of caves with paintings that have been discovered virtually nullifies the question of fraud. I found one myself a few years ago near the village of Montignac. Second, while it is virtually impossible to date the paintings, they have been found in caves containing artifacts which are clearly related to Stone Age Man. Finally, some of the caves could be dated geologically since they were sealed at the time of their discovery."

Indy was warming to the subject. "One of the caves was found by a farmer in Tayac as he was digging a potato cellar. Not only was the entrance sealed by rocks, but a painting discovered inside the cave had been covered by the crust of a stalagmite. So finally, by the turn of the century, the tide had turned. Even the most outspoken skeptics had conceded that they'd been wrong. The cave paintings were clearly the work of artists from the Stone Age."

Another student, a bespectacled man with a crew cut, raised his hand. "Can you tell us more about the cave you discovered?"

"Of course. One of the more interesting aspects of the cave is that one wall features a number of abstract signs, which were similar to drawings found in other caves. What this means is that a rudimentary system of writing was developing in the Paleolithic art. As a matter of fact—"

"Professor Jones?" The same student was raising his hand.

"Yes, George?"

"How did you find the cave?"

"By swimming into an underground river that led to the caverns," he answered, annoyed by the interruption.

"That must have been dangerous," someone else said.

"It was the only way I knew to get inside. Now about the writing system," Indy continued. "The symbols—"

"I don't mean to contradict you, Professor Jones, but I read in a journal that the man who discovered that cave was killed in it."

"Well, George, that's a matter of interpretation. I told the man you're referring to about the cave after I found an underwater entrance. But he found the way into the main chambers through another entry point about an hour ahead of me."

"But you should get the credit if you found it first," another student said.

Indy shrugged. "Thank you, Maybelle. I guess it makes a more interesting story with the explorer dying in the cave he discovers. But if you think about it, it's obvious that someone else was there to record the discovery or we wouldn't know what happened to Walcott."

"What did happen to him?" George asked.

At the request of the Sorbonne's archaeology department, Indy had never spoken in public about the details, even after the university credited the missing lab instructor with the discovery. "Walcott fell into an underground river. His body was never found."

A blonde raised her hand.

"Laura?"

"Professor Jones, do you have any plans to go back to the caves? I'd love to see those bisons and all the other paintings myself."

A twittering erupted at the girl's brashness. "I don't have any plans to go back right now. But I recommend the trip if you're interested."

"She's not, if you're not going," another girl said, snickering from the back of the room, and the class broke into laughter.

"I didn't mean it that way," Laura protested, turning red.

Indy didn't pay any heed. He kept his distance from his students. He knew that if he made one wrong move, his jealous colleagues would pounce on him. "Okay, we're going to take a look at some slides now of reproductions of ancient Stone Age art."

He moved away from the podium and pulled down a screen. "Would someone get the shades, please?" He switched off the light and moved to the rear of the room. The first slide was a painting of a mastodon from a cave near Montespan in the foothills of the Pyrenees. Bisons, bears, rhinoceros, reindeer, and lions followed. Some looked angered, their hair standing out in bristles, as if they were under attack. One mastodon was giving birth. Life and death.

Then he showed a slide of an animal that was not so readily identifiable. "Can anyone tell me what we're looking at?"

"That's no animal I've ever seen," a voice from the darkened room said.

"Deer antlers, a wolf tail, and a humanlike face," Indy said.

"Maybe it's a werewolf with antlers," someone else suggested.

"It's most likely a shaman wearing an animal skin, a mask, antlers, and a wolf tail. The painting was found in a cave at Les Trois Frères. It was located in a room twelve feet above the floor of the cave at the end of a winding corridor. This room might have been a place where shamans entered into trance to contact the spirit world for help in curing the sick or controlling the animal world. The painting could be an artist's rendition of a shaman transformed into an animal."

"Could they actually do that?" Laura asked.

"They apparently thought so."

"But could they really?" George asked.

A beat passed. "As a scientist, I'd have to say no. It's never been proved."

Laura raised her hand again. "But maybe they

could do things that we no longer believe are possible, just as we certainly can do things today that they would consider impossible."

"That's an interesting thought. But it would be impossible to prove."

Indy switched slides to one showing several markings on a wall. One looked like a barbed hook, another resembled a stringless bow, and a third looked like a window covered by a grid. "These are a few of the symbols I mentioned earlier. Any ideas on what they might mean?"

No one answered.

"Each one probably served a magical purpose. This is how written language began. Magical symbols representing the elements: air, fire, earth, water. Spirit, infinity, the eternal. The sun, the moon, the four winds. They all played important roles for the ancient magician or sorcerer or shaman, whose job it was to control the elements for the good of the community." Indy turned off the projectors and the lights came on as he walked to the front of the class. "Any questions before we move on?"

"Professor Jones, I've read about these shamans in ancient cultures all over the world from Siberia to Japan to South America. What's the connection? Why did they all do the same thing?"

Indy thought a moment. "Well, Christine, I guess it's the nature of being human to reach out to the unknown or at least to assign someone to do it for you, someone who could take control. The shamans made contact with the spirit world in order to cure the sick, improve the odds of the hunt, make rain, and even make sure the sun came up every day. They eventually became the priests and the astrologers. They tracked the stars and planets, the sun and the moon. They created calendars and wrestled with the problem of the relationship of the cosmos and man."

The bell rang. "Now there's magic for you. I just started talking and the hour is over."

As the students filed out of the class, Indy opened his telegram.

"I enjoyed your lecture, Professor Jones," Laura said. "I wish all of my classes were this interesting."

"She means all of her professors," another student said.

"Stop it," Laura said and hurried away.

Indy shook his head, but his smile faded as he read the telegram: INDY—SOMETHING'S COME UP. I CAN'T MEET YOU IN BLUFF. SORRY. MARA.

Indy crumpled it. "Thanks a lot, sweetheart. Guess we're going to miss the solstice together."

# 4

## CLIFF DWELLINGS

*Four Corners—A Month Later*

The fall morning was brisk, sparkling clear, the sort of day that Mara loved to spend hiking through woods and valleys, along lake shores and mountain trails. Today, she would descend into one of the most remarkable canyons of the American Southwest, or of anywhere for that matter. It was a place with an ancient history of human occupation, a place with a startling, dramatic architecture that had immortalized its mysterious inhabitants.

She had an excellent view from her position on the mesa top. The canyon was perhaps a half a mile across as the crow flies, and she could see a couple of miles up and down the valley, which was a forest of junipers, Douglas firs, ponderosas, and piñons. It was the far wall of the canyon, though, which interested her. Ancient dwellings grew out of the cliffs like stalactites in a cave. At first, she had difficulty spotting even one of them. Then her gaze settled on what looked like a group of buildings hanging in midair.

Mara reached into her pack and pulled out a telescope. She extended the tube to its full length and peered through it at one of the ruins. The stone buildings seemed to grow from the cliff wall. They rose two and three stories high and their rectangular windows looked out into the verdant valley. They were grouped tightly together under an overhang, a gaping mouth that seemed about to swallow the silent village. Even through the telescope, the place looked distant, eerie, frozen in time. And empty. The inhabitants had vanished centuries earlier, gone long before the arrival of Spanish explorers. But the Spanish hadn't found Mesa Verde. If they had, they'd left no record of it.

Mara's father was a young man in 1887 when two ranchers sighted the cliff houses while looking for stray cattle. Later, her father helped one of the brothers explore the ruins in Mesa Verde and other canyons. But she didn't want to think about her father. She hated the fact that she still depended on him financially, especially since he was no longer wealthy. It was the only way he'd ever helped her, and he never let her forget it. In every other way, he'd let her down. As if to remind her of his failings as a father, he'd refused to accompany her here, saying he didn't want anything to do with Mesa Verde anymore.

Mara lowered her telescope, then focused it on another of the cliff dwellings. Again no sign of life. She sighted a third in the scope, and carefully moved across the dwellings looking for some indication of a camp. She didn't know why Indy had left Bluff without her, but she was anxious to find him. She'd been looking forward to seeing him for a long time, and it seemed hard to believe that he was actually here.

She looked further down the canyon. It had to be one of these pueblos. "Sam, I don't see anyone out there." She turned to the Ute Indian, who'd guided her from Cortez. He patted one of the horses, set the feed down, and moved to the edge of the canyon. Sam, whose skin was a rich, burnished brown, was barrel-chested and slender-hipped with a slightly protruding belly. His black hair was streaked with gray, which was as much a result of the time he'd spent in the sun, she thought, as it was his fifty years. He quickly scanned the far cliff without the aid of the telescope, then pointed.

She followed his finger. "I don't see anything." She squinted, then raised the telescope. Barely visible in the shadow of an overhang far down the canyon was another site she hadn't seen. It looked as empty as the others. But then she glimpsed a wispy curl of smoke rising from one of the buildings. She lowered the telescope. "You've got darn good eyes, Sam. That's all I can say."

"It's Spruce Tree House. It's a big pueblo."

"How long will it take us to get down there?"

"We will be there by midday."

That was fine with Mara. The quicker the better. She'd felt edgy since yesterday afternoon when they'd reached the canyon region. It was almost as if she'd sensed someone following them. Then, last night at the camp, she'd noticed the way Sam had looked around and how he'd kept his rifle with him. She'd asked if something was wrong, but he'd just shaken his head and said that it was probably coyote. There were lots of coyotes in these mountains, he'd added, as if to convince himself as well as her.

As a child, during her first trip here with her father, she'd been surprised that the area was so wooded and green. Much of the Four Corners region was dry, desolate land like the Valley of the Gods or Monument Valley. While the cliff dwellings themselves were barren and rocky, above and below was a green, wooded land.

She was glad that Sam was willing to accompany her across the canyon. She knew that his family was preparing for a trip to their home pueblo for a celebration and he wanted to get back as soon as possible. But she wasn't sure of the best route to the ruins, and there was that nagging suspicion that they were being followed.

They rode another mile or so along the mesa top before Sam raised a hand. "We can walk from here. I'll lead your horse. Mine will wait here for me."

"Once we get close, you can head back if you like," she told him.

As they descended along the trail, Mara's excitement about seeing Indy again grew sharper, clearer. When he'd written that he was coming to the Southwest this summer, she knew she had to see him. She wanted to help him with his work and she hoped he would help her with hers as well. The solstice was approaching and, if all went well, everything would come together on that day. At least, that's what she'd been told.

A branch cracked somewhere behind her and she turned, scanning the forest. "What was that?"

"I didn't hear anything."

They moved on. Maybe it was just a deer or some

other harmless animal. Maybe it was a bear. The skin on the back of her neck prickled at the thought. Did bears follow you? She heard a swishing sound, maybe a branch snapping back into place. "Sam, I'm sure you heard that." He didn't answer. What was wrong with him? Indians were supposed to be aware of everything around them.

Then she recalled something her father had told her long ago. Indians were like everybody else. Some were skilled trackers and hunters; others were no better than average. Maybe Sam had great vision, but poor hearing.

"You wait here," Sam said. "I'll take a look."

She patted the horse on its side as Sam disappeared down the trail. Now everything was quiet. No sound of birds, no wind whispering through the branches, no chirring of insects. Perfectly quiet. Her uneasiness grew by the moment.

A sharp cry from just beyond the curtain of green broke the silence. "Sam?" Her voice sounded hollow, weak. Something was wrong, horribly wrong.

Noises. Crackling branches. A snorting sound.

She backed away and was on the verge of fleeing when she saw it. The palomino. Sam's horse. She felt relieved, but only for a moment. How'd it get there, and where was . . . "Sam, is that you?"

She saw a figure staggering near the horse. "Sam, what's wrong?" Then she saw the bib of blood covering his chest. He motioned her with his hand not to come to his aid, but to flee. She took a couple steps toward him. He shook his head. "Go, go," he gasped.

She leaped onto the back of her own horse, urging it down the path. She hugged its neck, prodded its sides. *Hurry. Move. Fast.*

Now the forest was the ally of her invisible en-

emy. Trees crowded her, branches whipped her, and
the trail was a hellish, green gauntlet. Her arms
and hands and cheeks and forehead were scratched
and bloody as they rushed on. She had no idea
whether or not she was being chased, whether she'd
lost the attackers or they were right behind her. She
just clung to the horse with all her strength and
kneed its sides, urging it on.

Finally, the terrible green assault ended. The trail
rose, narrowed. There were fewer trees, but the path
was so narrow, the horse's hoofs pounded just inches
from the edge. She wanted to get off and walk, but
there was no time. She continued climbing toward
the ridge and the sheltered cavern, Indy, and safety.

One of the horse's front legs suddenly buckled as
its hoof slid over the edge. It whinnied, rose up on
its hind legs, and tossed Mara through the air. She
was certain she was going to tumble down the cliff.
She landed hard on her back and rolled over onto
her stomach. Her legs dangled over the lip of the
cliff, her heart pounding, perspiration beading on
her forehead. She dragged herself forward inch by
inch away until one knee touched ground, then the
other.

Close. Too close. She pulled her legs under her,
stood, and winced as she felt the sharp pain of a
bruised rib. She told herself to keep going. She had
to get to the pueblo.

Voices. She must be near. She craned her head,
squinting. Three men rushed toward her from the
ruins. They stopped several feet away and stared.
"Where's Indy?" she asked.

None of them said a word. Something was wrong.
They looked like toughened ranch hands, not assis-

tants to an archaeologist. Then they stepped aside as another man moved forward.

"Hello, Mara. Welcome to Mesa Verde."

"Who are you?"

His wide-brimmed hat made it difficult to make out his features. He was a portly man whose khaki clothing was clean. He had a neatly trimmed goatee and a blue kerchief around his neck. She knew right away from the way he stood and carried himself that he was in charge.

"Don't you recognize me? Has it been that long?"

He spoke with an English accent, and there was something vaguely familiar about him. Then she knew, but she didn't know. It was as if the man were out of focus. Something wasn't right. He shouldn't be here. "I don't know who you are. Where's Indy?"

"You picked up some bad information, Mara. Jones isn't here."

"What do you want with me?"

"What do you think, Mara?"

"I don't know."

He laughed. "Okay, I'll spell it out. I want the ivory staff. Where is it?"

"I don't know what you're talking about."

"Of course you do. Don't you remember we talked about it back when we first met? The quicker you tell me where it is, the sooner you'll be on your way back home."

"Roland Walcott?" She could hardly believe it. "What are you doing here? You're dead."

"Do I look dead, Mara, dear?" He laughed. "Take me to the staff, and I'll tell you all about what happened to me."

"I don't know where it is."

"I don't believe that. You've hidden it out here somewhere, haven't you?"

"I've been out here drawing petroglyphs." He must have been watching her, she thought. Why else would he show up now when she was so close?

"Of course you were."

"Let me go and I'll give you some pots I've collected. They're in excellent condition. You can get—"

"Don't insult me. I don't want your bloody pots; I want the staff. It's worth a lot of money. You lead me to it and I'll sell it. We'll split the money."

Mara laughed. "You must think I'm a fool. Even if I knew what you were talking about, I'd never deal with you. Never."

Walcott sighed. "I can wait. I have the perfect place for you to think it over. Maybe your memory will come back. Unfortunately, you won't have a view of the canyon. No view at all."

"You can't keep me here!"

"I can do anything I want." Walcott looked past her and she turned to see two men approaching from the canyon. They looked as if they belonged with the others. "Well, what happened? Where's the bloody Indian?"

"He's bloody, all right. I had to stick him," a man with a heavy brow and recessed, beady eyes said. "He was getting too snoopy."

"I told you, Jimbo, I didn't want any needless violence."

"It was needed."

Walcott made a motion with his hand as if to dismiss the man. "Take her up. And be nice to her."

The man laughed, and she saw a mouth of jagged

yellow teeth. "I'll be real nice, boss man. Real gentle. You can count on me."

Far below the pueblo, the palomino nudged the man's face. Sam tried desperately to overcome the grogginess from his loss of blood. He attempted to stand, but the pain was too much. Then the horse bent down on its knees as Sam had trained it to do. The Ute crawled until he was lying across the horse's saddle. Sam eased a rope from the saddlebag and tied himself to his steed. He patted the horse, and the palomino rose to its feet and trotted up the canyon trail.

Sam felt the blood trickling over the saddle and down his horse's flank. His vision was blurred. He felt light-headed, woozy. He didn't know if he could make it, but the horse would take him home.

5

SAND ISLAND

Spellbound. That was how Indy felt as he stared at the cliff wall, a sandstone panel of the past. The ancient drawings at Sand Island on the shore of the San Juan River were in the heartland of Anasazi territory. Grand Gulch was to the west and Mesa Verde to the east. Tsegi Canyon was southwest of here and Chaco Canyon to the southeast.

Sand Island was a natural spot for him to start his investigation of rock art, and he'd driven out for a look not an hour after arriving in Bluff, which was just a couple of miles from the site. Not only was Sand Island easily accessible, but it was the largest exhibition of rock art in the Southwest with literally hundreds of depictions of animals, birds, and masks as well as geometric designs and abstract symbols, some dating back more than a thousand years. He suspected that the rock art of the Anasazis was a clue to the spiritual and magical aspects of the ancient Indian culture as much as the cave paintings of southwestern France were a key to the shamanistic influences of Ice Age Man.

At the moment, Indy was examining a spiral etched in the rock. The design might symbolize the sun, but he wasn't so sure about that. His thoughts were interrupted by the muttering from a few feet away. "What did you say, Jack?"

"I was wondering about these Anasazis. You never hear about them anymore. At least, I don't. What happened to them, anyhow?"

Indy turned to the tall, lanky redhead, who was unscrewing the top of a canteen. Jack Shannon was an old friend from Chicago, who now lived in San Francisco. They hadn't seen each other for a couple of years and when Indy had told him he'd be spending the summer in Four Corners, Shannon had made arrangements for a visit. They'd met yesterday in Cortez and had left for Bluff this morning shortly after Indy bought a '24 Ford. He'd seen it for sale on the main street, and had paid fifty-seven dollars and fifty cents for it, a fair deal, although Shannon didn't think so.

"The Anasazis vanished around the thirteenth century."

"Just vanished?"

"Not all at once. They reached a cultural high point here in the desert, then things took a turn for the worse. Maybe it was a great drought or invasions from nomadic tribes. Whatever, they left. Cultures are sort of like people. They eventually get old and die. Some live longer than others."

"But where did they go?"

Indy shrugged. "They probably moved south and became the tribes we call the Hopis and the Pueblos."

"I think the Anasazis were a little jaded myself," Shannon commented. "Maybe that's what finished them off. You know, like the Romans."

Indy looked at him as if he'd lost his mind. "What are you talking about?"

Shannon took a long swallow, and offered the canteen to Indy, who shook his head. Shannon was a jazz musician by profession and his knowledge of archaeology was minimal, but he always had an opinion. He pointed to a drawing on the rock face. It was a hunchbacked figure, who was playing a flute and exhibiting an enormous phallus. "If I played my horn on stage like that fellow, I know it would be my downfall."

"That's Kokopelli. He's a wandering hunchbacked flute player who seduced the nubile young girls in each of the villages he visited. He's a symbol of fertility. The hump might actually be a pack he's carrying."

Shannon considered what he'd said. "I can just imagine the sort of music he played; raucous and heady with lots of real reedy, suggestive riffs, you know. The kind of thing that gets you worked up, mesmerized."

Indy laughed. "You know, you just might have something there."

"He'd play to your soul," Shannon continued. "You'd do anything for that guy to hear more of the magical flute."

"If anyone asks, you're my ancient musical interpreter," Indy said, slapping his friend on the back.

"Hey, who're you calling ancient? You're pushing thirty yourself."

"I didn't mean it quite like that. C'mon. Let's take a look further down before we go back."

"You go ahead. I'll wait down by the car."

Indy knew that Shannon didn't have the tempera-
ment to stare at rock walls all day, but he was surprised at his lack of curiosity. They'd barely been
here half an hour. "What's wrong, are you tired already?"

"I've just seen enough. That's all. Anyhow, I
thought they were going to be colorful paintings, not
just these scratches on the wall."

"These *scratches*, as you call them, are petroglyphs. There are paintings at other sites, and
they're known as pictographs. It's all rock art."

Shannon shrugged. "If you ask me, most of this
stuff is probably the work of some kids who didn't
have anything else to do."

Shannon was trying Indy's patience, but Indy held
his temper. "It might look that way at first. But the
deeper you get into it, the more you realize there's a
pattern and meaning to it all. The Anasazis took their
rock art very seriously. It wasn't like drawing on a
bathroom wall in a public toilet."

Shannon glanced back at Kokopelli. "Well, I don't
know about that." He'd no sooner spoken when one
of his feet slipped out from beneath him and he slid
down several feet.

"You okay?"

Shannon brushed off his hands. "Yeah. I'm just
fine. See you at the bottom."

"I'll be with you in a few minutes," Indy called
after him as Shannon descended the cliff to the river
basin.

No matter what Shannon did with his life, he was
always the same to Indy. The sardonic edge of his
personality seemed to go with the jazz life, but he'd
been a true friend, in spite of everything. A few

years back, in the midst of a life filled with jazz and
gangsters, Shannon had taken up with a revivalist-
style church, which preached a literal interpretation
of the Bible. Since moving to San Francisco, he'd
found another similar church. Maybe Shannon just
seemed the same to Indy because he knew better
than to preach to Indy. But no doubt Shannon's Bible was tucked just out of sight.

As Indy moved along the ledge, he examined one
petroglyph after another. What fascinated him was
that the faint, nearly indistinct images were mixed
with sharper ones showing distinct differences in the
age of the creation. That meant that maybe six hundred years ago someone had stood here and etched a
drawing of a sheep next to a bird, which had been
drawn several hundreds of years earlier.

He could easily spend the rest of the day here
studying the drawings. But there were lots of sites
he would visit. One of the advantages in studying
rock art was that he wouldn't be tied to one site as
he would be if he were here for a dig. He'd travel to
all the major Anasazi ruins: Mesa Verde, Chaco Canyon, Grand Gulch, Hovenweep, and others. The
rock art was not in any one place, but in all of them.

It would be a good summer, even without Mara.
He'd considered writing her and suggesting she
come later, but she knew he was here. If she wanted
to see him, she'd find him.

Shannon walked over to the Ford, and kicked a rear
tire. He'd told Indy that he'd paid ten dollars too
much for the car, and he knew that Indy had been
thinking about it ever since. He enjoyed seeing Indy
again and reminiscing about old times, but he didn't
know how many days he could stand it out here in

the desert. Sure, the town was quaint and pictur-
esque with the bluffs and river, the big old cottonwood trees, and the houses with their sandstone
exteriors. But he'd hoped for something a little bigger than a village of two hundred. It wasn't just
Bluff, though. He missed Katrina, his wife, and their
fourteen-month-old son, and he already longed for
San Francisco and his North Beach hangouts. Maybe
it was a mistake saying he'd stay two weeks. He
dreaded the possibility that he was going to be bored
to death.

He sat down on the bumper and opened his canteen again. He and Indy had gone to a bar last night
in Cortez and he'd had a couple too many whiskeys.
His throat was dry and no matter how much water
he drank, he was still thirsty. But then Jesus had
spent forty days and forty nights in the desert. He
guessed he could manage less than half that. Maybe
some revelation would come to him. Yeah, that's how
he had to look at it. He needed to refresh his spirit,
to make a challenge of it. It was no coincidence that
Indy had invited him here. The trip was a prayer
answered. He needed a challenge.

Not that he was tired of San Francisco. He spent
four nights a week at the club, and was glad for the
work. But he knew he was getting stale. He was
playing the same music over and over again, and
each time it seemed there was less and less innova-
tion. He was afraid his music was turning to milk-
toast, and that it would soon take on all the elements
of the popular jazz musicians he'd always detested
for their lack of originality. It was almost to the point
that the only music he really enjoyed playing was on
Sunday nights when the gospel group got together

for a couple of hours. But while the gospel music revived him, it didn't pay the bills.

And there was Mother. She'd moved in with them six months ago, after selling the family house in Chicago. He loved her, but she got on his nerves sometimes, carrying on about how wonderful things had been in the old days and talking about his brothers as if they were still alive. At least she and Katrina got along, and Mother was great with the baby, which made it easier for Katrina.

He hoped the desert would bring new life to his music. He was already starting to play around with a tune that had come into his head after he'd seen Kokopelli blowing his flute. Maybe he'd get his cornet out, and work on it. He'd call it "Kokopelli."

He opened the trunk, and saw Indy's whip rolled up in the corner and his fedora next to it. Being around Indy had always brought something new into his life, and although some of the circumstances hadn't been what he would consider a great time, he didn't regret any of the experiences. After all, how many people could say that they'd stood on Mount Ararat and seen Noah's Ark? Not that anyone believed him, but it didn't matter. It was his experience, and he knew what he'd seen and where he'd been.

He placed Indy's hat on his head; it was a size too big. He picked up the whip, stepped away from the car, and tried cracking it. "Ouch!" The tip snapped his neck. *Now how does he work this thing so smoothly?*

A new Packard with a fine layer of road dust on its shiny, black finish eased down toward the river basin and came to a stop fifty yards from the Ford. "That's him right there playing with his whip," Walcott said.

"You sure?" one of the three other men in the car asked.

"Jimbo, there's only one archaeologist I know of who carries a whip around. Now go get him."

Jimbo frowned and his dark eyes seemed to recede further back into his head. "He must never use it. Doesn't look like he knows what he's doing."

"Don't let him fool you," the Englishman said.

"You gonna pick us up?"

Walcott stroked his goatee. "No, take his car. You know what to do with him. I'll catch up to you."

Jimbo scowled. "You're not coming right back?"

"Don't worry about me. Just do your job and you'll get paid when it's over."

"It's not safe there," Jimbo countered. "We already turned away two people, and they got those special park cops that come around. If they show up . . ."

"Don't worry. We're moving tonight. Now get going."

Jimbo stepped out of the Packard with his two companions. He signaled them to spread apart. Then, they closed in on the Ford.

Hey, that was better, Shannon thought as the whip cracked. It just took a little practice, that was all. The important thing was the right snap of the wrist.

"Hold it right there."

Shannon turned around to see three men with revolvers aimed at him. With their hats and kerchiefs, they looked like cowboys from the serials. He couldn't help laughing. "You worried I'm going to hit you or something?"

The one with the heavy brow cocked his gun. "Just drop the whip, Jones. Now!"

As far as Shannon knew, Indy didn't have any friends or enemies around here. But Shannon never argued with a gun. He patted the air with his hands. "Yeah, sure, okay. Take it easy."

"Get in the car." Eyebrows shoved him toward the Ford, knocking his hat off. One of the other men pulled the whip out of his hand.

"By the way, I'm not Jones, you know."

"Yeah? Then where is he?"

Shannon didn't want trouble, but he wasn't a snitch, either. "He's not here."

"We're not fools, Jones. Just get in the car."

Shannon scanned the cliff; Indy was nowhere in sight. Then he realized the whole thing must be a joke. Indy had set him up and now he was hiding up there, laughing.

"Indy," he shouted. "Real funny. Get down here."

The men stopped and looked toward the cliff. But if Indy was up there, he wasn't showing himself.

"Get him in there," one of the men said. The back door of the Ford opened and Shannon was shoved inside.

"This isn't funny anymore. You go tell—" Shannon never finished the sentence. A rag was stuffed in his mouth, his hands were tied, and he was pushed onto the floor.

Indy was pressed into a crevice between two slabs of sandstone. He'd been studying the depiction of a Spaniard and a horse from the days of the conquest when he noticed some markings on the wall about ten feet above him. He climbed up and found an arrow etched in the rock face that pointed toward a juniper tree growing out of the wall. He pulled a branch back and found an opening to the crevice.

He hoped he wasn't wasting his time, but now as he wedged further into the crevice, he saw what looked like another Kokopelli. He wondered why anyone would bother crawling in here to inscribe the mythical figure. It wasn't as if there were no other surfaces available to work. Then he realized he'd made a mistake. It wasn't Kokopelli, at least not the traditional version of the character. This figure carried a pack on his back, but there was no flute and no phallus. Instead, he was pointing toward the depths of the crevice.

Indy heard a faint call. Shannon was probably wondering what happened to him, but he could wait a minute. He wouldn't hear him, anyhow. He moved as far into the crevice as he could and stretched his hand until he touched the point where the two rock faces came together. He prodded with his fingers, moving them up and down along the joint of the rocks. He had an odd feeling that the rocks were claiming him, pulling him inward. He was turning to stone, joining the mineral world.

Finally, he withdrew his hand, and edged backward, shaking off the odd feelings. What had he expected to find, anyhow? It was a crevice and a dead end. Nothing more.

He thought he heard Shannon gun the Ford engine. "All right, all right. For crying out loud, I'm coming." He worked his way out of the crevice and around the bush. He'd just started to descend the cliff when he saw the Ford pulling away.

"Hey!" Indy skidded a few feet down. His hands slapped against the wall and he caught himself as his feet settled on a ledge. The Ford kept going. "Hey, what the . . ." He waved and shouted, but to no avail.

Indy continued working his way down the cliff as the Ford disappeared, kicking up clouds of dust that lingered in the air for several minutes. He wondered if Shannon had gotten concerned when Indy didn't answer his call. Maybe he was going to get help. Naw. That wasn't the sort of thing Shannon would do. If he was concerned, he would've come looking for Indy. He was probably just going for a joy ride in the new car, and would be back shortly.

When Indy reached the spot where the car had been, he bent down and picked up his whip and hat. Now why would he do that? Then it dawned on him. Shannon wasn't concerned about him. He was angry with him for taking his time, or maybe it was something Indy had said. But what? They hadn't talked about religion or anything Indy could think of that might anger his friend.

But now Indy was the one getting angry as he followed the road up and out of the river basin. When he was above the cliff, he gazed down the road back toward Bluff and east in the direction of Mexican Hat and the Valley of the Gods. Not a car in sight. He kept walking.

Anger was not the word for how Indy felt as he neared Bluff half an hour later. Usually, he could walk off his animosity, but this two-mile jaunt was another matter. With every step, he grew more and more irritated. He cursed Shannon under his breath. At first, he'd expected to see him drive up and make some snappy remark about how he'd gotten bored. But as it became apparent that Shannon wasn't coming back for him, Indy was no longer just aggravated, he was livid. He cursed Shannon with every invective he could think of, loudly, repeatedly.

What good did it do for Shannon to spend hours reading the Bible when he was so inconsiderate? He didn't even give Indy a warning. Nothing. Just drove away, and left behind his whip and hat, as if Indy would need them to get back to town.

An old man with a big white beard pulled up in a buckboard as Indy approached the boardinghouse he and Shannon had checked into when they'd arrived in town. "What can I do for you, sir?"

"You seen a 'twenty-four Ford around?"

"I've seen more than one around from time to time," the man said as he climbed down. "Any Ford in particular you looking for?"

"Yeah. Mine. My friend and I were just at Sand Island and he took off without me. I thought he'd be here."

"You staying here?"

"That's right."

"Are you Shannon?"

"No, Jones. How do you know Shannon?"

"Professor Jones?"

"Yeah, who are you?"

"I own the place. Name's Oscar Smithers. But you can call me Smitty. Everyone else does. The woman who checked you in was Rosie, my wife."

"Glad to meet you." They shook hands.

Smitty took off his hat, revealing a bald pate, fringed by long wisps of white hair. The man's sad brown eyes studied him. "What are you doing here, anyhow? I thought you were out at Mesa Verde."

"Who told you that?"

"My daughter. She went off looking for you."

Indy was more baffled than ever. "Who's your

daughter, and why would she know anything about me?"

"Her name's Mara. She said she was going to meet you here in Bluff."

"Mara Rogers?"

"That's right. After her mother and I divorced, the old lady moved to Santa Fe and took back her maiden name and gave it to the girl, too. Didn't want anything to do with me, anymore. I didn't see Mara again until she was eighteen."

Indy didn't want to hear the family history. More immediate matters were on his mind. "But I got a telegram from Mara saying she couldn't meet me."

"Don't know nothin' about that. I took her on my buckboard all the way to Cortez, and she got herself a horse and a guide to lead her into Mesa Verde."

"But why did she think I went there?"

"She just seemed to know. But to tell you the truth, Professor, the girl and I aren't on the best terms. I paid for all her schooling over in Europe, and even bought her a little place in Santa Fe when she came back. But she don't appreciate it. When she comes around, she usually talks more to Rosie than me."

Indy was exasperated. Smitty was no help.

"Now what's this about your Ford?" Smitty asked when Indy didn't respond.

With the news of Mara, he'd almost forgotten about Shannon. "I came here with a friend. He drove off from Sand Island with my Ford."

"So ya walked back?"

"Yeah, I walked."

Smitty shrugged. "Ain't a bad walk. . . . Say, there was a fellow here asking about you this morning. Didn't leave no name, though."

"What did he look like?" Indy asked.

"I'd say he was a few years older than you. Bigger than you. A round face with a goatee. Curly hair about the color of the sandstone and a turned-up little nose. Pushy fella. I took him for sort of a troublemaker."

"What did he want with me?"

"Didn't stick around to talk. Had some English way of talkin', too. Bloody this, bloody that."

Indy had no idea what was going on. None of it made sense. Everything around him had suddenly shifted into a strange twisted nightmare. It all started about the time he crawled into that crevice. And he had the feeling it was only beginning.

# 6

## WALCOTT'S CALL

Walcott inhaled deeply from his cigarette and blew the smoke over the head of the man in front of him. He had been waiting for a half an hour outside of the telegraph office in Cortez, and there was still no sign of his benefactor. He hated waiting for people, but he had no choice. Diego Calderone, after all, was going to pay him a fortune for the staff.

He lit another cigarette off the burning end of the last one, then crushed out the other with his heel. Two men entered the tavern across the street, and he wished he was with them. He needed a drink, and he'd get one when he was finished with Calderone. Maybe two or three. And why not? Their plan was working out just fine. They'd lured Mara to Mesa Verde, and now they had Jones. Tonight, they'd let them escape and Mara would do the rest.

Walcott had found out about the precious relic years ago when he was studying at the Sorbonne. He was working weekends in an antique shop when a

young woman walked in one day and said she
wanted to sell an old family document which pur-
ported to be proof of the 1798 sale of an alicorn, or
unicorn's horn, to an ancestor of hers. She said her
mother had recently died, and she'd found the paper
among her belongings. Walcott not only didn't believe in unicorns or their horns, but considered the
document worthless. But he liked the woman and
wanted to get to know her, especially when he found
out that she was also a student at the Sorbonne.

Walcott paid Mara Rogers five pounds for the document. She tried to get a couple more pounds out of
him, but he held firm. Instead, he invited her to
dinner. After a moment's hesitation, she'd accepted.
Over dinner, she talked more about the alicorn, and
its history. He was impressed when she said that it
had been owned by an emperor and later housed in
St. Mark's Cathedral in Venice, and that she could
prove it.

It occurred to Walcott that he might be able to
buy the relic itself from her for next to nothing. Mara
was being supported by her father, but not very
well. She'd no doubt be grateful. The alicorn was
probably just a piece of carved elephant tusk, but its
historical value might make it worth obtaining. Besides, he might even find someone who thought it
was a real unicorn's horn, and that would greatly
increase its value. But he didn't want to sound too
eager, or Mara would want too much for it. So he
hadn't said anything that first night.

But a week later, when he saw Mara at the Sorbonne, Walcott invited her to go see the cave paintings with him in southwestern France. On the
second day of the trip, he'd casually asked her about
selling the relic to him, but she hadn't given him an

answer. She said she would think about it. Well, she'd had years to think. Her time was up, and he was going to get it one way or another. Walcott blew out a cloud of smoke as the door of the tavern opened, and a man in a fancy wool suit stepped outside. *Calderone. So he's been over there drinking while I'm waiting out here. The bloody . . . Control yourself, Roland. Calderone's going to make you rich.*

The Italian walked with his head held high, and he carried a shiny, black cane even though he didn't seem to need it. He looked out of place in Cortez. It was hard to believe that someone with such an aristocratic demeanor was a leader of a resistance force. But Calderone was intent on overthrowing Benito Mussolini from power, and the two brawny bodyguards, who walked a few paces behind him, showed that he meant business.

Calderone never even looked at Walcott. But as he walked by, he uttered one word: "Inside."

Walcott followed him into the telegraph office and over to a high table used by customers for composing messages while standing. The two thugs stayed outside. "So how did it go?" Calderone spoke under his breath as he took out an expensive-looking fountain pen and opened the bottle of ink on the table.

Walcott stubbed out his cigarette on the floor. "Just like we planned. No problem."

"Are you sure?" Calderone was a handsome man with slicked back hair, a trimmed mustache, and a black mole on his cheek.

"I saw him get picked up myself."

"Good." He scrawled something on a piece of paper. "And our young lady friend?"

"She's not talking yet."

Calderone smiled as he scratched out a few words

and composed another line. "I didn't think she would. But now she's ready to go get it, don't you agree?"

"I think so."

"Good. Something has come up. I can't wait any longer. I have to leave for Rome today."

"But we're so close."

Calderone waved a hand. "It might take another few days yet. I can't afford being away any longer." He handed Walcott an envelope. "You'll find enough money here for your train and boat tickets to Italy, and expenses. When you get the staff, leave immediately. Don't waste any time."

In a deadly cold voice, he added: "And don't let me down. Do you understand?"

Walcott slipped the envelope inside his jacket. "Don't worry."

"So, how are you going to let them escape?" Calderone asked.

Walcott was so pleased about the money and the fact that Calderone wouldn't be breathing down his neck any longer that he had to think a moment to recall his plans. With Jones involved, he knew it probably wasn't going to take much for them to get away. "I was thinking I'd send one of my boys down into the kiva later tonight to get Mara. You know, let Jones think the worst. I'm sure he won't sit still for that."

Calderone chuckled to himself. "That's good. Make it someone who's guarding him. Do it after everyone else is asleep. But make sure Mara and Jones don't suspect anything. Maybe the guard should actually think he's going to get the woman. You know, as a bonus for good work. That'll make it real."

"What if he shoots Jones?" Walcott asked.

"So what? Just make sure he doesn't shoot her."

The Englishman nodded. Even though he thought Calderone was a fool for wasting his time chasing the staff, he had to admit that the Italian was a clever tactician.

Shrewd was the word. More shrewd than Walcott knew, or even suspected.

Indy paced under a cottonwood tree outside the boardinghouse. He wracked his mind, trying to make some sense of everything that had happened. Who was the guy with the English accent? Why did Shannon take off with his car? And why did Mara say she wasn't going to be able to meet him, and then arrive here anyhow, just to go off to Mesa Verde to look for him? Why Mesa Verde?

It was baffling. All of it.

"Professor Jones?"

Indy turned as Smitty stepped out of the house after taking a box of groceries inside. "I've been thinking. Maybe your friend just went for a drive while you were studying the rock drawings. He could be back there now waiting for you. We can ride down on the buckboard if you want."

Indy shook his head. "If that's the case, he can just drive back here himself when he gets tired of waiting for me." Even though Indy doubted that Shannon had simply stolen his car and gone off on his own, he couldn't imagine him hanging around Sand Island for long, either. Something else was going on, and the more he thought about it, the more he suspected that all the puzzling occurrences were somehow related.

"Smitty, if Mara went to Mesa Verde, spent a day

looking for me, then came back, would she be here yet?"

The old man ran his fingers through his beard. "Probably not for another day."

"Does she come around here much?"

"The last couple of years since she got back from Italy, we've been seeing more and more of her. Where did you meet her? She didn't say much about you."

"Paris . . . well actually it was in southwestern France on a field trip."

"I'll tell you one thing about her. She's an independent sort. Women never used to be that way, you know. This one goes off to Paris and Rome by herself to get more education than any woman needs. Sometimes she goes wandering around the desert alone, too. That's dangerous for a girl."

"Can I see the room where she stayed, and maybe talk to Rosie?"

Smitty shrugged. "Don't see why not. She's a little mad at me right now because she wants her old granddaddy to move in with us. He lives way out in the middle of nowhere. But I'm against it. We lose another room, and anyhow that old man can take care of hisself."

They walked into the two-story house and climbed the stairs. "You got a great house, Smitty."

"Biggest one in Bluff," Smitty said, matter-of-factly. "Most of the houses here were built around 1880 after the Mormons arrived. I'm not a Mormon myself. I like my booze too much. At least, I used to. Don't drink anymore. Decided to rent out the extra bedrooms, because people kept coming around all the time, asking if I rented rooms."

He paused at the top of the stairs. Then he added

in a quieter voice, "Besides, I needed the money. Most of what I put away from prospecting went right to Mara's education. I promised her mama that I'd pay as long as she wanted to go to school, and that girl just kept on going."

"Mara recommended the place in one of her letters," Indy said. "I'm surprised she didn't mention her father owned it."

"I'm not. That's the way she is with me. She only recommended it because it's where she figured she would be staying."

Smitty opened the door of a room and they moved inside. The room was clean and tidy. "Did Rosie find anything when she cleaned after Mara left?"

"Don't think so."

Indy looked under the bed and in the closet. He went through the dresser drawers, then walked over to a desk. There was a Bible and a copy of the Book of Mormon in one of the drawers. Nothing else. He was about to give up when he noticed a slip of paper in a trash basket next to the desk. It was a note to Mara's attention. Indy read it aloud.

*"I got here early, and went directly to Mesa Verde. Why don't you join me? I'll be at Spruce Tree House. Indy."*

"Well, I'll be," Smitty said.

"You didn't see it before now?" Indy asked.

"Nope."

Just then Rosie walked by and Smitty called to her. She was a Navajo, who looked to be in her midforties, probably twenty years younger than Smitty. Her long raven hair was tied in a braid. Her skin was bronze, and her face was round, with high cheekbones and dark eyes. "Do you know anything about this here note?"

She glanced at it. "I found it in an envelope a couple of days ago. It was taped to the outside door. I gave it to Mara when she arrived."

"Thanks for telling me," Smitty groused.

"Nothing to tell you," she shot back. "It was just an envelope."

"Did she say anything to you about the message?" Indy asked.

Rosie shook her head. "She just said she thought that she'd be back in a few days. That's all."

"Been many strangers around here lately?" Indy asked.

"Just your friend. Did he find you?"

"Jack? You saw Jack?"

"No, the Englishman," Rosie said. "I forgot to tell you about him when you checked in."

"I already told him about that fellow," Smitty interrupted.

"But he was back again. I told him you were at Sand Island. I thought he was going right out to look for you."

"I don't know what's going on," Indy said, "but it's starting to come together."

"What do you mean?" Smitty asked.

"I've got to get to Mesa Verde. I've got the feeling Mara's in trouble, and so is Jack."

"Well, let's hop in the buckboard and get on out there," Smitty said.

Kivas were never meant to serve as jails, Mara thought ruefully. The round underground chambers were the spiritual centers of Anasazi villages. They were places where the ancients gathered for sacred rites, where they supposedly journeyed into the underworld or transformed into wild beasts and prowled the desert or flew to distant places. But here she was, a prisoner, at the mercy of a man who she had thought died four years ago.

Even though it was abysmally dark in the kiva, Mara had explored every inch of it. It was about fifteen feet across and at least ten feet deep. Its single entrance, a hole in the center of the roof, was covered and of course there was no ladder to assist her in escaping. She had visited enough Anasazi ruins to know the layout of the kivas. Directly below the entrance was the ancient fire pit. On one side was a block of stone that had been used to deflect the heat and behind it was a ventilator shaft in the wall. Unfortunately, the shaft was far too narrow to even consider as an escape route.

Opposite the fire pit was the *sipapu*. It was a fist-sized hole in the floor, a symbolic opening in the earth through which the Anasazis thought their ancient ancestors had risen from the underworld. Mara wasn't one to believe in spirits and ghosts, but now she wished that the spirits of the ancients were around and could see what was going on. Maybe they would protect her from these horrible men, who had forced her into the kiva.

She figured she'd been here nearly twenty-four hours now. But how long could they hold her before the authorities showed up? Mesa Verde, after all, was a national monument, and Spruce Tree House one of the larger pueblos.

Yesterday had been the worst day of her life. Walcott and his brutish sidekick had climbed down into the kiva with her and had demanded to know where the staff was hidden. She kept telling him she didn't know. And each time, the heavy-browed goon had gestured obscenely with his torch. It wasn't hard to imagine what he had in mind for her. But Walcott, thankfully, held him at bay. She'd slept fitfully and she hadn't seen Walcott now for hours. Maybe he'd finally realized that she was telling the truth, and now he was trying to figure out what to do about it.

Mara heard muffled voices, and suddenly bright sunlight flooded the kiva. She squinted and held a hand in front of her face. A ladder was being lowered through the hole. As her eyes adjusted, she saw a confusion of arms and legs and shouts. Then abruptly a man dropped to the floor beside her.

"Have fun, Jones," someone yelled from above. Then the cover on the hole slammed shut.

"Indy?"

"Who's there?" a voice answered.

Even though she hadn't seen Indy for years, she knew immediately it wasn't him. It was a trick. "You're not Indy."

The man made a scraping noise as he moved. "Never said I was. Who are you? Where are we?"

"Stay where you are!" she snapped.

"I'm not going anywhere. My name's Shannon. Just tell me what's going on, and I'd appreciate it if you'd take off this blindfold and untie my hands."

Mara walked around behind him. Her eyes were adjusted to the dark; she could vaguely make out his shape. She pulled off his blindfold.

"Either I'm blind or—"

"It's dark," Mara snapped. "Why would Walcott think you're Indy?"

"Who's Walcott? What's going on anyhow? If this is a joke, it's not a bit funny."

"We're at Spruce Tree House in Mesa Verde."

"Tree house. It looks more like a hole in the ground."

"You're in a kiva."

"What's that?"

"I guess you're not an archaeologist."

"You got that right. Now who are you and what are we doing in this hole?"

"My name's Mara Rogers. And I don't know what you're doing here. I was expecting to find Indy, and ran into Walcott and his goons."

Shannon shook his head in exasperation. "Your name doesn't ring a bell anymore than Walcott's. How about enlightening me? How do you know Indy, and why would you think he was here?"

"I knew him in France when we were both students at the Sorbonne."

"Oh, is that right? I lived in Paris at the same time. I don't remember him ever mentioning anyone named Mara, and he didn't say anything about planning to meet a woman here, either. I'm not sure I believe you."

"You must be the old college roommate he mentioned in one of his letters. I left Paris a short time after we met. We've kept in touch by mail. But I'm surprised he didn't tell you we were going to meet here."

"He never said a word about you. I didn't know he had pen pals, either. Why would he keep in touch with you?"

"The usual reason, I suppose. We liked each other, and he was interested in my work."

"Which is?"

"I'm an art history professor at the University of New Mexico. I've also been drawing and cataloging Anasazi petroglyphs for the last couple of years."

"You mean . . ."

"Rock art."

"Yeah, I've seen Kokopelli."

"You've been to Sand Island," she said.

"How'd you know?"

"It's close to Bluff and it's got lots of Kokopellis."

"Okay, now that we know each other, how about helping me get my hands loose?" Shannon asked.

"Turn around." She went to work on the binding.

"What are they going to do with us?"

"I don't know."

"What's behind it?" Shannon persisted.

"You'd never guess, not in a million years."

"Give me a hint. Maybe I can help work things out with this Walcott. Who is he, anyhow?"

She stiffened, and edged away from him. Anger and fear radiated from her like heat.

"What's wrong?"

"Walcott put you up to this, didn't he? That's why I haven't seen him."

"I don't know what you're talking about."

"Maybe you're Indy's friend, maybe you're not," she said. "Either way, you can tell Walcott I don't know where it is. Period."

# 7

## ON THE ROPES

Shannon adjusted his legs as he leaned against the wall of the kiva. He'd been here several hours now, and in that time they'd heard twice from their captors. Once, someone had lowered a pot that contained a couple of boiled potatoes and bits of stringy meat. The other time the pot was removed, their chamber pot was emptied, and they were given a jug of water. He'd tried to talk with whoever was above, but to no avail. His captors still thought he was Indy, and Mara thought he was working for Walcott, whoever he was. And nobody was talking to him.

Mara kept scraping her foot against the ground, and the sound was bothering him. "What are doing, digging your way to China?"

She didn't answer.

He tried another tack. "If Indy was here, would he know why this was happening to us?"

She stopped scraping the ground. "No." After a

moment, she added, "He might think he did, but he wouldn't."

"What do you mean?"

"It's something that goes back to the time when I first met him."

"How'd you meet him, anyhow?"

She told him.

"Now I know who you are. You're the one Indy was with when the crazy prof tried to kill him in the cave."

"That's right. Walcott is the professor. He was going to kill Indy and me."

"But I thought he was dead."

"So did I."

"What's he want, anyhow?"

Mara didn't respond for several seconds. "A unicorn's horn. He's wanted it ever since I met him."

The setting sun cast an eerie orange glow on the landscape as Indy and Smitty turned onto the road to the ruins. They'd been traveling nearly four hours and Indy felt like every bone in his body was bruised. Smitty pulled back on the reins, slowing the buckboard to a stop. He jumped spryly to the ground. "Think we better stop here."

"How far are we from Spruce Tree House?" Indy rubbed his back as he climbed down.

"About a half mile. We walk from here. My guess is that we're dealing with more than one bad guy. Maybe a gang of them."

"Can you find the way from here? It's going to be dark before you know it."

"That's the best time to approach them," Smitty said. "I can find the way. Don't you worry about that, Professor."

"It sounds like you got this all figured out," Indy said.

"I'm just your guide. You're going to have to do the tough part yourself."

Indy had had the feeling all along that getting Shannon and Mara out wasn't going to be a picnic, and said as much.

Smitty grabbed a thick coil of rope from the back of the buckboard and handed it to Indy. "Not only that, but just getting in there is going to take a bit of serious monkey business. The easiest way to get to Spruce Tree House is to go down from the opposite side of the gorge. But that's like coming in the front door. Too dangerous. Even at night. Unless you had an army with you."

"What's the alternative?" Indy asked.

"We drop down on 'em from above. Or at least you do. That's where the rope there is gonna come in handy."

As they followed the trail through the growing darkness, Indy asked Smitty why he knew his way around Mesa Verde so well.

Smitty glanced back over his shoulder. "You ever heard of Richard Wetherill?"

"Of course. I'm an archaeologist, remember?" Wetherill's brother, Al, had been the first white man to see Mesa Verde. After the discovery in 1887, Richard dug out the cliff dwellings and went to the Chicago World's Fair of 1893 to display the artifacts.

"Well, when I was a young fella, I worked with the Wetherills. Their ranch wasn't far from here. That was before I got into prospecting. During the winter months, when there wasn't much to do on the ranch, I joined them in exploring the ruins here. I got to know Mesa Verde real good."

Indy was impressed. Mara had never mentioned that fact about her father. In fact, she'd barely mentioned him in her letters. "It must have been something, being the first ones to dig the ruins."

"Richard tried his best to do it the right way, too. When he went into Grand Gulch, he took lots of photographs before he ever lifted a shovel. He labeled everything he found, and he made a plan of the ruins. But you archaeologists crucified him."

Indy knew that many of his associates still considered Wetherill a vandal and a pillager because he lacked any archaeological training. In the early years, Wetherill didn't take any notes, sold relics to whoever would buy them, and destroyed sites beyond the point of further research. But Indy had always sensed some jealousy in those sentiments, because Wetherill had also made considerable contributions to Southwest archaeology.

"Fifty years from now his work will be recognized," Indy said.

Before Wetherill, no one had ever used stratigraphy, the means of dating artifacts according to the depth at which they were found. For twenty years, archaeologists scoffed at Wetherill's contention that an older culture, which he called the Basketmakers, had preceded the Cliff Dwellers at Mesa Verde, and called him a charlatan. In 1914, the Basketmaker culture was verified, but by then Wetherill was dead.

Smitty stopped as they reached an open area that led to the lip of a cliff. Indy was ready to walk out to the edge, but Smitty grabbed his arm and pointed across the opening. At first, Indy couldn't tell what he saw. Then he spotted the silhouette of a man seated on a rock. Indy glanced at Smitty and saw that the old-timer looked surprised.

"Be damned if I'm gonna get myself killed," Smitty grumbled.

Indy laid down the rope and motioned Smitty to stay where he was. He dropped to his hands and knees and slowly crawled forward, his .455 Webley holstered on his hip and his whip hooked to his belt. Fortunately, he'd left the revolver in his room before he and Shannon had gone to Sand Island. He moved silently forward; he was confident he could overtake the guard. The trick was doing it without alerting the others below. The guard unexpectedly stood up and looked around. Indy froze in a crouched position just fifteen feet from him. The man had huge, beefy arms and an inner tube of fat around his gut. He took several leisurely steps in Indy's direction, holding a rifle under his arm.

*Stop,* Indy ordered silently. Another couple of steps and the guard would spot him. *I'm a rock,* Indy said to himself. *He doesn't see me.*

The man was about take another step when he turned and stared across the opening. He shifted the rifle into his hands and started toward the path. *Swell. Smitty must have given himself away.* Indy loosened his whip and stalked his prey. The guard, unaware of him, continued forward.

Indy rose to his full height and, like a hawk about to dive on a rodent, focused on his moving target. He twirled the whip once around his head and let it fly. It snagged the guard in midstride, wrapping several times around his neck. He dropped his rifle and grabbed at his throat. Indy jerked hard and reeled him in as if he were landing an overgrown carp. The

surprised man gagged and struggled to reach his
rifle.

When he realized he couldn't get it, he turned and
rushed toward his assailant. Indy was caught by surprise, and the guard bowled him over and grabbed
him by his throat. Now they were both choking. The
man's hands were powerful and his thumbs pressed
deep into Indy's windpipe. Indy was about to pass
out when the thug groaned and toppled to the side.

"You okay there?" Smitty stood over him bran-
dishing the butt of his .45.

Indy sat up, rubbing his throat. "Just fine, Smitty.
But thanks for the help."

Smitty pulled a handkerchief from his pocket, and
quickly gagged the man as Indy reclaimed his whip.
"Thought I was gonna have to shoot him there for a
moment."

"Tell you the truth, I thought he was going to
shoot you."

"That would've spoiled my evening," Smitty muttered. "Okay, Professor, you—"

"Hey, do me a favor and just call me Indy, okay?"

"Indy. Right. You go on and take a look over the
ledge. I'll tie him up pretty as a Christmas package."

Indy nodded and moved to the lip of the cliff. He
dropped to his hands and knees and peered over the
side. A faint glow emanated from somewhere under
the overhang. Fingers of smoke curled upward,
swollen with the smell of cooking meat.

Then he spotted something else—a pinpoint of
orange light in the darkness. At first he thought it
was a firefly, but the movement was too repetitive,
back and forth with pauses on each end of the arc. A
cigarette. He figured it was attached to another
guard, even though he couldn't see him.

Indy imagined the rest of the culprits sitting around the camp fire, dinner plates in hand. He'd drop in on them and catch them by surprise.

"Hey," Smitty hissed. "Try this." He handed Indy the rope, which he had tied to the trunk of a nearby piñon. Indy tugged at it, then walked over to the tree. The pine seemed sturdy enough to hold his weight. He examined the knot. "You can trust my knots," Smitty said in a raspy whisper. "I used to rope steers."

"Never hurts to double-check." Indy patted the old man on the back. "Even the experts goof up once in a while."

"You better be ready for what's waitin' down there for ya. I'll take care of things up here."

"Yeah," Indy said grimly.

"We can always go back and get the sheriff."

"It's a little late for that. Mara and Jack might not make it till morning."

"Just checking on your nerve, Professor. I mean Indy." The truth was Shannon and Mara might already be dead, but Smitty didn't want to even think it, much less say it aloud.

"Let's get on with it. You sure I got enough rope?"

Smitty gauged the distance between the piñon and the edge of the cliff and nodded. "It's a little farther than I expected, but you've got a good eighty feet there to go down on. Don't worry about it."

"Okay. When I'm down, you better pull up the rope. I don't want it to give me away."

"Good thinking. I'll be watching for you."

"Just don't fall asleep on me," Indy said.

"Don't worry," Smitty answered. "I'm one of those somniacs."

"*In*somniac," Indy said as he headed to the edge

of the cliff. "Give me an hour. If you haven't heard anything from me by then, go get the sheriff."

"Will do."

Smitty unraveled the coil of rope as Indy stared down, looking for the telltale sign of the guard. But now there was no cigarette to guide him. What if the guard was standing right under the cliff? Then Indy glimpsed the flash of a match as the man lit another cigarette. He'd only moved a few feet. Indy threaded the rope through the loop at the end, slipped it under his arms, and tightened it.

"Here goes everything." He motioned to Smitty and sidled over the edge. At first it was just like walking down a steep, rocky hill with a safety belt. He stepped as lightly as possible, taking care not to loosen any rocks that would signal his approach. But after a few steps, the cliff fell off into a vertical drop. He touched his foot twice to the wall, then he was past the overhang and suspended in inky space.

Smitty fed the rope in lengths of two feet to three feet, and with each release, the rope bit into Indy's chest. He was a marionette dangling in the murky shadows, waiting for the black curtain to rise and the show to begin.

Down, down, down. The light from the camp fire drew his attention. It was coming from inside one of the buildings in the ancient pueblo. None of the structures under the overhang had roofs, so the light radiated through the open ceiling, producing a glow like a large, but weak, flickering flashlight.

Great. They wouldn't see him. He shifted his focus to the guard. He could make out his shape now and saw that his back was turned. Another point in Indy's favor. He considered taking him captive and using him as a shield. He decided against it. He didn't know if these guys had any sense of loyalty to their companions. If they didn't, his threat to shoot the guard wouldn't produce any results. Besides, the guard might give him away before he was ready to reveal himself to the others.

Then another thought occurred to him. What if Shannon and Mara weren't in the building with the others? Maybe they were being held in another part of the ruins. In that case, Indy might be able to get the information from the guard, then escape with his friends before the others were alerted. That sounded like a much easier alternative than fighting all of them. Besides, he didn't even know how many he was up against.

Suddenly, the jerking motion stopped. He waited and swayed, his feet still seven or eight feet above the ground. He felt a slight jerk, but this time he didn't go down any further and he knew that Smitty was signaling that he was out of rope.

There would've been plenty of rope if Smitty had found a tree closer to the edge. Now what was he going to do, just hang here until the guard found him? He jerked on the rope, but it had no effect. He couldn't even let Smitty know he wanted to be pulled up. Just swell.

Indy lifted himself up several inches, then, hanging by one hand, he worked at loosening the noose. If he could slide out of the loop and hang by his hands, he'd only have a few feet to drop. A *big* if.

He switched hands as the one holding his weight started to tremble, and the loop snapped tight again, constricting his chest, and knocking the wind out of his lungs. He waited until his arms were rested, then he started over again. This time he managed to make the loop nearly large enough to slip over his arms.

He worked one arm under the noose, but his other arm couldn't hold him any longer and suddenly the rope tightened around his neck and left arm.

He gagged at the pressure on his throat, kicked his legs, and pulled at the rope with his free hand. He couldn't get it over his head, and the rope pressed at his already sore windpipe. His fedora was knocked from his head and fell into the darkness. Finally, he groped at his belt and found his knife. He eased it between his throat and his trapped arm and sawed. He was almost through the rope when Smitty jerked hard and the blade nicked his forehead.

*Smitty! Please, don't pull. Not now.*

He sawed away again, desperate now, hurrying to finish. If Smitty started pulling him up, it was all over. He'd never make it; he'd either fall or choke. But that was exactly what Smitty started to do. As Smitty pulled him, the rope tightened even further. Indy gasped for air. Then the rope slipped from Smitty's hands; Indy fell a dozen feet. The remaining strands near his neck snapped. He dangled a moment by one hand, then dropped in a heap to the ground.

He raised his head, rubbed his throat as he drew in a deep breath, and looked around for the guard, for the whole gang. No one had seen him. He crawled over to a stone wall, grabbing his hat on the way, then cautiously rose to his feet. He looked over to where he'd last seen the guard. Gone, the guy was gone. Maybe he'd seen Indy hanging from the cliff and had left to get the others. But that wasn't Indy's only concern. Now, unless Smitty tied the rope to a tree closer to the cliff, his escape route was cut off. Worry about that later, he thought.

Indy edged away from the wall. A bright, plump gibbous moon was suspended above the trees. In its light he saw the guard strolling along the outskirts of the cliff dwelling. Indy breathed a little easier. But now it was time to act, and he did.

# 8

## SHOOT-OUT AT MESA VERDE

Walcott reeled down the trail as it descended into the canyon. Fortunately, there was a moon tonight and the path was easy to follow. He was in no condition to walk in daylight, much less in the darkness. When he was certain that Calderone had left town, he'd dropped into a tavern and bought everyone a round of drinks, then another. Before he knew it a couple of hours had slipped away. Now he had to get to Spruce Tree House as fast as possible, and make arrangements for Mara's escape.

A branch snapped in his face and he cursed. A soft mattress, even in one of Cortez's fleabag hotels would've felt real good tonight. But he prided himself on his ability to hold his liquor. He had responsibilities and he'd be damned if he'd let things get out of control. While he still had no idea where the staff was, he was closer now than ever, and he was confident of success. In fact, he'd assured Calderone that he would be on his way to Rome within days.

Walcott couldn't wait to see the look on Jones's face when he told him the tables had turned. It would be a pleasure to threaten him, to see how Jones reacted when he thought he was about to be killed. Walcott had thought a lot about Jones over the past few years, about how the brazen graduate student had ruined his career in archaeology. Yet, he'd known that someday things would work in his favor again, and when he'd found out that an archaeologist named Jones was joining Mara, he couldn't have been more pleased.

Walcott had survived his dive into the underground river because of air pockets between the water and stone. He'd been carried downstream, and when the river emerged from the hills, he'd pulled himself out. An hour later, he'd hopped onto a freight train heading north. He'd returned to London, and had hidden himself away for months. Finally, when he realized that no one was pursuing him, he went back to Paris and began looking for Mara. As it turned out, he found her in Rome, and then everything had started coming together.

He wondered what his boys were doing right now. They better not have touched Mara. If there was any trouble, he wouldn't pay them. Not a cent. He'd warned them.

He paused and reached into his pack to pull out a flask. He swallowed deeply, enjoying the burning sensation as the whiskey found its way to his stomach. He screwed the top back on, and stepped to the side of the trail where he opened his fly. A stream of urine splattered the bushes. He imagined himself as an ornery mountain lion marking his territory. "Nobody comes past this mark," he said aloud. "My territory."

He started as he heard the snap of a twig. What was that? Maybe a real bobcat. He buttoned his fly and hurried on. *Better get back before I'm somebody's supper.* The trail wound upward toward the ruins, and he trudged along as best he could.

There was something he was forgetting. Something important. The thought had been nagging him ever since he'd started drinking. He should know what it was.

He sat down on a log to rest a moment and gazed up through the trees toward the moon as a cloud passed over it. What was it? His mind was like the bloody moon glowing in the night sky and the whiskey was the dark cloud, obscuring his memory. He laughed aloud. *You're a silly old fart when you get drunk, Walcott, old chap. Now get up and march.*

The luck of the heavens was with Indy. The moon was shrouded now and it would be easier to move undetected through the ruins. He glanced toward the building where the men were eating. Orange light flickered through a small, square window. He decided to see if Mara and Shannon were there before he dealt with the guard. He moved quickly from one building to the next until he reached his target. He pressed his back against the wall and edged toward the window. He smelled coffee, and heard voices speaking over the crackling of wood.

"I don't know who the boss thinks he is. We do his dirty work for him and he runs to town."

"Yeah, he's probably drinking and whoring and laughing at us right now," someone answered.

"I say we go get the girl and have our own fun," the first voice said.

"Wait a minute. He said he wouldn't pay us if anything happened to her."

"Maybe we should wait," someone else put in.

"Don't tell me you guys are afraid of that limey. If he doesn't pay us, we'll take it from him. Now who's in with me?"

Indy peered through the window. He counted four grizzled faces around the fire. A man with thick eyebrows and a flattened nose glared at the others. Probably the one doing the badgering.

"I'm with you, Jimbo," one of the others said.

"Me, too," another echoed.

They all turned to the fourth man, who said: "All right, all right. You guys go on, I'll clean up here, and be right with you."

"You're gonna be last," one of the men said.

Jimbo grinned, displaying a mouthful of jagged teeth. "I guess he wants his coffee before dessert." He laughed like a maniac and they all stood up.

This was it. Indy pulled out his Webley as the first of the men emerged from the building. They were going to lead him right to Mara and Shannon, but after that it was going to get dicey. Real dicey. The others stepped outside. They were only a dozen feet from where Indy was crouched.

Suddenly the guard appeared. "Hey, I just saw the boss. He's coming up the trail. He'll be here in a minute."

Jimbo cursed under his breath. The clouds had drifted away from the moon and Indy could see the man's sunken, beady eyes. "Let's go meet him. We can still have our way and get our money, too. There's only one of him."

"What are you talking about?" the guard asked.

"We're gonna have a little fun with our lady friend."

"About time. I've been thinking about it myself for the last couple of hours."

As they walked away, Indy started to follow. But he accidentally kicked a stone. The men stopped and turned. Jimbo moved forward, and spotted him in the shadows. "Who's there?"

Indy raised the Webley and grinned. "I'm the guy with the big gun."

So far Smitty hadn't heard a sound from below. He didn't know what it meant. He crawled to the edge of the cliff and peered down. At first, he couldn't see anyone. Then in the silver glow of the moonlight, he spotted a man climbing the path leading toward the ruins. The man paused, opened a container, and took a drink.

Smitty heard a noise behind him and turned just in time to see the guard hopping toward him. He reached for his .45, but the beefy guard was already on top of him, and he was nearly smothered in the man's fleshy girth. Smitty struggled to say something to him, but the guard drove an elbow into Smitty's midsection, knocking the wind out of him. He forced Smitty closer and closer to the edge of the cliff. Rocks bit into Smitty's back, dust caked in his mouth. He knew that any second now he would tumble over the side and plunge to a certain death. He grabbed the guard around his throat with one hand just as the man shoved Smitty's legs over the edge. But his free hand found the rope.

"I'm too old for this nonsense," Smitty mumbled as he hung in mid-air. The guard forced Smitty's hand from his throat, but Smitty whipped the rope around the man's neck. As the guard struggled to move away from the ledge, Smitty's weight choked him. His eyes bulged, and looked as if they were about to pop from his head. But the more he fought, the tighter the rope got, and slowly, his resistance weakened until he finally stopped moving.

Smitty climbed up the rope and to safety, over the prone guard, whose neck apparently had snapped. "Sorry about that, big fella."

He started to stand up when the man's knees caught his foot and dragged him back down. "Hey, you're dead," he yelped. He pulled, but the guard's knee-grip tightened on his foot and the man rolled precariously close to the cliff. Smitty pulled his .45 and cracked it over the guard's head. The man went limp and Smitty pulled his foot free.

"Now, stay dead," he growled. He pushed his legs against the man's chest, and rolled him over the cliff.

Walcott wiped his forehead as he reached the top of the trail just outside the pueblo. He dug into his pack for his flask, and shook it. Just a few drops left. He unscrewed the top and took a swallow. Then he moved ahead into the pueblo and looked around. Now where were all his boys? No one was even guarding the entrance. Anyone could walk right up here. Angrily, he flung his empty flask back down the trail. He wasn't paying these guys to sit around the camp fire like a bunch of boy scouts. Hell, boy scouts would be more on the ball.

It occurred to him that they might've gotten ornery and gone after the woman. He hurried over to the kiva, lifted the cover, and peered down the hole. He couldn't see a thing.

"Who's down there?"

"Who do you think?" a man's voice answered in a surly tone. At first he thought the worst. He was too late.

"That's Walcott," Mara said. "Roland, let us out of here."

Walcott smiled. "What's wrong, Mara, not enjoying your company? Hello, Jones. It's been a long time."

"I've got news for you, Wally. I'm not Jones."

"That's right," Mara said. "It's his friend. You got the wrong guy."

Walcott was dumbfounded, but then he heard a hollow, metallic clang from just below the village. His flask. Someone had kicked it. He slid the wooden panel back over the hole in the kiva's roof, pulled out his revolver, and crept forward. Who was out there, anyhow?

In the moonlight he saw two men moving along the trail, then three more emerged from the shadows. All of them carried rifles.

A stray thought flashed through his whiskey-sodden brain. What happened to the body of the Ute his men had killed? He'd never seen it. That was what had been bothering him. The Indian must have survived and gotten away.

He scrambled back to the kiva, opened the cover, and lowered the ladder. "Get back. I'm coming down." He aimed his revolver into the hole. "One wrong move and you're dead."

"Everybody throw down your guns or pretty boy here gets it between the eyes," Indy barked as he stepped forward, keeping the Webley aimed at Jimbo.

"Do what he says," Jimbo ordered, and the men dropped their weapons.

"Okay, where are they, tough guy?"

"What are you talking about?" Jimbo answered innocently.

"My friends. I want them now."

Something glinted in the man's eyes; his lips pulled back from his teeth. "You made one mistake, big man."

A body flew like a missile from behind and slammed into the small of Indy's back. He tumbled to the ground; his gun fired harmlessly. He'd forgotten about the guy who stayed inside to clean up.

They rolled over and over, amid shouts, dust, and darkness. His gun was knocked from his hand. The man swung, but Indy blocked the blow, and flipped him over his head. Another of the thugs dropped on him, but Indy caught him with both feet and kicked him into the path of another assailant, knocking both of them to the ground.

Then Jimbo was on him, pummeling him with his fists. Indy groped blindly for the Webley, but just as his fingers tightened over it, a boot crushed his hand. He howled in pain, snapping his head up. Jimbo was glaring down at him, his beady eyes two beacons of hate. Indy was surrounded, and everyone was aiming their weapons at him. Blood dripped from a new gash on his forehead into a bruised eye. More blood oozed from his upper lip.

"Good try, buddy. Good try," Jimbo said. "Now we're gonna put some holes in you." Jimbo cocked his revolver, and that was when a rifle shot exploded behind them.

"Who are you?" Jimbo called out.

Several shadowy figures with rifles raised skyward

stood a dozen paces away. "You killed my grandfather," one of them said. "You're coming with us."

"That's what you think," Jimbo shouted and fired on the men.

Shannon had no idea why the Englishman had climbed into the kiva with them, but as he watched Walcott's eyes darting nervously toward the roof he realized that something must have happened. Walcott seemed frightened of whatever it was.

"What's going on out there?" Shannon asked.

Walcott waved the gun at him. "None of your business. Who are you, anyhow?"

"What's it matter to you, Wally?"

Footsteps trampled across the top of the kiva.

"Sounds like a parade," Shannon quipped.

"Shut up," hissed Walcott.

He'd no sooner spoken than a single shot was fired. Shannon started counting the seconds. He reached twelve when a flurry of gunfire erupted. From inside the kiva, it sounded like an explosion of popcorn kernels.

Walcott climbed up the ladder and moved the cover away. "Get up here, Mara!" She did as he said, and he pulled her out.

"What about me, Wally?" Shannon yelled.

"I'll take care of you." Walcott jabbed his gun into the hole and fired three times. "That should shut him up." He kicked the cover closed, and hustled Mara away.

Everyone was scrambling for cover and firing wildly. The man closest to Indy was hit in the neck; blood spurted as he reeled in a circle, crumpled to his knees, and fell on top of Indy.

The gunfire lasted several seconds, then turned sporadic and distant. Indy lost track of time. The man on top of him groaned and shuttered; Indy felt his death like a black rose wilting, shriveling, and crumbling. He smelled blood and a horrible stench of death. He pushed the body away from him, no longer caring what awaited him.

Indy raised his head, still dazed from the beating he'd taken. He crawled a few feet, then slowly stood up. His head was spinning. He felt sick. Besides the man who'd fallen on him, he saw three other blood-soaked bodies.

Beyond the scene of death, pale beams of moonlight illuminated the pueblo. A light breeze rippled through the ruins, as if to carry off the spirits of the newly deceased. Indy stepped over bodies and moved out toward the edge of the cliff. He heard a couple more shots from the valley as the gun battle continued.

"Jones, Jones!" called an eerie voice from above. He spotted Smitty leaning over the cliff. "By God, you're alive."

"What happened?"

"I saw it all. I wanted to warn you, but there was nothing I could do."

"Who were they?"

"Utes. Musta had a real good reason to go rampagin' on like that."

"Indy!"

He looked around for the ghostly voice; he heard it again. It was muffled, but unmistakably Shannon's and it seemed to be coming from somewhere below him. Then he saw the ladder lying on the ground. He walked over to a trapdoor, and pushed it aside. He stared into the dark hole of a kiva.

"Jack?" Indy saw a head of wild red hair as a ray of moonlight penetrated the kiva. Then he glimpsed Shannon's soiled face. It was smeared with blood.

"What happened? Are you okay?"

"I'm all right. A bullet hit my arm. Passed right on through. It's not bad."

"Where's Mara?"

"Gone. He took her with him."

Indy lowered the ladder and helped Shannon out as best he could. "Who took her?"

"Walcott. Your old English caveman buddy from Paris."

"Walcott?" It took a moment for the name to find a face . . . and an unpleasant memory. "Roland!" Somehow, he wasn't surprised.

More distant shots rang out. "I've got to help Mara."

"Wait a minute!" Shannon yelled. "Watch out for—" But Indy vanished from sight before he could say another word.

Indy bolted down the trail leading away from Spruce Tree House. Knotted roots conspired to trip him. Branches slapped at him with a vengeance, and tentacles of vines reached out to strangle him. But nothing was going to stop him. He hurried on and on through the gloomy, nightmarish landscape.

He'd run for a couple of minutes before he realized that his Webley was in his hand. But he had no recollection of picking it up, or even any memory of carrying it. He had to find Mara and get her away from the crazed Walcott. That was all that mattered.

He'd no sooner fixed his mind on the thought when he burst into an open space, and there she was. Her bloodied, lifeless body lay in the moonlight. He rushed forward, but suddenly his feet were pulled out from underneath him, and the world flipped upside down. He was caught in a snare—a man-made trap.

Abruptly, as if on cue, an inverted figure darted out from the shadows, a knife in hand. Indy fired the Webley and the man fell to the ground. Another followed, then another. Indy fired twice and the would-be assailants collapsed. He heard a yell, and twisted around to see more of Walcott's henchmen. He fired and fired, emptying his revolver; the attackers dropped one after another. But still more rushed toward him. He swung the butt of the gun at the first one, striking him squarely between the eyes; the gun fell from his hand. Another thug stabbed at his throat, but Indy grabbed the man's forearm and struggled with him, wrenching his arm back until he dropped the knife. Then he threw an awkward, upside down punch, and his fist landed squarely against the man's forehead.

Indy unhitched his whip as someone else dashed toward him. He snared the man around the ankles, sending him to the ground, but more followed. How many were there, anyhow? He hurled the whip over his feet and onto a tree limb. He quickly climbed hand-over-hand, grabbed the branch, and pulled himself up. He reached for his knife and started sawing at the leather snare around his ankles. But then he looked down to see that he was surrounded by a horde of armed men. Ten times more than he'd seen at the ruins.

"Guess you guys win."

Just as the thugs raised their rifles, Mara stepped out of the forest and reached a hand toward Indy. "Please, help me. Please."

"Help you? What about me? Hey, wait a minute . . ." Something was wrong here. Very wrong.

"Please, Indy. I need your help." She vanished as if she were never there.

"No, wait!"

The guns exploded, and his body shuddered. Then the nightmare started all over again. . . .

9

MARA'S MESSAGE

The gray-haired doctor in the Cortez hospital peered over his wire-rimmed glasses as he carefully dug his forceps into Walcott's shoulder. In spite of the morphine he'd been given, the pain was excruciating. Rivulets of perspiration ran down his forehead, into his eyes, and over his cheeks. He was on the verge of passing out when the doctor held up the forceps.

"Got it." He slapped the bullet into Walcott's palm. "There you go. A momento."

"Thank God," the Englishman said.

"That one wasn't too bad. I've been pulling out lead for nearly forty years. I've seen it all." As he bandaged the wound and fitted a sling over his arm, the doctor told him a couple of gunfight stories, but Walcott wasn't paying any attention. He just wanted to get out of there as fast as possible.

"You won't be able to use this arm for at least a couple of weeks," the doctor said as he finished.

"I don't have to stay in bed, do I?" the Englishman asked.

"Well, you definitely won't feel like dancing tonight, young man. You can expect some pain for awhile, maybe a little fever. Just take it easy. Okay, stay right here. The sheriff's deputy will want to get your story."

"I told you, it was just an accident. You see—"

"Sorry. You've got to talk to the deputy. I just pull out the bullets and patch the holes." The doctor walked out of the room.

Walcott didn't want to talk to the law. They wouldn't believe that he'd accidentally shot himself, especially after they found out about what happened at Mesa Verde.

Two orderlies garbed in white outfits walked into the room and helped him into a wheelchair. "Where you taking me?"

"Out," one of them said.

There was something familiar about the two men, Walcott thought as they quickly wheeled him down the corridor. Both were hulking men with Mediterranean features. Calderone! They were his bodyguards. Walcott turned in his seat and started to say something, but one of the men made a quick motion with his hand silencing him.

He rolled out the front door. A car was waiting; doors opened; hands lifted and guided him. "Watch the arm. Ouch!" Doors closed, and less than five minutes after the bullet had been removed, Walcott was out of the hospital and speeding away.

"Mr. Calderone!" he exclaimed to the man sitting in the back seat with him. "I—I thought you had left."

Calderone tapped the head of his black cane

lightly on Walcott's knee. He cleared his throat, and the mole on his cheek twitched as he spoke. "I thought it best if I stayed a bit longer to see how things went. I wanted to make sure that you didn't run off . . . or go on a drinking binge before your work was completed."

"We ran into trouble. We were attacked."

Calderone waved a hand as if he didn't care to hear about it. "Where is she?"

"I don't know. Everything went bloody crazy. But I'll find her, I promise."

"Indy, wake up."

He blinked open his eyes. He was sweating and gasping for air. But he hadn't been shot. He was in bed, aching all over, and Shannon was standing next to him. "What happened? Where am I?"

"Take it easy," Shannon said. "You were yelling in your sleep."

"Wait a minute. We were at Mesa Verde. I didn't dream that."

"You bet you didn't dream it. You fell into an open kiva and knocked yourself out after you heard the shooting in the valley."

Indy touched his brow and felt a gauze pad and tape. He saw that Shannon's forearm was bandaged. "How long ago was that?"

"Last night."

Indy winced as he sat up. A sharp, piercing pain lanced through the back of his head; he felt a lump at the base of his skull. He looked toward the darkened windows. "What time is it now? Where is the sun?"

"It's almost midnight. You slept most of the day."

"I was getting worried, but the doc said to just let you sleep. Remember when he examined you?"

A hazy image of a dark-haired man with a mustache and a black bag came to mind. "Yeah, sort of."

Indy leaned back on the bed, resting on his elbows. "How'd you get me back to Bluff?"

"Don't ask. Smitty and I had a time of it getting you out of that hole. We finally tied your whip around you and pulled you out. Then we carried you for nearly a half a mile up a trail to the top. He is one strong old man, I'll tell you that."

That probably accounted for part of his dream in which he was caught in a snare and held upside down. But he was more confused than ever. "What happened to Mara and Walcott?"

"We don't know. Smitty wanted to look for her, but I talked him out of it. Too many crazy cowboys and Indians for me, and I wanted to get you out of there. I thought you might be really hurt."

"You just left her down there?"

"We went back this morning. Rangers were all over the place. They'd heard about the trouble, and found five bodies. But no Mara, no Walcott."

"What was it about, anyhow?"

"The grandfather of one of the Utes was stabbed by the same guys who caught me and Mara. I told you all this before. Don't you remember?"

Indy rubbed his face. "It's all sort of a blur." He noticed a piece of gauze taped on one side of Shannon's neck. "What's that? I thought you were hit in the shoulder."

"Turns out I got hit twice, just grazed on the neck, and a superficial wound to the shoulder. I'll live."

"You're lucky."

"The good news is we found your Ford. I drove you back here."

Indy could care less about the car. He recalled Mara being dead, then alive, then vanishing in his dream. What had she said? *Please help me. . . .*

"You think she's alive?"

Shannon shrugged. "Like I said, there's no body."

Indy swung his legs over the side of the bed, ignoring the piercing pain in the back of his head. "We've got to find her, Jack."

"Not tonight, we don't," Shannon said.

Smitty walked into the room. "The darnedest thing I ever heard. Well, Indy, you're back among the living. How are you doing?"

"I'm getting better by the second. What were you talking about a moment ago?"

"One of the sheriff's deputies told me that a doctor at the hospital in Cortez treated a guy with a minor bullet wound who fit Walcott's description. But by the time the Cortez cops got there, he was gone."

"What about Mara?"

"There's a posse looking for the Utes. Seems they might've taken her."

"What's this all about, Indy?" Shannon asked.

"You're asking the wrong person, Jack. You probably know more than I do."

"Can I get you something to eat, Indy?" Smitty asked.

"You sure can. I'm starving."

"Okay, a bowl of my favorite mutton soup coming right up. I got some bread and lard, too."

"Sounds good, but you can save the lard."

"Suit yourself," Smitty said, and he walked off.

"He's been cooking the mutton soup all day. It

beats beef jerky and boiled potatoes, which was what I got in that kiva."

"Sit down, Jack." Indy nodded to the chair next to the bed. "Why were you and Mara kidnapped and put down there?"

"It was supposed to be *you* and Mara. Not me," Shannon said, emphatically. "And I can't figure that woman out. But she's right up your alley, I'll say that much. You two should do real well together."

Indy hadn't even seen Mara yet, much less gotten involved with her. Yet, he was involved and he didn't even know what it was about. "Tell me about it."

"She's up to her eyeballs in the same sort of stuff that's always getting you into trouble."

"Can you be a little more specific for once, Jack?"

"Sure. Your old buddy Walcott was after some weird artifact, and thought she had it."

"What is it?"

"She didn't want to talk much about it, but she called it a unicorn's horn."

Indy repeated what he'd said as if to make sure that he'd heard right. "No such thing. Unicorns are myth. They don't exist; they never did. Why, they weren't even a myth in America. There are thousands of Indian legends and myths filled with animals that talk and reason like people. But there's not one single unicorn in any of them."

"I'm just telling you what she said."

Indy touched the back of his head again as he felt another sharp shoot of pain. "She must have been joking."

"It wasn't the time or place to joke, Indy."

"Maybe it's a horn from a mastodon."

"She said unicorn. How's your head feel?"

"It could be better. What else did she say about this horn?"

"It had something to do with her family, but she didn't go into details."

"Did you say anything to Smitty or anyone else about it?"

"No, I thought I'd wait and tell you first."

Indy smiled. "That's what I like about you, Jack. You know how to play your cards."

Shannon shrugged. "I almost forgot. There's something else she told me." He smiled gamely. "A message, just for you."

"Yeah, what?"

"She said that if I got out alive and she didn't make it, I was to tell you . . ."

"Go on, what did she say?"

"I'm thinking. I memorized it. Okay, this was it: the letters A, M, N, H, and the numbers seventy-three and nineteen-twenty. And then the letters N, C, N."

"Huh?"

"She said you would know what it meant."

"I'm glad she was so confident. Why didn't she just tell you what it meant?"

"She said if I knew what it all stood for, Walcott might get it out of me, and she didn't want him to know."

"Anything else?"

"That's about it. I thought she was going to tell me something more, but then she just said that it was ironic that we were being held captive in a kiva so close to the 'underworld.' "

Indy flopped back down on the bed. "Write those letters and numbers down for me, will you? I'll have to think about it."

"Wait a minute. There was something else. I almost forgot."

"What's that?"

"The letters B, T, B, H. That goes at the end of the message."

Indy rolled over. "Swell."

Smitty opened the trophy case filled with Anasazi artifacts in his sunny library and picked out a piece of corrugated pottery. He ran his fingers over the wavy ridges of a bowl that was probably more than a thousand years old. He held it in both hands at arm's length, as if supplicating a god. "Why do you think they made the pots so rough on the outside like this one?"

Indy looked up from the overstuffed chair in the corner. A notebook rested on his lap, and written on it was the combination of letters and numbers that Mara had given Shannon. It was midmorning and he felt well enough to be out of bed, but he was still suffering from a recurring headache. Meanwhile, Mara was missing, and Indy was left only with her cryptic message. "Probably so it would be easier to carry a wet pot after it was filled with water."

"Maybe. But there was a guy staying here who was with some museum of natural history a few years back, and he thought they made 'em like this so they'd look like woven baskets. You know, me and Wetherill found lots of stuff from the Basketmaker people, who were here first. So maybe the Anasazis thought that clay pots were more practical, but they liked the looks of the old baskets. You see what I mean?"

"Yeah, I get it, Smitty." Indy wondered whether Smitty really had done everything he'd said. Maybe he'd been with Wetherill, maybe not. But what bothered him most about Smitty was his cavalier attitude about his daughter's disappearance. If he was worried about her, he didn't show it. "There's something I don't understand, Smitty. You don't seem too worried about Mara. Why aren't you out looking for her?"

Smitty put the pot back in the cabinet, then took a step toward Indy, his fists tightening into balls. "Tell me where to look. I'm ready to go. I handled all the police questions while you were upstairs snoozing. I've done everything I can. Doin' my best, and she ain't been much of a daughter to me, either."

"I'm sorry. It's just that . . ." Indy tapped his pencil against the notebook. "I'm not getting anywhere fast with this thing and I hate just sitting around."

"I'd like to help with that puzzle, but those letters and numbers don't mean a thing to me, and as far as sitting around goes, that's not for me, either. If all this hadn't happened I'd be out hiking in the canyons. That's where my life is."

"I'd like to be there with you. By the way, what do you know about a unicorn's horn?"

Smitty turned his attention back to the glass case and seemed to be studying his collection of artifacts. "What are you talking about?"

"That's what Mara said Walcott was after."

"She did? Nobody told me about that." The old prospector shuffled his feet. He knew something.

"C'mon, Smitty. What's it about?"

"Don't know nothin' about any unicorns."

"How about a mastodon horn?"

"Well, I used to have a staff that was made of ivory. A pretty thing with a silver tip and a beautiful silver handle. Mara's mother called it a unicorn's horn. I didn't see whose head it came from so I can't rightly say what it was made out of. She left it here when she ran off with the girl."

"What did it look like?"

"Ivory, straight, and sort of swirled."

"What do you mean by swirled?"

"It looked like a piece of ivory that had gotten soft and someone had twisted it."

Exactly what the mythical unicorn's horn was supposed to look like. "Does Mara have it now?"

He shrugged. "Don't know. If she does, she never told me about it."

"Well, what happened to it?"

Smitty waved a hand and grimaced. "Oh, years back, when I was drinking, I pawned it at the trading post. I needed the money. Besides, Rosie wanted me to get rid of it. She thought the thing had something to do with my drinking."

"How could that be?"

Smitty laughed. "Don't ask me. She's just superstitious. Anyhow, I ain't never seen it since."

"Could Mara have picked it up?"

"No, I asked Neddie about it once a few years back. He's the fella who runs the pawnshop. He said some old Indian he didn't know came and took it off his hands."

"Maybe he knows who the Indian is," Indy suggested.

"Tell you what, why don't we go on down and see what Neddie can remember."

Indy was ready to get out of the house. His headache was just a dull throb unless he turned his head too quickly. "Good idea. We can see what's taking Jack so long, too." Shannon had gone to the trading post to buy butter to replace Smitty's lard, and a few other things. He'd been gone more than an hour.

He looked at Mara's message again as he stood up. It didn't make a bit of sense.

The trading post was a combination dry goods store, grocery store, clothing store, and pawnshop. You could buy a fifty-pound sack of flour, a black, high-topped, flat-rimmed hat like the Navajos wore, or a turquoise-and-silver bracelet. But as Indy walked into the trading post, his attention was immediately drawn to the rear of the store and the source of a horrible, ear-splitting racket. He moved through a crowd of apparently deaf spectators and spotted Shannon playing a saxophone with a shriveled old Negro, who was blowing on a set of bagpipes. The result was an eerie cacophony that sounded like a marching tune for an army headed to hell.

Maybe it really wasn't so bad. Maybe it was just his headache. The throbbing had started again.

"What do you think?" a voice yelled in his ear. Indy turned to see Smitty grinning and pointing at Shannon and the old man.

"I've never heard anything quite like it."

Indy caught Shannon's eye and made a sour face. Shannon winked, then waved a hand like a conductor bringing a performance to a close. The old man continued through the signal, playing several more squeaky notes before he stopped.

Smitty applauded, and several people followed his lead. Shannon bowed dramatically and the old man laughed.

"I didn't know you could play a saxophone, Jack," Indy said as he moved forward.

"I can blow a few notes, I guess. You must be feeling pretty good if you can listen to us."

"Yeah, sort of. Who's your friend?"

"This is Neddie Watson. He runs the pawn shop here in the trading post."

"Oh, so you're Neddie." Indy shook his hand as Shannon introduced him to Watson. "Where did you learn to play the bagpipes?"

Watson set the bagpipes down on a chair as Shannon returned the saxophone to its case. "Well, I'm still learning. This here instrument was pawned back in 1914. It sat here for six years. Then the day I turned eighty, I said I'm gonna give meself those pipes and learn to play 'em. Like I said, I'm still learnin'. Maybe if I'd had that saxophone here then, I would've tried it instead."

"How did you end up in Bluff?" Indy asked.

"That's what everyone always asks him," Smitty said, joining them.

"That's right," Watson said. "They sure do. I was in the army in 'sixty-three and 'sixty-four when we rounded up all the Navajos in Arizona and walked them from Fort Defiance all the way across New Mexico. It was a waste of time, and a lot of lives. The Navajos wouldn't put up with that treatment, and I don't blame them one bit. A lot of them just died, and finally the army released them and gave them some of their land back."

"Yeah, I've heard about it," Indy said.

Smitty clasped his friend on the shoulder. "Neddie, you remember that old ivory staff I pawned back ten years ago or so?"

"That was in 'eighteen. I remember. It was a very strange and beautiful thing. 'Cept it gave me the creeps. I didn't like it around here, and I was glad when I finally got rid of it."

"Why didn't you like it?" Indy asked.

"We had two fires here while that thing was hanging on the wall, and we never had one before or after it was gone."

"Ah, Neddie. That's nonsense," Smitty said. "I never had any fires when I had it."

"Listen to you. Maybe you didn't have any fires, but you almost drank yourself to death, and if I recall right you sobered up for good after you got rid of that thing."

"Now you sound like Rosie," Smitty said.

"So who did you sell it to?" Indy asked before Smitty could respond.

"Some old Moqui. I remember thinking that he must have pawned most of his turquoise jewelry to get it. He wanted it real bad. Don't know why."

"What's a Moqui?" Shannon asked.

Indy remembered hearing the term when he was a kid. "It's a word for Hopi, I think."

Smitty laughed. "Neddie calls any Indian who doesn't live around here a Moqui."

"That doesn't narrow it down much," Indy said.

"It's a funny thing you should ask about that ol' piece of ivory," Watson said. "Some Englishman was asking about it the other day."

"What did you tell him?" Indy asked.

"Nothing. I just told him I couldn't remember anything about any ivory stick." He grinned slyly. "Us older folks can get away with lies about our memory, you know."

"What about Mara? Did she ever ask about it?" Indy persisted.

Watson glanced at Smitty, then nodded. "Back a

couple of years ago, she did. She wanted to find that Moqui real bad. Don't know if she ever found him, though." He looked down at the floor, then up at Smitty. "I do hope she's okay."

"Hear anything new?" Smitty asked.

"Those fellows who were holed up there at Mesa were no-good bandits."

"Holed up?" Shannon said. "Let me tell you about being holed up."

"Jack, let him finish," Indy interrupted.

"Yeah, they say a couple of 'em were wanted by the law. Some of the ranchers are even sayin' the Utes did us a good turn getting rid of 'em."

"They didn't do me no good turn running off with Mara," Smitty said darkly. Then he glanced at Indy and added: "She's the only daughter I got."

Watson nodded. "I heard something else, too. Don't know if it's true, but a Moqui passing through just this morning said he heard that those renegade Utes didn't *take* your daughter. She went with them on her own."

# 10

## SHAPE-SHIFTER

As they unloaded the supplies from the buckboard, Indy mulled over what Watson had said, both about Mara's disappearance and about the staff. If she wasn't being held by the Utes, then what had happened to her? Was she hiding on her own, still fearing that Walcott was after her? Maybe she thought that someone else was involved in the Englishman's misadventures, and she wasn't sure who it was.

The staff was another matter. Why would Walcott go to all this trouble to get his hands on it? Did he really think it was a unicorn's horn? If Mara knew where it was, why would she endanger her life to protect it? "Smitty, how much do you think that staff was worth?"

The old timer seemed surprised by the question, but only for a moment. "Depends, I guess."

"On what?"

Smitty threw a sack of oats for his horses over his shoulder as Indy grabbed a box of groceries. "On

whatever someone would pay for it. That's what the
fella from the natural history museum told me when
I asked him what it was worth. He said it was definitely ivory. He thought it might be a carved elephant tusk or from some sort of arctic whale called a
narwok."

"That's a narwhal, and it's a good guess. The male
has a long, straight, spiral ivory tusk."

"Yeah, you got it. Can't remember that fella's
name now. He did a lot of exploring around here for
the museum."

"I'll get the door for you guys," Shannon said.

Indy snapped his fingers. "Wait a minute. That's
the American Museum of Natural History, right?"

"I guess so," Smitty said as he lugged the oats
toward the house."

"That's it!" Indy rushed to the house with the groceries under his arm and Smitty trailing after him.

"Hey, what's it?" Smitty dropped the sack of oats,
and hurried after him.

Indy didn't answer. He set the box on the kitchen
counter. "I think I've got it, Jack."

"Got what?"

Indy sprinted into the library. He snatched up the
notebook where Shannon had written: A.M.N.H 73
N.C.N. 1920 B.T.B.H. "Yeah. I was right."

"What is it?" Shannon asked as he and Smitty
stopped in the doorway to the library.

"I'll show you." The young archaeologist pushed
past them and headed for the stairway, climbing the
steps two at a time. He disappeared into his room,
and dug into his bag until he found his reference
books. "Here it is." He held up a slender book.
Shannon and Smitty moved into the room and
waited for him to explain.

"This is a catalogue of Anasazi sites." He flipped to the introduction, then tapped the page. "Here we go: *This survey was conducted in 1920 by Nels C. Nelson of the American Museum of Natural History. Nelson led the expedition in an effort to identify Richard Wetherill's numbered sites and so document the artifacts in the possession of the museum. He was guided by John Wetherill, Richard's younger brother, and accompanied by B.T.B. Hyde.'*"

"I still don't get it," Shannon said.

"Okay, in Mara's message, the A.M.N.H stands for American Museum of Natural History. N.C.N. is Nels C. Nelson, of course. B.T.B. Hyde is B.T.B.H. and 1920 is the year that they carried out the survey. That leaves the number 73." He paged through the catalog. "Here it is. Site No. 73. It's called Junction Ruin. It's located in Upper Grand Gulch."

"Well, what do you know," Smitty said. "That Nels Nelson is the museum fella who stayed here. Right in this room, in fact. I offered to guide him on that survey, but he decided to go with Wetherill's younger brother. I didn't like that one bit, either."

"It doesn't matter now, Smitty," Indy said. "You can lead *us* to Junction Ruin. I think that's where Mara's hiding out."

"Hm . . . Maybe so, but that's rugged territory," Smitty said. "You gotta go through Kane Gulch, which is no easy hike. She'd have to know what she was doing, and I don't know where she'd get her food and water."

"I'm pretty sure she's been there," Indy said. "I remember her writing me about the rock art in Upper Grand Gulch."

Smitty shrugged. "All right. If you think we might

find her hiding out there, I'm more than willing to go take a look."

"I don't know what else her message could mean," Indy said. "Unless she's got the staff, and hid it there."

"That's what I was wondering," Shannon said.

"Well, let's go look," Smitty said.

"Are you sure you can find Junction Ruin?"

"Of course, I can," he scoffed. "It's right at the junction of Kane and Upper Grand."

"Sounds like we can drive there," Shannon said.

"Huh, that's what you think. Like I said, it ain't easy. When I was with Wetherill back in 'ninety-seven, we had a real tough time in Grand Gulch. I've even got a copy of the notes from the trip. Come on downstairs, I'll show you."

Shannon tugged on Indy's arm as they started to descend the stairs. "Do you really think she's hiding in that ruins? I mean, even if that's what she intended to do, there's no way of knowing that she's actually there."

Indy thought of his dream of Mara pleading for help. "You're right, but we've got to try."

"Indy, take a look," Smitty called from downstairs.

They found him in the library where he'd opened a bound notebook to a page near the front. He pointed to his name listed as Wetherill's assistant.

Indy took the notebook from Smitty. "That's you all right. I never doubted it for a minute." Smitty, it seemed, was looking for recognition that he'd never received. Indy paged through the typed notes, wondering momentarily if Wetherill had bothered to mention the rock art. Since it wasn't anything you could date and carry away, both archaeologists and pot hunters had pretty much ignored it. He paused to read a passage. "I guess you didn't have much luck with horses on that trip."

"Grand Gulch can be rough on 'em," Smitty said. "Real rough."

"What're you reading?" Shannon asked.

"It's about horses." Indy read it aloud. " '*We had several extra ones on the way down to use in case of accidents which proved of frequent occurrence. One animal fell off a bridge and broke its neck. Another fell off the trail where it wound about a ledge, going into the cañon, and was killed instantly. Another fell off a cliff with the same result.*' "

"They got bridges out there?" Shannon asked the question nonchalantly, but Indy could tell it wasn't the bridges that concerned him.

"There're some natural arches," Smitty replied. "They're something to see."

"I bet," Shannon said, unenthusiastically. He touched his injured arm. "Don't you think someone should stay behind, you know, in case Mara turns up around here?"

Indy nodded. "That might be a good idea."

Shannon raised a hand. "I volunteer."

"Don't worry about it," Smitty said. "Rosie will be here. She can hold down the fort."

"Smitty, with my luck it wouldn't be a horse who would break its neck," Shannon said. "Just the name, Grand Gulch, sounds like a place I'd want to avoid."

"Suit yourself." Smitty sounded disappointed. "It's really not that bad. You just gotta be careful, and watch out for rattlers. There's plenty of them out there."

Indy handed the notebook back to the old pros-

pector. "That's good to know. Maybe a good rattler
bite will take care of my headache."

Just getting to the trailhead proved to be an adventure in itself. The road, open a few months of the
year, was rugged and every bump the Ford hit
seemed to reverberate through Indy's head, feeding
the dull pain. He was getting concerned about the
prolonged headache, and as the day wore on, his
vision blurred more than once. Although he didn't
complain to Smitty, he could tell by the way the old
man watched him that he knew the headache was
still bothering him.

By dusk, Indy was starting to feel numb from the
drive. Finally, Smitty told him to stop. The landscape was dry and desolate with clumps of sagebrush
rising every few yards. Distant, dark hills were sil-
houetted against the pale, blue-gray sky.

"Where are we?"

"Right here."

"Yeah. I can see that. Are we taking a break, or
what?"

Smitty simply nodded toward the west. "Don't
you see it?"

Indy peered into the growing darkness and saw a
hogan, an eight-sided, dome-roofed adobe structure
that nearly blended into the landscape. A wisp of
smoke rose from the smoke hole in the center. It was
hard to believe that anyone lived in this desolate
terrain. They hadn't seen another building for at
least an hour.

"What are we doing here?"

"Getting horses. The road ends just up a ways."

Indy remembered that Smitty had said they would
arrange for horses when they got to the canyon, but

he'd assumed they'd do it tomorrow. "So what are we waiting for?"

"It's the polite thing to do. You don't just go barging in on the Navajos."

It was nearly dark when Smitty stepped out of the car. "Wait here. I'll be right back." He slammed the door and headed toward the house.

After a couple of minutes, Indy opened the door and stretched his legs. He rubbed the back of his head, trying to ease the throbbing pain, and wondered why Smitty had gone alone. He moved away from the car and strolled down the dirt road with his hands in his pockets. As soon as the sun set, the temperature dropped; he could literally feel it falling degree by degree. He enjoyed this time of day when, for a few minutes, it was like being caught between two worlds, the one of daylight, the other of night.

He suddenly stopped. Three antelope stood perfectly still not a hundred feet away. They could have been statues, except for the soft glow of their eyes. Suddenly, a large bird swept low over his head, shrieking as it furiously beat its wings. He ducked, and as he did, the antelopes dashed across the road, vanishing from sight.

"Wild out here," Indy muttered, and he headed back to the car.

He leaned against the fender and rubbed his arms against the cold. "C'mon, Smitty. What're you doing in there?" A faint light burned from a window of the hogan. Another few minutes, he thought, then he'd go investigate.

He stared up at Venus, bright in the western sky, then tried to count the stars that had popped out. When he'd found seven and saw several more materializing, he decided he'd waited long enough. He pushed away from the car and headed toward the hogan.

When he got within twenty feet of the building, he paused. He heard a low growling that sounded like it was coming from right under him. His eyes darted about until he spotted a dog laying in the dirt a few feet away. It was medium-sized with short, tan fur. An Indian dog. He'd seen plenty of them as a kid. They all looked as if they were from the same litter. "Easy, boy. Easy," he whispered. "I'm not going to hurt you." Indy moved past the dog and looked back to see the animal trailing him, wagging, rear-end wriggling.

He knocked on the door. No one answered. He knocked again, then moved over to the window on his right. Its shutters were partially open, and through them he saw the flickering of candles. "Hello? Smitty? You there?"

No answer. He looked back at the dog. "Where'd they go, boy?"

"Indy! Don't you have no manners?"

Indy nearly jumped out of his skin, but it wasn't the dog talking. Smitty stood by the corner of the house. "Where were you?"

"Out back. Picking out our horses. I was just coming to get you."

Indy thought he glimpsed a small, wiry man standing in the shadows behind Smitty, but when he looked again, the man was no longer there. "Where're we staying tonight?"

"Right here. Let's go inside. Aguila is making a cup of tea for you. He says it will help your headache."

Indy followed Smitty into the hogan. A fire was

burning in the potbelly stove and a black pot rested on top of it. "Sit down."

He settled into a lumpy chair that was made of a rough wooden frame and two gunny sacks filled with straw. Smitty picked up the pot with a rag and poured the steaming tea into a ceramic cup that looked like a bowl with handles on either side. "Here you go. Drink."

Indy took the offering, and blew on the tea to cool it. He felt uneasy sitting in a stranger's house, drinking his tea, without the man being present. "Where is your friend?"

"He's around. Don't worry about him. Just relax. He's sort of shy."

"Maybe he doesn't want company. Why don't we get the horses and go find a place to camp for the night?"

Smitty laughed. "What's wrong with you? Aguila's glad to have us here, otherwise he wouldn't have offered to make the tea. It would be an insult to leave now. Besides, he says he knows you."

"What?"

Smitty smiled. "He said he went out to greet you by the car. Didn't you see him?"

"No one came out there."

Smitty laughed. "You must be tired after all the driving. He said you didn't recognize him."

As Indy sipped the tea, perspiration beaded on his brow. The faster he finished it, he thought, the quicker he could go outside. Everything Smitty had said about the man who lived here made him uneasy. He felt as if the walls of the hogan were closing in on him.

Smitty settled back on a cot. "How's the tea?"

"It tastes like hot water with a slight metallic flavor, maybe from the pot. You sure the tea's in here?"

"I hope so."

"Why don't you have some?"

"Aguila said it was only for you. You're the one with the headache."

Indy took several swallows, and the tea nearly scalded the inside of his mouth. "Your friend . . . Aguila . . . says he knows me, but . . ." He laughed. ". . . But I don't know . . . anyone named . . . Aguila." He laughed again as if what he'd just said was uproariously funny.

"Are you okay?"

Indy laughed again. "Never felt better." He settled back in the chair and rested his head against the earthen wall. Now his mood shifted again and he felt drowsy.

"If you're tired, there's another cot over there." Smitty pointed toward one of the corners.

Indy realized he'd closed his eyes. He blinked them open, rubbing his damp forehead. A drop of sweat rolled over his cheek. He felt flushed; his skin tingled. "No, I don't want to stay here." How long had it taken him to reply? He didn't know.

Just the thought of spending the night in the hogan sent a shudder through him. He wasn't so sure he wanted to see Aguila, or anyone else either. Not tonight. He sat up straight and swallowed the rest of the tea in two huge gulps, then set the cup on the woven rug, which covered part of the hard-packed dirt floor.

"Did your headache go away?" Smitty's voice bubbled across the hogan. It sounded as if he were talking with his mouth in a bowl of water.

"Headache, what headache?" Indy's voice echoed

around him. He laughed and the sound assumed a life of its own.

"You seem like you're having a good ol' time over there," Smitty said. "Maybe I should've tried that tea." He yawned, and stretched his arms.

"What was in it, anyhow?"

Smitty laid back on the cot. "Just some herbs. Aguila is a medicine man. He's very wise about all of the plants in these parts. In fact, he helped me stop my drinking with one of his potions. Said he could see my doom hovering near me, and if I wanted to chase it away, he could help me. At first, I laughed and offered him a drink from my flask, but he looked at me in such a strange way that I almost sobered up right on the spot."

Indy couldn't help laughing again. "You mean this old Indian just walked up to you and said you were going to die if you didn't let him help you?"

"Well, you gotta understand that he's Rosie's granddaddy. She'd had enough of me, and had gone off when he showed up."

"Oh, now I get it. So what happened?" Indy couldn't tell whether he had just thought the question or actually spoken it. But it didn't matter, because Smitty kept talking. He explained that Aguila gave him a pouch with some powder in it and told him to take a spoonful of it every six hours with a glass of water until it was gone. He stuck around until Smitty took his first dose, then he left.

"He wasn't gone for fifteen minutes when I got out my flask. But you know what? I couldn't drink it. I took just a little taste and my gut heaved so bad that I nearly died right there. Then after several hours I figured the stuff had worn off and I could take a drink, but I no sooner reached for the flask when Aguila was at my door again. He showed up every six hours for three days. I don't know where he went, but each time he was suddenly there. By then, I was too afraid to tell him to leave me alone."

"So it worked?" Again, Indy couldn't tell whether he'd spoken or not.

"It did the trick. I ain't had the desire for a drink in nearly ten years now."

"That's an interesting story," Indy remarked when Smitty didn't say anything further. "You think Aguila is coming back tonight?"

Indy heard a soft snoring; Smitty was fast asleep. As he stood up, intending to wake him, he heard a wheezing sound outside the hogan. He figured it was probably a horse. Aguila must have brought their horses to the front of the hogan.

When he didn't hear the noise again, he decided to take a look. If Aguila was out there, he'd thank him for the tea and horses and tell him he'd sleep inside his car. He stepped outside and looked around. What in the name of God was in that tea? A tingling sensation that he'd felt earlier was now even more intense. It spread over his hands, feet, face, crept down his neck, and over his chest, up his arms, and all over his legs. Sweat trickled over his brow and into his eyes. He wiped his face with the back of his hands, and when he opened his eyes nothing looked quite the same. It was pitch dark, but he was seeing things—things he never knew were there. It was as if he could see the air itself. It formed a graphic texture that one moment was like a three-dimensional jigsaw puzzle, then shifted into a million dots, which created some pattern that he couldn't quite comprehend.

Indy realized he wasn't alone, but all the dots

made it hard to focus. Then they seemed to take on shape and dimension, swirling about in a cocoonlike form. "Aguila, is that you?"

Indy squinted, trying to bring the image into focus. Then he realized it wasn't a man at all. *What was it?* He leaped back. It was some sort of creature with four wings and the body of a snake, with green luminescent scales and the head of lizard.

He opened his mouth to yell, but no sound came out. He blinked and looked again and realized he was mistaken. It was a huge bird with a prominent beak. An eagle. *All right, that's better.* It was perched on a three-foot-high stack of rock slabs. Probably a pet, he thought. Its left eye stared intently at him; its gaze was penetrating, assessing. "Are your wings clipped?" Indy whispered.

As if in response, it flapped its wings in a graceful slow-motion movement, creating a spectacular series of ghostlike images. Then the bird rose from the stone pedestal and soared skyward.

Indy followed its flight and felt a yearning to go with it. He knew this bird; it was his bird, his guardian. Years ago, he'd been led on a vision quest with an old Indian. He'd spent three days on the top of a mesa waiting for his guardian creature to appear. When he was on the verge of giving up, and had conceded that no animal would approach him, that it was ridiculous that he'd even thought that one might, an eagle had soared overhead and landed on the stone shelter where he'd spent the three days.

Since then, the eagle had appeared to him several times. He'd seen it in Greece at Delphi, again in England at Stonehenge, and another time in the Amazon. In each instance, it had appeared at a time of great need. He wasn't even sure eagles lived in those

places, but the circumstances under which he'd encountered them were not exactly normal.

But nothing had ever happened to him like what
he was now experiencing. He felt a soaring sensation. He could see the stars above him, but the
ground was no longer below him. His arms were
moving and he realized they were wings. Indy was
inside the body of an eagle; he was an eagle. He was
possessed by its abilities, its nature, its essence.

Below him, he saw mountains and ridges. His
night vision was spectacular. In spite of the darkness, everything seemed to glow and pulsate, the
mountains and boulders and stones seemed as alive
as the luminescent trees and shrubs. He felt no fear
of falling, no fear at all. What he was doing was natural, expected. He was with the bird and of the bird,
but yet the bird was its own being as well.

Then Indy realized he wasn't alone. Another eagle
glided above him. The moment he was aware of the
other bird, it descended until it was a few feet away
from him. "Now you fly with Aguila."

The eagle was talking to him, talking inside his
head. "Where are we going?"

"You will see."

"Do I know you?"

"Of course. Your vision is improving in more ways
than you realize."

At that moment, Indy realized that Aguila was the
Indian who took him to the mesa on a vision quest
when he was eighteen. It wasn't the name he'd used,
but somehow he sensed the eagle and the Indian
were one and the same.

It was hard to say how long they glided through
the night or the direction they took, but then the
other eagle hurtled downward and he followed. The

desert here was barren and forbidding. Yet, he was aware of the small animals, his prey, which were hiding or scurrying for cover. He could feel the presence of rabbits, snakes, mice, and prairie dogs. He'd never been aware of an animal in such a way. He sensed their fear, smelled their blood, and tasted their flesh.

Suddenly, the hungry animal that he was dived for the desert floor and its talons seized a rattler. The snake twisted back and forth. Indy felt sinewy flesh beneath its skin, and a lump that he knew was a small rodent the snake had recently swallowed. The eagle shrieked and his beak caught the rattler behind its head. He bit hard and the snake's spine snapped. It shuddered and stopped moving as the eagle clipped off the rest of the head . . . and feasted.

When he rose from the desert, he carried part of the snake with him. "Now you know your eagle nature, and that you can outwit even snakes in human skin."

It was the other eagle, Aguila, speaking. Again it was more of an impression of a thought than spoken words. As soon as he looked for the eagle, he saw it plunge again and he followed. This time, human things lay below him. Stone towers in ruins rose from the desert. They passed one cluster, then another. They circled a third set of towers, then landed on a precariously narrow ledge on the surface of a huge rock. The remains of the rattler skidded down the rock to the ground.

"Look!" Aguila ordered.

Indy didn't know what he was talking about, but then he realized that he or the eagle or both were peering down into an opening in the rock and he could clearly see three circular petroglyphs. The center one was a series of concentric circles, and on either side of it were identical spirals.

Two thoughts simultaneously mixed in his mind. To the bird, the symbols were meaningless, unworthy of attention. To the man, they were important, but he didn't why or how. And then they were flying again, soaring through the night. On and on, and all thoughts of symbols were left behind as the simple joy of flight overcame all else.

After a timeless journey, the two eagles dropped down again into a canyon and swooped under an overhang above a network of stone shapes that made no sense to his bird self. His human awareness had to struggle to subdue the control of his bird nature that saw walls as nonsensical forms. They lighted upon the edge of a round depression, and Aguila hopped to the floor several feet below him. He clawed at the ground, then pecked viciously at his own tail. A single feather fluttered to the ground, and the bird then leaped back up to the rim.

"There is your last revelation of the night." With that, Aguila soared away. The bird that was Indy let out a sharp squawk and beat its wings in pursuit.

# 11

## GRAND GULCH

"Wake up, Jones. Now what are you doing up there?"

The voice tugged Indy from a deep sleep. He didn't want to hear it, didn't want to be bothered. But it was insistent. *Wake up . . . wake up.*

"All right," he mumbled without opening his eyes. He recognized the voice as Smitty's and remembered . . . What did he remember?

Slowly, he roused himself from sleep. He was chilled and damp. His mouth was dry and his eyelids felt as if they were glued together. He blinked, and rubbed his eyes; the gray glow of the dawn spread out from the horizon. He must have slept outside, he thought, then realized he was several feet off the ground, lying on something hard and shiny.

The car roof.

"What am I doing up here?"

"That's what I asked you," Smitty said. "I woke up and looked out the window. Couldn't tell what was on the car. Thought it was some big animal. Hardly believed it when I came out and saw it was you."

Indy sat up and looked around. Two saddled horses and a pack horse were hitched to a pile of sandstone slabs in front of the hogan. He stared at the slabs, thinking there was something significant about them. "I don't understand it. Don't know how I got here."

"Musta been something in that tea you drank."

At the mention of the tea, a shudder ran through Indy; he felt sick to his stomach. A memory lapped at the back of his mind like a tide edging higher and higher. He recalled bits and pieces at first, and tried to fit them together in a way that made sense.

"Aguila is an eagle," he muttered.

"What's that?" Smitty gave him an odd look.

Indy studied the stone slabs again, and this time he remembered the eagle had been perched on them.

"Aguila is an eagle," he repeated.

"You mean in Mex'can?"

Indy realized the obvious. *Águila* was Spanish for eagle. It hadn't even occurred to him. But that wasn't the point. He dropped down from the roof of the Ford. "He *is* an eagle and he turned me into one."

"Oh, boy." Smitty laughed. "He must have really given you a good dose of something in that tea."

Indy was about to argue, but he realized what he was saying was preposterous. It was one thing to have an eagle as a guardian, a creature who supposedly watched over you. It was something else to turn into one and fly over the desert.

"Did you see him turn into an eagle?" Smitty asked.

"Well, no. But I just knew it was him."

"C'mon, let's go ask him about this eagle stuff."

As they headed toward the hogan, Indy's stomach knotted. "Maybe we shouldn't bother him."

"Why not? You want to see him in his own skin, don't you?" Smitty laughed again, and tugged on his arm.

Indy didn't have an answer, but he fought a growing sense of foreboding all the way to the hogan. The door was partially open, and the aroma of warm tortillas wafted through the air. Smitty stuck his head inside. "Aguila? Mind if Indy and I join you?"

He stepped away from the door and shrugged. "He must be out back."

They moved around the side of the house and the dog Indy had seen last night trotted after them. He was surprised to see a pasture and a solid row of ponderosa trees amid the semiarid landscape. How different the place seemed during the day. Then he saw the stream and realized that Aguila had an abundant source of water, no doubt the reason he'd settled here.

Smitty called out to the old Indian, but again there was no answer. "That's strange. He was here a few minutes ago. Let's go inside and get some chow."

"Did he say he was leaving?" Indy asked.

"He mentioned something about going up in the hills to pick his herbs, but I didn't think he'd leave so fast." He shrugged. "Then again you never know what to expect with that old man."

"I'll agree with that."

Indy decided he wasn't going to take a single bite of Aguila's food. He'd been drugged and the old Indian wasn't going to do it again.

"Sit down and eat," Smitty said as he bit into a cornmeal tortilla made with a spicy meat sauce.

"I'm not really hungry. I'll just have some of the beef jerky from our supplies."

"Suit yourself, but you're missing a good meal." Smitty took another bite. "Maybe eagles don't eat this kind of grub."

"Okay, I guess I must have dreamed the whole thing," Indy said, interrupting Smitty's laughter. "You know how dreams can seem real sometimes?"

"That's what I thought, but I wasn't going to say it. I think we'd all like to fly like eagles."

"The thing that bothers me is that I don't know how I got on the roof of the Ford."

Smitty polished off his second tortilla. "I remember you saying that you didn't want to stay here in the hogan. I bet you fell asleep on the cot, and then got up during the night."

"I don't think I've ever sleepwalked in my life. And even if I did, I think I would've slept on the car seat, not the roof."

"Then maybe you were flying in your sleep," Smitty said with a chuckle.

"Right."

"By the way, how's the headache? You haven't said a word about it."

Indy hadn't given it a thought. "It's gone. I guess the tea did its job." And then some.

Smitty got up from the table. "Maybe we'll run into Aguila when we get back."

Shannon had just poured himself a cup of coffee and sat down when the kitchen door opened and Rosie greeted him. "Good morning. Did you sleep well?"

"Like a block of sandstone, Rosie. Ten hours. Must be because Indy's gone."

Rosie's long black hair was tied in a braid and decorated with green ribbons. Her dark Navajo eyes gazed down her aquiline nose. "Why do you say that?"

"Oh, I don't know. Sometimes when I'm around him, I get the feeling the roof is about to fall in."

"Does he have lots of accidents?"

"He has a way of attracting trouble. But don't tell him that or he'll tell you that I'm the one who draws the troublemakers."

"Maybe it's both of you, when you are together."

"No, I don't think that's it. We each manage to do it on our own, too. Cup of coffee?"

She shook her head, then noticed the Bible on the kitchen table. "Do you read it?"

"All the time. Well, not really, but I was looking up some passages last night on unicorns."

She pushed up the sleeves of her colorful, patterned sweater and started cleaning up around the sink. "In the Bible?"

"Sure. You want to hear what I found?"

Rosie picked up the broom and started to sweep the floor. "Okay."

Shannon sipped his coffee, and flipped to one of the pages he'd marked. "Let's see. This is Isaiah thirty-four, verse seven. 'And the unicorns shall come down with them, and the bullocks with their bulls; and their land shall be soaked with blood, and their dust made fat with fatness.'"

"What's that mean?" she asked. "It doesn't sound good."

"Well, it's about something that happened a long time ago." He turned to another page, and cleared his throat. "Here's another one. 'Save me from the lion's mouth; for thou hast heard me from the horns of unicorns.' That was Psalm twenty-two, verse twenty-one."

"Why are you studying these words about unicorns?"

"It's a long story. Here's another one. Psalm ninety-two, verse ten. 'But my horn shalt thou exalt like the horn of the unicorn; I shall be anointed with fresh oil.' "

Rosie turned to face him. "I don't like this. Please stop it."

"Sorry." Shannon closed the Bible. "If you don't want to believe in unicorns, that's all right with me."

Rosie nervously wiped the counter. "That staff has caused much evil. It'd be best if Mara just left it alone."

"You know about the staff?"

Rosie set the broom down and leaned against the counter. "Of course. It was here in this house, you know."

"Do you know what happened to it?"

She nodded.

Shannon could hardly believe it. "Where is it?"

"Hidden away. The man who bought it from the pawnshop is a healer, a medicine man. Some people call him a witch, but I've seen him heal. He saved Smitty's life. He said that staff was killing Smitty and that I had to get it away from him."

"Sounds like he wanted it for himself."

"No, Aguila wanted to take the evil from it."

Shannon had no idea why a unicorn's horn would be considered evil, but that didn't matter. "Did you tell Smitty who bought it?"

She shook her head. "Aguila said it was best not to say anything to him. I've kept my word."

"What about Mara?"

"She knows."

"You told her?"

"Aguila did. But I don't think he told her where it is."

"Where does this witch, or healer, live?"

"Near Kane Gulch. I'm sure that's where Smitty and Professor Jones stayed last night."

Rosie had listened to many of the conversations about the events at Mesa Verde, but had said very little. Now it seemed she knew more than she was letting on. "Any chance that Aguila might know where to find Mara?"

"It could be that he knows, but he doesn't know."

Shannon shook his head. "You lost me."

"Sometimes people know things, but they don't realize it until the right question is asked."

They rode horseback for most of the morning before the land opened up like a scar and they descended into Kane Gulch. Indy was sandwiched between Smitty and the pack horse, and the trail quickly turned perilously narrow, twisting and turning along ridges that plunged hundreds of feet, just inches from the hoof marks they were leaving behind.

"Good job, Chico, good job," Indy said, patting the horse as they made it around another bend.

Indy kept thinking of Richard Wetherill's notes about the fate of their horses. When he'd read it, he wondered if the party had been drinking. How else could they have fared so poorly with their animals? Now, he realized that no one in his right mind would drink on this route. The miracle of Wetherill's expedition had been that not one of the explorers had died. He thought of Shannon, who didn't like riding horses, and knew that his friend had made a wise decision not to join them.

"How're you doing back there, Indy?" Smitty called.

"Fine. I'm glad I didn't have any of Aguila's tea this morning, though."

"I told you it wasn't gonna be easy. But at least we've got an extra horse with us."

"What reason did you give Aguila for our trip to Junction Ruin?" Indy asked.

"The truth. I told him my daughter was missing and she might be out there. That's all."

"Does he know Mara?"

"Yeah, I think she's used him as a guide. I was hoping he'd seen her, but no such luck. Makes me think that she might not be at Junction Ruin."

"We've got to take a look, though," Indy said.

If Smitty answered, Indy never heard him. Indy's horse hit a spot of loose gravel and its front hoof skidded over the side. It panicked, reared up on its hind legs, and tossed Indy out of the saddle. He hit the side of the packhorse, then struck the shoulder of the trail. His momentum took him over the edge and his fedora sailed out ahead of him. He rolled over a couple of times, then slid downward. He dug his heels into the dirt and stones, but he couldn't stop. He sent a shower of rocks and dust in front of him.

Finally, he slid into an anchored rock and came to a stop. That was *close. Too close.*

"Indy! Watch out!" Smitty called.

A boulder bounded down the steep slope, heading directly at Indy. He rolled over to one side, and started sliding again; he clawed at the ground, desperately trying to stop his fall. He hooked an arm over another rock, but he was still in the path of the careening boulder.

Indy was about to dive to one side when the boulder broke into two pieces. One chunk veered toward the spot where he was about to dive; the other rocketed right at him. He flattened himself on the ground, squeezing his eyes shut. He felt the rock graze his buttock and his heels, and then it was by him. He raised his head, then ducked again as pebbles and dirt showered down on him.

He let out a sigh; he'd survived. But the instant he'd relaxed, the rock he was holding pulled loose and he skidded toward the cliff. This was it. He was going over. But at the last moment the crook of his elbow caught a clump of sagebrush. He didn't move, didn't dare. When the dust settled, he still clung to the dry bush, but his legs hung over the side of the cliff.

"Indy, hang on! Hang on!" Smitty yelled somewhere above him.

"Sure," he said between gritted teeth. "Why not?"

But then the roots of the sagebrush started to give way. Inch by inch it lost its hold on the dry earth, and Indy moved closer and closer to falling over the edge of the cliff. He looked around for something else to grab. There was nothing but dirt and loose rocks. He couldn't last but a few seconds longer.

"Catch!"

A rope dangled a few feet to his right. Smitty snapped it, attempting to flip it over to him, but the rope only snaked in place. Indy groped for it, but the roots of the shrub pulled loose. He lunged for the rope . . . and missed by inches.

* * *

When Walcott heard the pounding on the door of his
hotel room, he knew it was either the law or Calderone. He wasn't sure which one was worse. The cops
would arrest him, but if the Sicilian's impatience had
turned to anger, Walcott knew Calderone would kill
him without a moment's hesitation. A day and a half
had passed since he'd been shot in the skirmish below Mesa Verde, and he was still in pain, and he was
feverish.

He climbed out of bed, hobbled over to the door,
and opened it a couple of inches. "Who is it?"

Calderone pushed his cane through the opening.
"Why are you still here?" He walked into the room,
followed by his two hulking bodyguards.

"I have a fever. I need some medicine."

"This is not the time to lie in bed. You need to find
Mara and the staff."

Walcott watched Calderone's mole twitch. "All
right. I'll find her, and if she's got the staff, I'll get it.
First, I've got to find my car. I left it at the hospital."

Calderone smiled. "It's parked in the back of the
hotel waiting for you."

"Thank you. I appreciate it. The police might have
gotten it, and—"

"Do you still have the money I gave you, or did
you drink it all up?"

"No, I have it. Most of it, I mean. I'll get it for
you."

The Sicilian held his cane out in front of Walcott.
"Keep it. I'm leaving today. My people need me."
He nodded to one of his bodyguards, who passed
him a long and slender polished teakwood box.
Calderone opened it, revealing a red velvet lining.
"You will place the staff here and bring it to Rome."

He walked to the door, and the bodyguards followed. "If I don't hear from you, I'll send someone to finish the job for me."

The door slammed. Walcott had a good idea what Calderone meant by finishing the job, and he didn't like it. He couldn't wait any longer. He had to find Mara, and the way to her now was through Jones.

# 12

## THE THREE CIRCLES

Mara stoked the fire in the stone shelter high on a canyon wall as she warmed up leftover rabbit stew from the night before. She had escaped with the three surviving Utes after Walcott had been wounded, and had convinced them to take her to this remote canyon. She felt safe here, safer than if she had gone to Cortez or Bluff.

Walcott, she was convinced, was not the only one involved. Someone had been feeding him information, and until she found out who it was, she was in danger. But now she had to leave. The solstice, the day of promise, was just a sunrise away, and she knew she must go in search of Aguila. She'd leave as soon as she finished eating.

At the thought of the solstice, a fragment of a recurring dream came to mind. She bent over, and picked up a stick. Somehow, she knew that it was a dream that had recurred over and over and she had been repeatedly forgetting it. This time she'd re-

member. She scratched three circular symbols in the
dirt. The one in the center was different from the
other two. It was a series of circles within circles,
what she considered to be an Anasazi sun symbol.
The other two were spirals. She'd seen them too, but
had heard varying interpretations of their meaning.
The most common was that they meant a journey of
some sort. The three symbols were somehow related
to her quest for the unicorn's horn. That much she
knew.

Ben, the grandson of Sam, the Ute guide who had
been killed by Walcott's thugs, sat across the fire
watching her. She pointed at her drawing. "Have
you ever seen these three symbols together?" Ben
stared at the drawing, then shook his head. "What
do you think it means?" she asked. "I saw them in a
dream."

"Then your dreams have been invaded by a wolf,"
he answered.

She knew the kind of wolf he meant, not the animal, but a witch, an Indian who could transform
himself into the shapes of wolves or other animals
and even fly. Many Indians feared them, and believed they would cause illness or even death
through evil magic. It surprised her that Ben had
made the observation. Aguila was considered by
many to be a wolf.

Ben suddenly stirred as if he'd heard something.
A moment later, the two other men rushed into the
stone shelter. They spoke excitedly in Shoshoni as
Ben scrambled to his feet.

"What's going on?" she asked.

"Someone's coming."

"Who?" She pushed past them, stepping out of
the shelter for a better view. To her surprise, Aguila

was walking along a path leading directly toward their hidden shelter. He was a small, wiry man, barely over five feet tall, with graying hair that fell to his shoulders. Even though he was at least seventy, he was fit and never seemed to tire. He walked among the rocks with a baffling gracefulness, as if he knew exactly where to take every step without ever having to look down.

"It's okay," she called out. "I know him." But the Utes were already darting away among the boulders as they headed toward the top of the canyon wall. She shrugged and moved down the path. "I was going to look for you today," she said. She knew from experience that looking for Aguila and finding him were two different matters. "How did you know I was here?"

His peculiar green eyes seemed to literally glow. Those eyes alone were enough to convince anyone who suspected that the elfin old man might be a witch. "Your father and a young man are looking for you. I knew this is where you would be."

"Then they got my message."

"So your father said."

Indy dropped straight down over the cliff, and before he had time to even think about what was going to happen next, his boots struck a flat surface, and he found himself seated on a narrow switchback in the trail. He'd only fallen about fifteen feet, but just a yard away the cliff fell another two hundred feet.

He wiped a hand over his face, and tried to catch his breath. His body was still locked in an emergency survival mode, the sort that allowed him to take considerable punishment without feeling immediate pain. But now, as he realized he'd survived the fall, he mentally checked over his body. No shots of pain, signaling serious injury, responded to his call. He was scraped and bruised, but had suffered no broken bones.

His fedora rested atop some sagebrush growing from the side of the cliff just below the trail. He crawled forward, carefully reached out, and snatched the hat. He pressed it firmly over his head, and as he did, his gaze turned upward. For an instant, he thought he'd spotted an eagle circling high above him. Then he realized it was a vulture, actually several of them. "Sorry, guys. No cleanup crew needed today."

"My God, Indy, you're alive!"

He looked up to see Smitty on his horse, careening around a bend at a dangerously fast trot. The two other horses trailed after him. Indy used the wall to brace himself as he stood up. "I took the shortcut down."

Smitty stared in amazement. "I thought you were a goner for sure."

"I don't go away that easily." Indy mounted his horse and grimaced as the back of his shirt rubbed against a patch of raw skin.

The path soon narrowed even further. Now the girth of the horses was actually wider than the trail. But to Indy's surprise Smitty stayed in the saddle. He was about to suggest they walk when Smitty's horse reared up and then tap-danced on the tightrope-like ledge.

"You slimy devil!" Smitty growled. But the horse wasn't the object of his anger. Smitty pulled out his revolver and fired twice at the ground.

The horses pranced nervously and Indy thought they were all about to hurtle into the abyss. He reined in Chico as best he could. "Whoa! Whoa, boy!"

"Got him!" Smitty shouted, and he urged his horse forward. The beast hesitated, then moved ahead.

Indy felt Chico's wariness as the animal spotted a six-foot rattler laying lifeless in the center of the trail. "It's okay, boy. Go on." But nothing that Indy said could persuade the horse to step over the dead snake. He finally unhitched his whip and with one swipe knocked the rattler over the ledge. "There, that suit you?"

The horse snorted and they moved on.

In spite of the treacherous terrain and lurking vipers, the remainder of the journey to the ruins came off without incident. As they arrived at the junction of Kane Gulch and Grand Gulch near midday, Indy glimpsed the ancient Anasazi pueblo, their destination. Like the cliff dwellings of Mesa Verde, the stone structures had been built under an overhang.

"Mara!" Smitty yelled. His voice echoed in the canyon, and seemed to violate the sanctity of the ruins. "Mara!"

No answer.

The overhang was nearly ten yards deep and curved so that they couldn't see all the buildings. The ones closest to them faced east, while those at the other end looked south.

"Well, if there's anyone here, they certainly know we've arrived," Indy said, not exactly pleased by Smitty's shouting.

"It's deserted. Just as I thought."

Indy got down from his horse. "Let's not give up so quickly. Maybe she's out getting water. Or maybe she's gone and left us a message."

Smitty didn't answer, but Indy could tell that he was disappointed. The old prospector didn't have much to say about Mara, but his concern was etched in his dark expression.

As they climbed into the ruins, Indy was immediately enchanted by the silent village. He imagined what it had been like when the village was alive and thriving. He closed his eyes a moment, and could literally hear the sound of children playing, of women grinding corn, of men gathering for a hunt. But he forced himself to focus on his search for Mara. He noticed markings on the rear wall, not rock art, but the message Mara had passed to Shannon: No. 73 AMNH 1920 N.C.N. and B.T.B.H.

Seeing it now made Indy even more intent on finding out why Mara had wanted him to come here. Maybe she'd intended to meet him here, but hadn't made it. Or hadn't made it yet. The only other alternative was that this was the hiding place of the staff. But where would he look? It could literally take weeks for him to scour these ruins to find a buried artifact, even one that was only recently hidden.

"I'll go down to the other end and work my way back," Smitty said, and he disappeared around a wall.

Indy moved from room to room, making a quick inspection of each one. He passed an open-topped kiva. Its log ceiling had vanished long ago, and its interior had been filled with rubble. When he came upon another desecrated kiva, he bent down and picked out a pottery shard from the rubble. He brushed the dirt from its exterior, revealing a network of dark lines that had been painted over the original pale orange hue. He dropped it back into the kiva and continued on.

He stopped to examine a handprint left behind in the mortar of a wall. When he placed his own hand over it, his fingers measured nearly an inch longer than the person who had made the impression. It gave him an odd feeling to think that the person who had made the impression had been dead for at least six hundred years. In spite of his experience in ruins much older than this one, the handprint made the place utterly human. It told him and everyone who would ever see it that people had lived and died here, and that they were not so different from anyone else. Even though the village had been excavated by Wetherill and others, Indy knew that if he spent the summer here he would no doubt learn much more about the people who had lived here. Maybe some other time.

As he walked on without finding any indication that Mara, or anyone else for that matter, had been here recently, he became more and more frustrated. If the point was for him to find the staff, then why hadn't she been more specific? He wished Shannon were here now so he could question him about Mara's exact words. She must have given some hint about where she had expected him to look. But maybe it was obvious.

He asked himself where he would hide something in these ruins if he wanted an archaeologist to find it. He thought about his question as he examined a small storage room that gave no hint of any hidden secrets. He couldn't think of a single place. He wracked his mind. There was something else that Mara had said to Shannon: *"It's ironic that we're in a kiva and so close to the underworld."*

The underworld. What better place to hide the staff? Shannon had thought she was changing the subject, but Mara actually was giving him another clue. The Anasazis' connection to the underworld was the *sipapu*, the small hole in the floor of a kiva. Maybe that was what she'd done with it. But the kivas he'd seen so far had been littered with rubble nearly to their rim.

"Any luck?" Smitty called out as he ambled toward Indy.

Indy shook his head. "How about you?"

"I didn't find Mara, if that's what you mean, or any sign that she's been here."

"Did you see any kivas?" Indy asked.

"A couple."

"Full of rubble?"

Smitty motioned with his hand. "One of them was. The other one way back was fairly clean."

"Show me where it is."

The kiva in question wasn't exactly uncluttered, but it would be possible to clear away the rubble without much trouble. Indy lowered himself over the side. The early morning sunlight would reach back here, but by late afternoon the kiva was shrouded in shadow. "I've got a feeling about this kiva, Smitty. I want to find the *sipapu*."

"The hole to the underworld," Smitty said, chuckling. "You think that's where the answers are?"

"We'll see."

"Tell you what, I'm gonna get the lantern. It's dark back here, and my eyes aren't so good anymore. Then I'll give you a hand."

By the time Smitty returned, a pile of rocks was growing outside of the kiva as Indy tossed one after another over his shoulder. "Watch where you're throwing," Smitty groused. "You almost hit me."

He lit the lantern and passed it down to Indy, who

held it up to see if there were any signs of the *sipapu*. Most of the rocks he'd removed had come from the center of the kiva and now an indention in the floor was visible. But the depression was too large for the *sipapu*. "This must be the firepit." He held the lantern up to the wall and circled the kiva until he found another indention. "Okay, here we go."

"In the wall? I thought the hole to the underworld was in the floor."

"It is in the floor," Indy said as he paced across the kiva. "That was the ventilator shaft." He dropped to one knee and reached for a rock. "Right about here is where we should find the—"

"What is it?" Smitty asked.

Indy's thoughts had flown back to his eagle dream. "It's a feather, Smitty, an eagle feather," he said. "Ain't that something."

"So what?"

"It just reminded me of something. Doesn't matter now." Indy quickly removed rocks, sifting through the loose dirt beneath the rocks. His anticipation grew with each stone he pulled away. Then he felt something. "It looks like a piece of canvas, Smitty. Can't tell yet, but it might be a bag."

# 13

## DEPARTURES

From her perch atop a boulder, Mara had an excellent view of Sipapu Bridge, one of three natural sandstone formations that arced gracefully over White Canyon. The bridge and the entire canyon were bathed in a pale yellow light as the sun hovered over the canyon wall in its slow, orderly descent. She imagined Indian priests patiently watching the sun day after day, year after year, noting where the sun rose and set, calculating the hours and minutes and seconds, and precisely marking the change of seasons.

It wasn't the first time Mara had been here, but the view of the bridge still enchanted her, left her with a sense of eternity. The bridge connected the distant past with the present and the future. The events of her life, which seemed so overwhelming right now, would take place in a minuscule speck of time in the geological sense of things. The thought was at once comforting and frightening. Comforting in that her trials would be over before she knew it, but frightening because she sensed the immensity of time and space and her relative insignificance. She was like a moth, with a life span measured in hours instead of years. She'd bat her wings a few times, then vanish from the world.

Mara looked around, wondering what had happened to Aguila. She'd wanted to leave right away to meet Indy and her father at Junction Ruin, which was only a few miles, away. But Aguila had told her that was unnecessary. Everything was unfolding as was intended, and there was no reason to rush.

Her gaze shifted to the valley floor where three men on horseback moved single file at a fast trot. She raised a hand and waved. The Utes had remained out of sight ever since Aguila had arrived, and she'd assumed they feared him because they thought he might be a scout for the law. But when she found Ben filling his skins with water, he told her that they couldn't stay here with the Navajo witch and were leaving. They feared him even more than the law officers who were searching for them.

Mara had never felt the slightest apprehension around Aguila. Maybe it was because she'd grown up in a culture where witches were a superstition from the past, while her Ute friends saw them as real and dreadful. She had met Aguila after she'd begun her search for the staff. Rosie had steered her on the right path, but she'd warned Mara that Aguila was a strange man. She'd said that he'd hidden the staff and would never sell it to her.

So Mara had visited him under a pretext. She'd made a couple of dozen drawings of rock art, and her plan was to ask him to help her understand the meaning of the drawings for a book she planned to write. But just making contact with Aguila had been an unusually difficult task. Even though Rosie had told her where he lived, finding the exact site was nearly impossible since no one she asked would admit that they had ever heard of him. Finally, Mara had found the hogan, just as Rosie had described it, near a stream and a row of Ponderosa trees that served as a windbreak.

Even then, Mara couldn't find Aguila. She waited two days and finally left. The second time she made the trip she stayed three days, and only when she was about to leave did he finally show up. He stepped out of his door as if he'd been there all along and asked what she wanted. Mara was sure the place had been vacant and that he must have snuck inside when she wasn't looking.

Aguila had studied her drawings, and then told her that she needed more drawings in her collection before he could say anything about them. She'd sensed that he would tell her nothing about the staff if she asked, so she'd left and returned a month later with several new drawings of petroglyphs and pictographs.

At first, Aguila seemed impressed that she had done what he said, but then he told her he would take her to a place where she would find many more rock paintings and etchings. They walked for several hours until they reached a place she later learned was known as White Canyon. Aguila said it was a special, sacred place and that she could always find sanctuary here. He showed her ancient pueblos tucked under overhangs that had been perfectly preserved. Even their wooden beam ceilings were intact. He also showed her where there were springs with clean, cool water bubbling from the earth.

Mara spent hours carefully copying paintings and carvings of shape-changing shamans, animals, and mysterious symbols. Finally, when she presented her drawings to Aguila, she said she had a special request, and told him that she was interested in recovering the unicorn's horn, the staff which he'd bought at the pawnshop. Aguila had acted as if he didn't hear her. He'd simply examined her drawings, then remarked that she was still missing an important one that she would have to find on her own.

"But what about the staff?" she'd asked in frustration.

"When you find the rock drawing, you will have the key to your quest," he answered. "Then the staff will be yours for the taking." She persisted, asking where to look and what to look for, but he only told her that she must find it on her own.

After returning to her home, she found out what a truly unusual place she had visited. It was not until 1883 that the first non-Indian had entered White Canyon. A prospector named Cass Hite had passed on tales of the huge stone bridges and ruins he'd discovered. Then in 1904, a *National Geographic* expedition visited the canyon, and four years later Theodore Roosevelt proclaimed the area a national monument. A short time later the names of the bridges were changed from Edwin, Augusta, and Caroline to the Hopi names: Katchina, Sipapu, and Owachomo. Although the Hopis had never lived in the canyon, it was thought that they were descendants of the Anasazis.

Mara had written Indy about her experiences and drawings, but she hadn't mentioned Aguila. He was an important contact and she didn't want to do anything that would endanger her relationship with the old Navajo. She'd said nothing about him to anyone, with the exception of Rosie, in whom she'd confided everything.

Suddenly, Mara's thoughts were interrupted by a voice from behind her.

"Come with me now."

Aguila stood on top of another boulder ten feet away. In spite of the steep incline and loose rubble on the canyon slope she hadn't heard him approach. But that didn't surprise her. She was used to Aguila's peculiar way of coming and going. She hadn't seen him for a couple of hours and had assumed he'd wandered off on one of his inexplicable jaunts.

"Where have you been?"

"I wanted to give the Utes a chance to leave. If I were here, they would've been too afraid to show themselves."

"Do they have reason to be fearful?"

He laughed. "Not today."

She didn't like his answer. "Do you hurt people with your magic?"

He looked out at Sipapu Bridge for a moment. "There is an old story of two witches who ascended from the underworld at the time when mankind was young. One of them brought corn to feed the people; the other brought death so that the earth wouldn't be overpopulated. But death, or even the thought of it, caused such horror that all witches became evil in the eyes of the people."

"But you're saying that some do evil and others don't?"

"What you call evil and good is not as easy to understand as some might think. What about you? Are you good or evil?"

"Well, I don't think of myself as an evil person, if that's what you mean."

Aguila chuckled softly. "All of us have the dark and the light within us. But remember this: the wolves who get into trouble are usually weak and inexperienced. Most are greedy and cast spells to make themselves rich at the expense of others. The dark rules their weaknesses and eventually brings them to their knees."

Mara nodded. "There's a saying: A little knowledge can be dangerous."

"Exactly. The powerful wolves work with the natural forces rather than against them. No brute force or exhibitions of power are necessary, only magical nudges."

"And you are one of the powerful ones?"

"Sometimes, I do display certain powers to wake people up." Aguila started walking back toward the ruins where Mara and the Utes had been camped.

"Are we going to find Indy and my father now?"

"We'll meet them at my house."

"What about the staff?" Mara asked. "Tomorrow is the solstice."

"You will have it at sunrise, if you know where to look."

"What? Aguila, that's not fair. You said you would take me to it on the solstice."

"Have you found the sacred drawing?"

"Yes." She hurried past him and into the shelter. She pointed at the floor as Aguila peered through the doorway. "Here!"

He looked at her drawing. His expression gave no indication of what he thought. Now, suddenly, she wasn't so confident. "Well, am I right?"

He nodded. "The right symbols, but the wrong location. You still must find them."

"But I don't know where to look."

He shrugged. "Keep looking."

With that, Aguila left the shelter and climbed the path toward the mesa top and the horses.

Mara was furious. "Wait. Where do I look? I don't have any idea. It's too late."

When he didn't answer, she hurried after him. "Aguila, please, don't do this to me," she pleaded. "I don't have time for these games."

Aguila mounted his horse. "You have plenty of time, if you don't waste it."

Indy cleared the rubble carefully away from the small canvas sack. He had no idea what was inside, but he knew it had something to do with Mara. Quite a coincidence. He'd dreamed of seeing an eagle lose a feather, and now he'd found one at the spot he was supposed to look. A lucky feather. He'd leave it at that.

"What is it you got there?" Smitty asked as Indy lifted a small canvas sack from the *sipapu.*

"Don't know."

"It ain't that ivory staff. I can tell you that right now."

Indy opened the bag and found a rectangular object inside that was wrapped in cloth like a mummy. Whatever it was hadn't been here long, because the cloth was in good condition. He carefully unraveled the cloth until he was holding a leather-bound book. The leather was brittle and cracked, and Indy opened its cover as if he were handling the wings of a butterfly.

"It looks like a journal of some sort," Indy said as

he sat on the floor of the kiva. Smitty moved closer, holding the lantern over his shoulder as Indy quickly paged through the book. It seemed to be a family history, but the ivory staff was at the center of it. "Mara's made some notes here at the end."

"Let me see that," Smitty said, grabbing for the book.

Indy held it out of the old prospector's reach. "Hey, take it easy. What are you doing?"

"If that's my daughter's diary, I should get it. Until she shows up, I'm the rightful owner." Smitty's fists were clenched and he looked as if he were about to punch Indy.

"You told me your eyes aren't very good. I'll do you a favor and read it aloud."

Smitty hesitated, then nodded. "Just get on with it."

What was wrong with him, anyhow? Indy wondered. He held the journal up to the light and started with Mara's notes.

*Now you've read the history of my family's association with the unicorn's horn. I discovered this record among my mother's possessions after her death, and of course I became curious about what had happened to the mysterious staff. I looked everywhere, but couldn't find it. I remembered seeing it once as a child, and recalled my mother scolding me, telling me never to touch it. She called it an alicorn, a word that I'd never heard. She said it had been in the family for a long time, but that it was best left alone. I never saw it after that day.*

*When I didn't find the staff anywhere in the house, I went to Bluff and asked my father about it. He was gruff with me and said he didn't know anything about it, and not to bother him about such trivial matters. He denied ever having it, but I didn't believe him. We argued, and I brought up all the old stuff about him never being around when I was young, that his drinking was the reason my mother left him, and how he hadn't even responded when I telegramed him of Mother's death.*

*He stormed out of the house, and I went to my room to pack. I decided to leave right away for Rome and my last year of study, even though I'd planned to stay another week. Maybe it's an unfair comparison, but at the time I thought that even Mussolini seemed more reasonable and compassionate than my own father.*

"Well, I'll be damned," Smitty muttered. "She compared me to some no-good dictator. I suppose I should've told Mara right out what I'd done with it, but she put me on the defensive and I got a stubborn streak."

"Listen to this," Indy said, and read the next line.

*That was when Rosie knocked on my door, and told me Smitty had pawned the staff, and that she knew who had bought it. She'd never told Smitty, even when he'd started to ask about it. She was afraid that he would find it again and everything would go bad.*

Smitty kicked a stone and cursed. "I can't believe that woman. My own wife. She knew all along and never told me. Who bought it from Neddie? Does she say?"

Indy found the name. "Yeah, she does. It's Aguila. He's the one."

"For crying out loud. Let's go back and have a talk

with that old Indian. He's been playin' games with us."

Indy wanted to keep reading the journal, but he knew Smitty was right. He had the feeling that Aguila was not only the key to finding the staff, but also the key to locating Mara, and that's what mattered most.

"Neddie, I think we need a little more practice before we go onstage together," Shannon said as he laid the saxophone down in its case.

"What do you mean? Look, we've already got an audience."

The wrinkled shopkeeper gestured toward the dozen or so people, mostly Navajos, who watched them as if they were wild animals in a cage. Shannon didn't blame them. The combination of the old man's bagpipes and his saxophone created a sound that could be mistaken for the call of a couple of strange beasts in heat, or maybe the howl of a rabid creature, or both.

"Well, they didn't have to pay to hear us," Shannon said. "On the other hand, we didn't have to pay them to listen, either."

"That's the spirit, young man. Now are you ready to try another one?"

"That's it for me, today, Neddie." Shannon had walked over to the trading post nearly two hours ago to get another opinion on Aguila. But if Neddie or the others knew him, they weren't letting on.

"What's your hurry, Jackie?"

"I've got to go see about dinner. Rosie promised to make me something special."

"Probably Navajo pizza. That's her specialty. It's like a pizza on fried Indian bread."

"Sounds good," Shannon said. "It'll be a nice change from Smitty's mutton soup."

When he reached the house, he noticed a dusty Packard parked on the street. It hadn't been there when he left, and he wondered if another boarder had arrived. As he approached the back door, the smell of frying dough wafted through the screen door. "Let me guess," he called out, stepping into the kitchen. "Navajo—"

Rosie was sitting at the kitchen table and a man was clutching her braid near the back of her head. He held a revolver in his hand, and he was pointing it at Shannon's chest. "—pizza . . . What's going on?"

Shannon recognized the man as one of those who'd accosted him at Sand Island, the one with the heavy brow and flattened nose. But his attention shifted as another figure stepped forward from the parlor. "What's it look like, a bloody picnic?"

Walcott. His left arm was in a sling and a cigarette hung from his lip. "What are you doing here?"

"What do you think, Shannon?"

"I don't know, but I've had enough of this."

Walcott pointed to the table, and winced as his bad arm slid to one side. "Sit down!"

Shannon glanced at the thug and revolver, then did as he was told. "What do you want from us?"

"Where's your pal Jones?"

"He's gone."

"We already know that. He's looking for Mara. Where did he go?"

"I don't know."

"I think you do, and we'll wait right here until you tell us."

"We can beat it out of him," the thug said.

"We'll do this my way, Jimbo," Walcott said. "I've been waiting for years, and I can wait a little while longer."

"I find it hard to believe that you're running around the desert looking for a phantom unicorn's horn," Shannon said in a derogatory tone.

Walcott smiled and nodded to the Bible that Shannon had left on the counter. "If you believe in the Bible, then you must believe in unicorns."

"Maybe they existed once, but they're long gone now," Shannon responded.

Walcott blew smoke toward Shannon. Perspiration beaded on his forehead; he looked flushed. "All except for one certain legendary unicorn's horn, and it's going to be mine."

"What do you want with it?"

"You could say it's been an interest of mine for some time now, and considering my past experiences with Mara and your buddy Jones, I think you can understand why I might go the extra step to get the artifact."

"Where did it come from?" Shannon asked.

"First tell me where I can find Jones, and I'll fill you in on all the details."

"He doesn't know where the horn is," Shannon shot back.

"But he knows where Mara is, doesn't he? And she knows where it's hidden."

"I already told you," Rosie insisted. "She doesn't know where it is any more than Professor Jones does. Now just leave them alone, and leave us alone."

Walcott adjusted his arm in the sling. "How can you be so sure she doesn't know?"

Shannon suddenly realized he might know a way

to get these guys off their backs. "Why don't you take a shortcut and ask an old Indian named Aguila?" Shannon said. "He probably knows where the staff is. He's the one who bought it."

"No!" shouted Rosie. "He's my grandfather!"

Walcott dropped his cigarette on the kitchen floor and crushed it. "Now we're getting somewhere."

Jimbo shoved Rosie's head toward the table. "Start talking, squaw. Where do we find Grandpa?"

"Easy, Jimbo, easy," Walcott said.

"You won't be able to find him," she said, gasping for breath as the ranch hand loosened his grip.

"Either you take us to him now, or you both die." Walcott's voice was cold and hard and Shannon didn't doubt that he meant what he said. "What's it going to be?"

"Leave my grandfather out of it. I'll take you to where the staff is hidden. I know the place."

"So the truth finally comes out!" Walcott crowed. "Where is it?"

"Hovenweep."

"Ah, hidden in an Anasazi ruin," Walcott said. "How clever. You knew all along and you didn't even tell ol' Smitty."

The way Walcott talked about Smitty, as if he were a friend, bothered Shannon. But then, everything about Walcott bothered him. "Okay, now you know. So leave us alone."

"Not quite, Shannon. We've got an archaeological excavation ahead of us tonight, and you and Jimbo are going to be my excavators."

# 14

## THE JOURNAL

As the sun vanished over a ridge in the distance, its rays created an aura around Aguila's darkened hogan. Near the front door, the dog yelped at Indy and Smitty, and a couple of chickens pecked in the dirt. But there was no sign of Aguila. Still, they waited by their horses at what Smitty considered a respectable distance.

"I don't think he's here," the old prospector said.

Somehow, Indy wasn't surprised. He was exhausted from the trip and was sure Smitty must've felt the same way. But he was also relieved that they'd managed to negotiate the harrowing trail out of the canyon without a single slip up, so to speak, and it would've taken only one to ruin a perfectly good life.

Smitty held the reins of both horses. "I'll take them out back and look around," he said.

"While you're doing that, I'll wait in the car and

catch up on my reading." Indy patted his pocket, which held the journal.

Smitty hesitated a moment. "The rest of it's stuff about the past, right?"

"Looks that way." Actually, Indy hadn't finished reading Mara's entry, but no need to tell Smitty.

"You come across any more references to me, you let me know."

Indy chuckled. "Will do, Smitty."

It felt good to ease behind the wheel of the Ford again. Yesterday at this time, he didn't care if he ever saw the car again. But that was before his horseback ride through Kane Gulch. He took out a candle from his pack and lit it. Then he opened the journal to the first page. The entry was dated October 24, 1798.

*My name is James Rogers and I am beginning this diary to record all that I know about a certain relic from antiquity which came into my possession in the year 1787. I am speaking of an unusual ivory sceptor, which, if one is to believe its previous owner, was made from an alicorn, that is, a unicorn's horn. In appearance, the relic is straight and slender, rather than curved as one would expect from an elephant tusk. It also has peculiar ripples along its entire shaft, which creates the illusion that it is twisted. The staff measures forty-two and a half inches in length from hilt to point, which is capped in silver. It is approximately one and three quarters inches in diameter at its hilt and gradually narrows to a point.*

*In addition, the sceptor bears a silver-gilded handle in the design of a double-headed eagle. The emblem is probably Hittite in origin and perhaps was brought to Europe by the crusaders. Whatever its origin, it was adopted by the Romans in the fifteenth*

century. *The handle also bears a Greek inscription:*
Ἰωάννης Παλαιολόγος βασιλεύς + Ἑλικόρνις
ἀντιφάρμακον.

I interpreted the inscription before I purchased the staff, and was very pleased to discover that it read as follows: John Palaeologus, Emperor. Alicorn good against poison. I believe that the emperor in question was John VI of the Palaeologus dynasty who ruled as Emperor of the East from 1425 to 1448. I should also mention that the lower portion of the staff had been dipped in a vermillion dye, and etched in the dye were Greek and Arabic phrases, no doubt intended to increase the power of the alicorn.

Needless to say, I bought the sceptor, and at a bargain price, I might add. Over the next several months, I spent many hours in the British Museum Library and St. Mark's Library in Venice studying the lore and history of alicorns, and I now can say that I know as much of the hazy history of this relic as can be learned.

The alicorn in question was said to have been taken at the fall of Constantinople in 1204 and became part of the Venetian share of the spoils. Two centuries later, as I said, it was in the hands of John VI, the Emperor of the East. During his reign, he visited Venice to seek help for his crumbling empire. He may have brought the alicorn with him on this journey, and parted with it. Whatever the reason, it appears that the alicorn fell into the hands of a wealthy jewel merchant named Giorgio Belbava. Records at St. Mark's Library show that in 1488, this alicorn was given by the son of Belbava to Doge Barbarigo, and the Doge turned it over to the procurators of the cathedral. The man I bought it from had no idea how his father had obtained the relic, and when I bought it, I confess, I did not press for a full explanation.

Approximately one year after my purchase, I journeyed to America with my family and settled in Massachusetts. The alicorn came with me. Within a decade, I became a rather wealthy landowner and a few weeks ago, I found the opportunity to travel back to England for the first time since my departure.

To my surprise, barely a day after my arrival I happened upon the very man who had sold me the alicorn. His name is Jonathan Ainsworth, and he was the office manager of an enterprise which rented carriages to visitors in London. At first, he did not recognize me, but when I refreshed his memory, he asked with undisguised curiosity about the fate of the alicorn and its influences upon my life. I told him that it was quite safe at my residence in Boston and that I had no idea what he meant by influences upon my life.

Oddly enough, he seemed relieved by my response, then proceeded to tell me that his father had wanted the alicorn destroyed, rather than sold, and that near the end of his life the elder Ainsworth had become convinced that the relic was responsible for his downfall. I told him of my good fortune and that his father's calamitous end was lamentable, but it had nothing to do with the staff. I was, however, curious about how the alicorn had come into the family's possession, and asked what he knew of it.

He explained that his father had written a letter which answered that very question, and when I requested permission to read it, he not only agreed but said I could have it. We met the following day at his office where I took possession of the letter. I found the historical information fascinating and new to me,

*but I must admit I was somewhat disturbed by Ains-
worth's dire commentary. Before I said farewell to
the younger Ainsworth we both agreed that it was
good that the old superstitions were dead.*

*For historical purposes, I will now copy Michael
Ainsworth's letter word for word. In the not too distant future I can imagine that the history of these
mysterious alicorns will fade from memory. So, with
that in mind, I am preserving this tale from the past.
Although I have strong doubts about the supposed
mystical nature of the alicorn, I have no reason to
believe that the related material is untrue. You, dear
reader, can judge for yourself.*

Indy looked up and saw that Smitty hadn't returned. He was probably rubbing down the animals.
So Indy decided to keep reading and see what Ainsworth himself had to say. The letter was dated
March 16, 1785.

*Dear Jonathan,*

*When you read this letter, my son, I hope you are
in good health. I hold no such hopes for myself as I
see my life rapidly deteriorating. I want to tell you
why it is happening, and how you can prevent falling
upon a similar fate.*

*My story begins when you were a young child and
I was at the start of my career as a barrister. At that
time, I was hired by a rather unusual organization
called the People of the Horn, which functioned in a
stately manse in Mayfair. In spite of its name, the
organization's sole purpose, of all things, seemed to
be directed at disavowing belief in unicorns, and it
was my job to keep their legal matters in order. I
should say they were having quite good success. The*

*unicorn's horn or alicorn, as it is known, had been recommended by physicians to ward off poisons, and infectious diseases, particularly the Plague, for centuries. In fact, powder of alicorn was listed as an official drug by the English Royal College of Physicians for many years. Then in 1746, as the People of the Horn began loudly ridiculing the drug, the Society dropped it from their approved list.*

*Out of curiosity, I began looking into the organization's background, as I had access to many of its papers, and soon discovered that they were an ancient order that was started in the twelfth century by an Arab mystic who had taken up residence in London. It became apparent that at least at the onset, the People of the Horn were very much inclined to believe in unicorns and were intrigued in particular by the unicorn's horn. From their documents, I learned that by the year 1600, they were aware of at least a dozen alicorns in Europe and England, which they were convinced were actual horns of unicorns. Most were kept in great churches and monasteries. They were regarded as sacred objects and were sometimes used as pontifical staffs. Two of them, I recall with certainty, were stored in St. Mark's Cathedral, another in the Tower of London's lower Jewel House.*

*I found this all rather amusing until I accidentally came upon secret documents, which revealed much more than I really cared to know. It seems that the People of the Horn had been actively involved in raiding the treasure houses of the clergy and royalty in search of alicorns, the very objects that they professed did not exist. There has been much looting of church treasures in the last century, and it seems that the People of the Horn were not the least of those involved.*

*I was dismayed that I was working with an organization which had secretly participated in criminal activity, but I was also curious about its motives. After all, the unicorn's horn of lore was supposedly a benevolent object with magical properties of healing and protection against poison. So why would the People of the Horn turn against the alicorn?*

*I continued my study of their records, and discovered that it was during the middle of the last century that the organization became concerned about the alicorn, claiming that its properties were no longer effective for healing and, in fact, were possibly detrimental. They conjectured that after a certain time, separated from the animal itself, the horn's magical properties reversed themselves. They pointed to several deaths in rather peculiar circumstances, in which individuals of considerable wealth and stature, who were the owners of alicorns, had fallen victim to a poison of one sort or another, or had lost their fortunes or status. As I read on, I became more concerned. I discovered that the People of the Horn, as recently as five years earlier, had robbed a visiting sheik of his staff. After the crime, they ruled that the artifact in question was merely an elephant's tusk carved to the likeness of a walking stick.*

*To continue my own story, late one night as I perused the secret records that were kept in a vault in the library, I heard voices coming from the main office. I quickly put away the file I was reading and secreted myself among the shelves. At first, I was going to announce my presence and make some excuse for working past midnight. But as Fate would have it, before I knocked I overheard several members congratulating themselves for committing a crime. They apparently had entered a nobleman's treasury and stolen what they believed was an alicorn.*

*More members joined in the celebration and from what I overheard, I learned that they believed the relic in question was the last true alicorn in existence. It apparently had been among the treasures of St. Mark's Cathedral for more than two centuries, along with another alicorn. But when the treasure chests were invaded seventy-five years ago, only one alicorn had been discovered. The other one had been apparently absconded with earlier, and until recently its whereabouts had been unknown.*

*I trembled as I listened, both fearful and fascinated. It seemed they were planning to keep this alicorn, since they doubted they would ever encounter another one. They believed that their knowledge of the horn would protect them from its dangers. They would be like the owner of a poisonous snake, who cares for the creature, but respects its deadly quality. It would be a symbol of power for the organization and a reason for them to continue their secret existence as true-believers in unicorns into the nineteenth century.*

*I remained hidden while they argued about who should be the temporary caretaker of the alicorn until a permanent home was decided upon. The man who had heard about the nobleman's alicorn wanted to be in charge of it; so did the man who carried out the break-in, as did the one in charge of internal security. Finally, everyone agreed that no one was to remove the alicorn from the room. It would remain there until the following day when an emergency meeting of all members would be held and a formal decision made on its disposition.*

*When they had all wandered off for the night I*

crept into the darkened room where their celebration had been held. At first I didn't see the alicorn. But after a thorough search, I found what appeared to be a staff tucked inside of a cloth rifle case on a shelf in the corner of the adjacent cloakroom. I never thought twice about it. I walked out the door with the alicorn and took it home.

In the days following my daring theft, chaos reigned among the People of the Horn. One secret meeting after another was held and I was told it involved matters that did not pertain to my work. Later, I heard that three members had been purged from the group, and I suspected they were the three who had wanted to take charge of the alicorn. I found the entire episode extremely amusing, and, in fact, I had decided to return the alicorn to the cloakroom to further the drama and intrigue. But before I acted, a chilling tragedy occurred. All three men who had fought for control of the alicorn died quite suddenly of arsenic poisoning, and their possessions were pillaged.

At that point, I wanted nothing further to do with the organization, and looked for ways to resign without drawing attention to myself. About this time, I met Frederick Mathers and we formed our own legal firm. Soon our business was flourishing, and I had no time for the People of the Horn. I resigned my position and no questions were ever asked. I never told Frederick about the alicorn, nor did I think that it had anything to do with our immense success. But I did come to think of it as a good luck charm, and kept it in my office.

Later, I found that when I held the staff and made a specific request, more times than not my request would be fulfilled. After this happened on several occasions, I began to regard the alicorn as a talisman possessing magical properties. At times, I wondered why the People of the Horn had gone about destroying alicorns. If any others were as endowed as my own, their destruction had been a great disservice, a tragedy.

You know most of the rest, Jonathan. In spite of my wealth, I was never satisfied. I always wanted more. You were old enough to understand when I seemed to lose my judgment and made one poor business deal after another until our wealth was depleted. Whenever I held the staff, I felt ill, as if my life had been poisoned, and soon another dose of bad luck followed.

Mathers carried on by himself, leaving me desperate and near destitute. When we moved to Yorkshire, hoping to start anew, I put the alicorn away for good. Yet, I could not bring myself to destroy it. Things became even worse as I accepted clients who did not pay me. Finally, completely disheartened, I schemed with one of my criminal clients to defraud a house of charity, and I was caught.

If I only could do it all over again, I would never have touched that cursed staff, the unicorn's horn. I blame its bad magic for the twists and turns of my life. So please, take my advice and destroy it. Break it into a thousand pieces and spread it over the city. Then pray to God that none of its evil will ever touch your life. That's all I ask.
Your father,
Michael Ainsworth

Indy looked up from the journal. It was dark now and he could see nothing outside of the car. "Swell story," he said aloud. If it was true, they ought to just leave the staff where it was. But Mara obviously had her own ideas about it. He blew out the candle and peered toward the hogan. He noticed a flicker of light in one of the windows. Smitty, he hoped, was preparing something to eat.

There wasn't much more left to read so he lit the candle again and returned to the journal. The next entry was dated in 1862, and immediately caught his attention.

*When my grandfather, James Rogers, returned to America he discovered that in his absence a series of misfortunes had befallen him. Most of his land had been confiscated because his accountant had not paid taxes and had stolen a large sum of his money. Less than a year later, heavily in debt, he died suddenly of a heart attack while eating an apple.*

*Years later, my grandmother told me that she thought the apple was laced with poison and that he had killed himself. She said that Grandpa was convinced that an evil power had ruined him, and she thought the same power might have forced him to commit suicide. Grandma never explained this evil power, and I'm not sure she knew what it was, but I believe I discovered what Grandpa was talking about.*

*I found the unicorn's horn, along with Grandpa's diary, in a steamer trunk behind a false wall in the attic of the family house in 1852. I was sixteen. I played with the strange staff for awhile, then put it back in the trunk when Mother called me. I didn't read the diary until many years later. As far as I can tell, my father never knew about the unicorn's horn, and if Grandma did know of it, she never told him.*

*When I was eighteen, I felt inspired to move to the*

*West. I took the steamer trunk from the attic and packed my clothing and a few belongings. I took the staff and unread diary along with me as family mementos. I traveled for months, finally settling in Escalante, Utah. There, I married and started a family on a small ranch.*

*Just today I opened the old steamer trunk and rediscovered the strange staff and diary. After I read the diary, I put the staff back into the trunk. I don't like what I read about this alicorn. I never even knew unicorns were real creatures. But I'm not superstitious so I'm not going to worry about it.*

It was signed Peter Rogers. Maybe he lived happily ever after, Indy thought. There was still more, and he continued reading. The next entry was written four years later, but it was in another handwriting.

*I never knew my husband could write such a nice piece as that. It was about that time that Pete started prospecting some. I didn't mind it none, but then the last couple of years he started gowen off for weeks at a time without saying nothing to us.*

*Six months ago, he left and this time I ain't expecten him back. He's done left me and Sara behind. I don't write too good, but I wanted to put this down on paper so Sara knows her pappy turned bad. Don't know nothing about this pretty ivory walking stick, and don't care none about it.*
*Lorraine Rogers*

Another entry followed. Indy kept reading without pause.

*My mama didn't have to write that down because I found out on my own that Daddy had gone bad. Mama died when I was twelve. That was about six years after Daddy disappeared. I later heard from a rancher that Daddy found a rich vein of gold and then took up with some young bar floozy. But he wasn't ever able to enjoy his wealth for long, because he died while cleaning out chunks of gold. They use arsenic for that, you know.*

*Anyhow, I was adopted by a Mormon family, and this cursed staff and diary were about the only thing left of my past. For better or worse, I've kept them. They are a part of me. But many times I've wondered if my Fate affected others in a bad way.*

*When I was nineteen, back in '79, our family joined a wagon train of two hundred and fifty Mormons for a journey into the southeast part of Utah to start a mission. It was a horrible trip. The trail was no good for wagons and we couldn't go back because of the snow in the high country. We took a vote and everyone agreed that we should go on and build our own road. Somehow, we finally made it through that terrible canyon they call Grand Gulch and when we reached the San Juan River, we stopped. None of us wanted to go any further, and that became our town. It was called Bluff. But the mission there just never took hold. It was all over a year later, but most of us stayed on.*

*The next spring I met Oscar Smithers, who was about the only non-Mormon in town. He worked with the Wetherill brothers on a ranch, and talked of getting his own spread. A year later we got married and I soon had Mara. We lived with my stepparents, because the house was roomy, and besides, Smitty spent a lot of time at the ranch.*

*Things were good for a few years. But I'll be
damned if he didn't get the prospecting bug just like
my daddy. He did real well for a few years, and I
made him promise me that he would pay for Mara to
go to college because all her teachers said she was
quite exceptional. That was what I heard over and
over. But then Smitty found the bottle, and it got so
bad that I decided to leave. I took six thousand dollars Smitty had hidden inside the mattress, and I
went to Santa Fe with Mara. I never felt bad about
taking the money, not a bit, because Smitty got the
house. And I left him something else, too. That unicorn's horn.*

*I didn't want Mara to inherit it or have anything to
do with it. Someday, Mara, you'll read this diary, and
understand about our family's history. But for now
I'm keeping it hidden. You're young and hopeful, and
I don't want any ideas of curses hanging over your
pretty head.*
*Sara Rogers Smithers*

Indy was about to close the journal and join
Smitty, but he remembered that he hadn't completely read Mara's entry. He turned to the last para-
graphs.

*In spite of everything I know about the staff, I am
intent on finding it. Although the coincidences are
numerous and unfortunate, I am a modern person
and don't believe in superstitions. I want to find this
unique artifact, and Aguila understands my interest.
However, he has offered very little in the way of a
clue to its location. It's a game with him, I think, and
I'm playing along. I have thought a great deal about
what I will do with the staff. At first, I only wanted to*

*keep it for myself, but I changed my mind. Once I have it in my possession, I will quickly donate it to a museum. I want it studied so we know exactly what it is. But I want to make sure it gets displayed. That way, everyone can share in the magic of our past.*

*But now I'm concerned. Aguila told me that my life is in danger because of the staff. In a couple of weeks, I'm supposed to meet my friend Indy in Bluff, and I wish it were sooner. I feel the danger nearby. I'm afraid that my father might be the source of it, but maybe I'm wrong. Anyhow, I'm hiding the journal, because I fear it will be stolen if I don't.*

*There's one thing I suppose I should add. My mother, Sara, killed herself. She put prussic acid in her food. Maybe she felt she had no choice. She believed in Fate, and the power of the unicorn's horn.*

Indy snapped the journal closed, and blew out the candle as he mulled over what he'd read. Even though Mara didn't believe in curses, she now found her own life in danger as a result of the alicorn. If that wasn't ironic enough, she also found herself on an extraordinary treasure hunt being directed by an Indian shaman. Yet, she had continued her pursuit. Something about it didn't quite make sense.

"Indy! Indy!"

He tucked the journal under the seat of the Ford, where it would be safe, then stepped out into the darkness. "What is it?"

"Mara is here! Come on. Get your butt over here."

# 15

## HOVENWEEP

The Packard came to a stop at the end of a dirt road. Darkness had blanketed the desert, obscuring the ruins. Walcott stepped out of the car, taking care not to jar his injured arm. Jimbo opened the back door for Rosie and Shannon, and his revolver followed Shannon's every move.

Walcott saw the shadow of a building that looked like a tower. So this was Hovenweep. Now, time for the truth. "Okay, where is it, Rosie?"

"We have to walk from here," she answered.

"How far?"

"Maybe an hour, maybe a little longer."

"An hour?" Walcott felt weak and feverish. But he couldn't stop now. Not when he was so close.

"You better be right," Jimbo growled, "or you're going to be one dead—"

"That's enough," Walcott snapped. "We don't need to make threats as long as everyone is cooperating. Rosie knows we're not playing games. Don't you, Rosie?" He pulled out a knife and cut the cloth that bound her wrists. As he moved over to Shannon with the knife, he told Jimbo to get the shovels and lantern from the trunk.

Walcott knew that Jimbo didn't like being admonished in front of the two captives, but the burly ranch hand did what he was told. He'd been out of jail only a couple of weeks when Walcott had met and hired him and a couple of the others at a bar in Cortez. This afternoon he'd found Jimbo back at the bar and had given him seventy dollars. Walcott needed the help, but he had to watch the ranch hand. Like right now, he thought, as Jimbo handed Shannon one of the shovels.

Walcott jerked it out of Shannon's grasp, and thrust it back at Jimbo. "You carry them both."

"Why can't he carry one?" Jimbo said.

"Think about it, my friend. Do you want him to carry your gun, too? I didn't say I trusted them, Jimbo. I only want to make sure they don't stumble on the rocks and hit their heads. We need Rosie to lead the way, and Shannon to help you dig. Now get my box for me. Please."

Walcott hitched his sling, adjusting his wounded arm, and shook a couple of cigarettes loose from his pack. He lit one and stuck the other behind his ear. The longer he was around Jimbo, the less he liked him. But it would be over soon. They'd have the ivory staff and that would be that. He'd pay off Jimbo, and never see him again. Of course, the other possibility was that he could knock off the ranch hand and the other two as well and be done with the lot of them. As he saw it, they were all expendable. The fewer the witnesses, the better.

Jimbo handed him the long wooden box for the

staff. "I gotta carry the lantern, too?" Jimbo complained.

The brute was like a little child, Walcott thought. He closed his eyes a moment, wishing away his fever and the pain. Then he glared at Jimbo. "Put the two shovels over your shoulder and hook the lantern over the handles. That way you'll have a hand free just in case you need to reach for your gun."

They followed a trail along the rim of the canyon, passing more stone towers. Some were circular, some square, others oval. What the devil were these Indians up to around here? In his years as an archaeology student and instructor, Walcott had never even considered North America as territory worthy of consideration. The ruins were minimal, recent, and impoverished. The gold artifacts came from South American cultures, not the nomads of the North.

But the more time Walcott spent in the Southwest, the more his opinion was changing. The Anasazis may not have had the material wealth of the Aztecs, but their ability to survive in a harsh environment astonished him. Mesa Verde was an architectural masterpiece, and these towers, what he could see of them, were another mystery. Maybe after he cashed in on the ivory staff, he'd come here and just enjoy himself. Besides, there were probably other treasures hidden here he didn't know about. But the staff was all that mattered now and the future was up for grabs.

They descended to the bottom of the canyon and continued walking. Before they'd covered a mile, Walcott started to wonder if Rosie was leading them into a trap. The box he was carrying was getting heavier and heavier as they covered a second mile, then a third. He did his best to stay alert and ready to draw his .38.

Finally, Rosie stopped, and Walcott realized they were standing below more ruins. A full moon had risen above the canyon wall and the illuminated towers looked eerie and unearthly. "Here we are," she said.

"Which one of them is it?" Walcott asked, gazing up at the structures.

"None of them. It's down here. Right in front of us." She pointed to a massive rock that backed against the base of the canyon wall. It rose at least fifteen feet high and was twice as long. "I don't see anything," Walcott said.

Rosie walked around the end of the rock and Walcott drew his gun as he hurried after her. She paused in front of an opening in the rock, and pointed at the cavity. "In there."

"Are you sure?" he asked.

She nodded. "I came here with my grandfather one morning at sunrise. We sat in front of the rock with the unicorn's horn for a long time, maybe an hour. Then he told me to wait. He went in through that crevice. When he came out, he didn't have it anymore."

"How long was he in there?"

"Maybe fifteen minutes."

"Then it shouldn't take too long to find it," Jimbo said.

Walcott turned to him and Shannon. "That depends, Jimbo. That depends."

"What do you mean?"

Walcott could see that Jimbo didn't like his superior attitude, but he didn't give a damn what Jimbo thought. "Did your grandfather have a shovel with him, Rosie?"

She shook her head.

The Englishman smiled. "See what I mean, Jimbo?"

"I don't get it. How did he bury it then?"

"If he didn't have a shovel," Walcott explained, "it means that the old man must have come here in advance and dug a hole. In that case, he could have spent a long time digging it."

To his surprise, Jimbo challenged him. "Why would he come here twice? It doesn't make no sense."

Walcott looked at Rosie for support. But if she agreed with him, she didn't show it.

"The first time was for the work, the second was for the sunrise ceremony," Walcott explained. "He went inside, dropped it in the hole, and kicked the dirt over it. Am I right, Rosie?"

"I don't know what he did in there," she answered. "I didn't look."

Jimbo scowled at Walcott. "What're you trying to tell me, that it's buried deep, or what?"

"Maybe he didn't bury it at all," Shannon said. "Maybe he just left it in there."

"Shut your mouth," Jimbo snapped, taking out his frustration. "Nobody's asking you."

Walcott lit the lantern. "I'm going to take a look. Watch them closely."

Walcott entered the crevice and found a corridor about three feet wide. The staff could be buried anywhere in here, he thought. They might have to dig up the entire floor.

He stopped and held up the lantern as he spotted a rock carving. He moved closer and studied the three circular symbols. He touched a finger to the one in the center, which was a series of concentric circles. He drew a line to the ground and scratched an X with his fingernail. "Right here."

He stood up, brushed his hands off, and smiled smugly to himself. This might not take so long after all. He moved ahead and found another way out at the far end of the corridor, then retraced his steps. He passed the lantern to Jimbo. "It's too narrow for more than one person to work at a time. But you can start digging in the floor right where I made an X below the marks on the wall."

Walcott lit the cigarette he'd been saving behind his ear, and set the box down on a rock next to him. "Well, what are you waiting for? Go to work."

Jimbo nodded toward Shannon. "He should do it, not me."

Walcott blew a cloud of smoke over Jimbo's head. "You're bigger and stronger and you've got something to gain. You can do it faster and better. When you're ready to be relieved, I'll supervise Shannon."

Jimbo grunted and headed back into the crevice. He was not a happy treasure hunter.

"Is that really you?" Indy asked.

Mara's blond hair was short, and in the darkness in front of the hogan, Indy couldn't be sure. Then she smiled and her face lit up and he had no more doubts.

"Hello, Indy." She took a tentative step closer to him.

He reached out and took both of her hands in his own. "It's been a long time."

She hugged him. "I was starting to wonder if I

was ever going to see you again. God, I'm glad you're here . . . and I'm here."

"I know what you mean. The Old West has been pretty wild lately."

She stepped back from him and seemed embarrassed. "I'm sorry I've caused so much trouble."

"Don't worry about it. I'm just glad to see you alive. How did you get here, and where were you?"

"Aguila and I came together on horseback from White Canyon."

Smitty cleared his throat. "Why don't we go inside. I've got fried potatoes and corn on the stove, and if you don't mind beef jerky, I've got plenty of that with me."

"I'm starved," Mara said.

"Hey, wait a minute," Indy said. "Where's Aguila? I haven't even met him yet. . . . At least, I don't think I have." His voice trailed off.

Mara and Smitty exchanged glances. "When we were less than a mile away, he told me to go on. He said he had other things to do, and would get here as soon as he could."

"Busy guy," Indy commented. "He knew where you were hiding, didn't he?"

"He guessed. C'mon." She took his hand and led him toward the hogan.

He liked the feel of her cool hand in his and thought how odd it was to see her just after reading what she'd written. "I found the journal."

"I know. Dad told me," she said as they stepped inside. "I just knew you'd figure out the message. The last thing I wanted was for Walcott to get his hands on my family history. He'd probably sell it to the highest bidder."

"We headed back as soon as we found out that

Aguila knew more than he was saying. But I guess if you're here, and you're all right, it doesn't matter where he is."

"I'm afraid it does," she said.

"What do you mean?"

"Dad, can I help with the meal?"

"No. You two just sit down and talk."

They took seats at Aguila's rustic wooden table. "What it means, Indy, is that if Aguila doesn't get here soon, he's not keeping his promise to me. He said he would show me on the solstice where the staff is hidden, and that's tomorrow."

"Then we've got a whole day."

She shook her head. "I don't think so. We may only have until morning."

"Why do you say that?"

"According to Aguila, the ancient ones, the Anasazis, were astronomers. Most of the pueblos had special, sacred places that were aligned with the sun so that the beginning of each season, at sunrise, they could be observed by the priest-astronomers."

Indy nodded. "That's possible, but what's it got to do with finding the staff?"

"I'm not sure, but Aguila made it clear that day-break was important."

As Smitty carried plates of food to the table, he offered his own opinion. "Maybe it's hidden in a spot you can't see unless the sun hits it just right."

"That could be, Dad. If you've got some hot water there, I've got some tea. It's a special type that Aguila made for me."

Indy nearly choked. "None for me, thank you. I've sampled Aguila's tea."

Mara looked puzzled. "You've had some already?"

"Did he ever," Smitty said with a chuckle as he

examined the bag of herbs Mara had passed to him. "It cured a bad headache, but made him crazy for awhile. He thought he went flying like an eagle."

"I'm sure this is different tea. It's very mild. I've had it before."

"I don't think I'll have any of that tea, either, if you don't mind," Smitty said.

As they ate, Indy couldn't help thinking about his dream again. Mara's mention of the tea had triggered his memory, and he was amazed how well he could still remember it and how real it had seemed. Dreams were supposed to be fantasies and nonsensical jumbles of nonevents, but he was convinced his flying dream had been a premonition that he would find the spot where Mara had hidden her journal. There was more to the dream, and now he remembered the eagles had landed at a place with petroglyphs.

"What are you thinking about?" Mara asked.

"Circles."

"What do you mean?"

"I saw them in a dream I had after I drank the tea."

Smitty laughed. "Oh, boy, here we go again."

"Tell me about it," Mara said, her curiosity aroused.

Indy recounted how the dream had started, how it felt to fly and how he'd talked with the other eagle, who was Aguila. Then he jumped to the end of the dream, and explained how the two birds had landed by a kiva and one of them had dropped a feather.

"You mean the eagle feather was actually there?" Mara asked.

"Right near the *sipapu*."

"It could be any old eagle feather," Smitty said.

"That's true," Indy conceded.

"Tell me about these circles," Mara asked.

"That was somewhere else. I saw them on a wall like petroglyphs." He proceeded to describe the three circular engravings.

Mara looked as if she could barely restrain herself. "Where did you see them?"

He shrugged. "I don't know. It was a dream."

"Was there anything else you could identify?" she persisted.

"Wait a minute. There was something. Towers. It was a ruin with towers."

"Only one place around this territory with old towers, and that's Hovenweep," Smitty said. "It's about an hour out of Bluff when the roads are good. When it rains, you can't even get there by horseback."

Mara leaped to her feet. "That's it! That's where the staff is hidden. We've got to get to Hovenweep and find those circles before sunrise."

"Hold it! Why are you so blasted sure about this, girl?" Smitty asked.

"Because last night I dreamed the same thing. Not about the eagles, but the symbols. That was Aguila telling me where to look. He did keep his promise."

Shannon and Rosie sat side by side on a flat rock as Walcott smoked and watched them from a few feet away. The Englishman kept his revolver holstered, almost as if he were challenging him to make a move, looking for an excuse to gun him down. Even though his hands were tied, Shannon was tempted to jump him. He was waiting for Walcott to relax and turn his attention away. With one arm in a sling he was vulnerable, and besides that he looked ill. Shannon wasn't going to pass up any chances to turn the situation in his favor. He couldn't just wait and play Walcott's game; he sensed there was no future in that. Not for him, and not for Rosie, either.

"So you never told Mara about this place?" Shannon asked Rosie. He kept an eye on Walcott.

"I respected Grandpa too much to tell Mara. I always thought he would show the unicorn's horn to her himself."

Walcott tossed the burning butt of his cigarette at Shannon's foot. "If you want to talk, talk to me, not between yourselves."

It was just what Shannon wanted. If he could engage Walcott in conversation, he might catch him off guard. "So do you really think this ivory staff is a unicorn's horn?"

"It used to be."

"What's that mean?"

"Unicorns are a myth, but the staff is from the time when people believed in them." Walcott smiled as trails of smoke wafted from the corners of his mouth.

"It's either a unicorn's horn or it's not," Shannon said.

Walcott's hoarse laughter turned into a spasm of coughs. "Stick to your Bible, Shannon, if you want absolutes."

"You said you were going to tell me about the history of it. I want to hear about it."

Walcott glanced toward the rock, then back to Shannon. "Why not?" He took another cigarette from the pack in his pocket, then began talking about an ancient secret order called the People of the Horn.

"Why did they destroy these horns?" Shannon

asked. Walcott was getting caught up in his talk and paying less heed to him. Just what he wanted. Shannon's eyes darted for a moment to the shovel that lay a few feet away from Walcott, and estimated how long it would take him to reach it and hit Walcott with it.

"Because they became frightened of the horns. Things had reached a breaking point between what was real and what was not, and when they saw that the horns were losing, they appointed themselves as the ones to destroy them. Think about it. If people aren't going to believe in unicorns, you can't have any of their horns around. Somebody had to get rid of them, and they took the job."

"That doesn't make a bit of sense to me," Shannon said.

"No, I don't suppose it would."

"Well, were they unicorn's horns or weren't they? Tell me that."

"It doesn't matter."

Shannon realized that if he was going to act, he should do it soon. Once Walcott got the staff, Shannon and Rosie were expendable. "How do you know all of this stuff?"

Walcott flicked away the burning cigarette butt. "Mara told me all about the order." He reached into his pocket for his pack. "That was back when we were friends in Paris."

Shannon, seizing the opportunity, dashed toward Walcott and drove his head into the Englishman's injured arm. Walcott howled in pain, and tumbled over. Shannon reached down and grabbed the shovel with his bound hands just as Walcott drew his revolver. Shannon slammed the shovel against Walcott's hand. The .38 flew through the air, landing at Rosie's feet. She snatched it up and aimed it at the Englishman.

Shannon stood with the shovel raised over Walcott's head. "Give me the gun, Rosie. Quick." He glanced toward the rock, wondering if Jimbo had heard the ruckus.

"Don't listen to him, Rosie," Walcott said. "I won't hurt you. You do want to get out of here alive, don't you?"

Shannon realized that Walcott was stalling for time. He grabbed the Englishman by the back of his collar, jammed the shovel handle under his jaw, and spun him around so he faced the rock wall, which was about fifty feet away. Still no sign of Jimbo. Then he spotted the ranch hand peering out from the opposite end of the rock.

"Rosie, get down!"

Jimbo fired and Rosie dropped to the ground with a groan. Shannon dragged Walcott with him as he edged toward Rosie.

"Give up, Shannon. It's all over." Walcott struggled to get away, but Shannon squeezed the Englishman's injured arm and Walcott's knees buckled. They both toppled to the ground, but Shannon was exposed to Jimbo's aim of fire. Another shot exploded and the bullet glanced off the steel shovel.

Shannon instinctively ducked down and Walcott rolled over on top of him, pressing the handle of the shovel against Shannon's throat. Shannon twisted his head, taking the pressure off his throat. Blood streamed down Rosie's face as she reached toward Walcott's gun, which had fallen from her grasp. Her hand dropped on the weapon just as another shot fired from the rock. Her body jolted; she clutched her chest as blood spilled over her hands.

Shannon shoved Walcott away, but the Englishman rolled over and snatched the .38 and leveled it at Shannon. "Get over here!" He motioned Shannon away from Rosie, but the musician didn't care what happened any longer. He cradled Rosie in his arms and tried to stop the bleeding. When he raised his head, the barrel of the revolver pointed at his face and behind it, Walcott grinned like a maniac. Rosie was dead, and Shannon knew he was about to join her.

But Walcott was distracted as Jimbo screamed and flailed his arms against the assault of a huge bird, which had swept out of the dark sky and sunk its talons into his throat. It pecked at his face and tore into his throat as if in retribution for killing Rosie. Walcott took aim at the eagle. He fired; the bird let out a wild screech and flew off. Jimbo staggered a moment, but he was dead before he struck the ground. Walcott's bullet had struck him in the center of the forehead.

"Nice shot," Shannon rasped.

# 16

## SUN DAGGERS

There was only an hour left before sunrise as the Ford bounced over the rugged dirt road. The ruins were close by now, but Indy didn't think the prospects of finding the staff were particularly encouraging. Even if the location was right, there were several clusters of towers at Hovenweep, and the first problem was locating the right one. Even then there was no guarantee that they'd find the three enigmatic symbols. Mara had even visited Hovenweep about a year ago in search of petroglyphs, but said she was certain she hadn't seen that particular set of symbols.

"What's that?" she asked, leaning forward as Indy slowed to a stop.

"It looks like a '27 Packard."

"Oh, my God. He's here," Mara groaned.

"Who?" Indy asked.

"That car belongs to Roland Walcott. He escaped from the Utes in it after he got shot."

"Well, ain't that somethin'," Smitty mumbled from the back seat. "He beat us here. How'd you figure?"

Mara pounded the dashboard with a fist. "How could he know it was here?"

They stepped out of the car and took a look at the Packard. Smitty bent down and picked something off the ground. "The bastard."

"What's wrong?" Mara asked.

"He's got Rosie with him." Smitty held up a piece of cloth. "She always tied the bottom of her braid with a green ribbon."

"If Walcott has Rosie, that means he's probably got Shannon too. And I bet Walcott's not alone," Indy said.

"Rosie must have known all along where the staff was hidden," Mara said. "She never told me."

"You? What about me? I'm her husband!" Smitty growled and threw down the ribbon.

"I didn't know you wanted it back." Mara sounded surprised by Smitty's anger. He didn't answer. Instead, he headed along the rim of the canyon, taking yard-long strides as he went.

Mara hurried after him and Indy trailed behind, his mind probing new questions. He couldn't tell whether Smitty was more angry because Walcott had abducted his wife, or because Rosie had never told him where the staff was hidden. Why was he suddenly so interested in it?

They moved along the dry, scrubby mesa top. The moon illuminated the trail, and cast shadows from the tall stone towers. Every time they came upon a tower, they quickly looked it over, then walked on. Indy was impressed by the stone structures rising out of desert, and wished he were there under different circumstances. The only thing he could recall reading about Hovenweep was that very little, if any, archaeological work had been undertaken here, and no one seemed to know why the Anasazis had built the towers. But there was little time to consider such questions. As far as Indy was concerned, locating the symbols and the staff was now a secondary matter to finding Rosie and Shannon. But he had the feeling that when they found one, they would find all.

"Do you know what Hovenweep means?" Mara asked, pausing at the point where the trail descended into the canyon.

"Can't say I do," Indy answered.

"It's Ute. It means deserted valley."

"It's lived up to the name so far," Indy said.

"They've got to be here. We've got to find them," Mara said impatiently.

"We'll find 'em." Smitty's voice rang with determination as he followed the trail toward the bottom of the canyon. "If I remember right, there's another set of towers about three miles up the canyon."

"That's right," Mara said. "The Holy Group."

Three miles. Indy knew it would be close to sunrise when they got there. Very close.

Shannon tossed a shovelful of dirt out of the crevice. A faint glow illuminated the horizon. It would soon be daylight and he wondered how much longer Walcott would be willing to continue on. As Shannon figured it, the staff might have been here once, but it wasn't anymore. He was exhausted from digging and hauling dirt, which was all he'd done since he'd moved the two bodies behind a boulder. He couldn't see what difference it made whether the bodies were out in the open or hidden. There was no one around for miles. But Walcott apparently was the sort of person who liked everything neat and tidy with no loose ends, and Shannon knew that he was one big loose end. The only reason he was still alive was that Walcott couldn't dig with one arm.

He considered making a dash for the nearest boulder, but he knew that Walcott was standing near the other side of the rock with his revolver in hand. Even if Walcott missed, Shannon's chances of getting away, now that it was nearly morning, weren't very good. He should've made his break when it was still dark, but it was too late to think about that.

Walcott had been considerably more cautious since Shannon had attacked him. His revolver was never out of his hand and he stayed far enough away from Shannon so that he couldn't very easily throw dirt in his face or hit him with the shovel. If he tried it, Walcott had promised to shoot him dead before the dirt or shovel hit its mark.

As he slowly moved back down the corridor, Walcott let him know he was close by. "It's got to be here somewhere, Shannon. It's just a matter of finding where that place is. Keep digging."

Following Walcott's direction, Shannon had dug down to a depth of about four feet, then moved a couple of feet and started over. But other than pieces of broken pottery, nothing else had turned up, and he'd had enough. He threw the shovel into a hole. "You're going to have to find it on your own, Wally. I'm done. Finished. I don't work overtime, especially when the only payment I can expect is to be shot at sunrise."

Walcott moved into view at the end of the corridor. "Oh, you might live to see many more sunrises. That is, if you keep at it. But if you don't, I'm not going to be very pleased with you. Now pick up the shovel and get back to work."

Shannon considered walking away, but he knew he'd never make it out of the rock alive. He had to play on the hope that Walcott wouldn't carry out his threat. Or that his gun would jam. Or that a miracle would happen. He hadn't forgotten about the bird that had attacked Jimbo. Anything was possible.

"I'll give you to the count of five to pick up that shovel and start digging," Walcott said. "One . . . two . . ."

The muzzle of the gun was pointed at Shannon's heart. He thought of his wife and infant son. He couldn't give up. He had to find a way out of this.

". . . Three . . . four . . ."

Shannon stepped down into the hole.

"That's better. Now dig."

He snatched up the shovel and was about to slam it into the ground when he heard a muffled call.

"Rosie . . . Rosie . . . you here?"

It was Smitty.

"Out of that hole," Walcott growled. "Now. Get over here, and drop the shovel."

As Shannon worked his way across the honey-combed floor, he heard Indy's voice calling for him. Walcott pressed the gun to Shannon's head and pushed him toward the entrance. He heard Indy saying something about splitting up to check the three towers.

"Don't say a word or I'll blow the back of your head off," Walcott hissed. When they reached the entrance to the crevice, Walcott ordered him to get down on his knees.

Shannon dropped down and craned his neck, but he couldn't see either Indy or Smitty. He knew they were probably heading toward the towers, and away from the rock.

"Okay. Stand up." Still holding his .38 to Shannon's head, the Englishman peered out into the dawn. "When I say go, you run for those boulders. I'll be right behind you. And don't forget, open your mouth and you're dead."

The first rays of sunlight spilled over the canyon wall as Indy climbed toward one of the towers. As in the ruins they'd already visited, there was no sign that anyone was here. Yet, Indy sensed something was wrong. He felt that familiar tingling along his spine that had always warned him when he was in danger. It was a feeling that he trusted and had learned not to ignore.

He touched his empty holster. He'd given the Webley to Mara when they'd split up, but now he wished he had it. The truth was they were all equally susceptible to an attack and it might come at any moment.

Suddenly, a shriek split open the silence of dawn. He dropped to the ground, and twisted around.

"Rosie, my God, Rosie."

Mara. Indy scrambled over the rocks until he reached her side. Rosie's bloodied body lay lifeless, and a few feet away was another body. At first, Indy thought it must be Shannon, but the body was too large. He moved closer, turned it over, and winced. He recognized the face as one of the men from Mesa Verde. Jimbo. His neck looked as though it had been ripped open as if by an animal, but a bullet hole punctured the middle of his forehead.

"Oh, no! Not Rosie!" Smitty moaned, dropping to his knees beside his dead wife. But his sorrow quickly shifted to anger as he leaped to his feet and pulled out his .45. "Where are you, Walcott? Get out here where I can see you." His voice echoed in the canyon. "You coward. You bastard." He fired the .45 in the air. "You said we were partners. Is this what partners do?"

"Partners?" Mara said. "I should have known."

Smitty charged away, yelling for Walcott.

Indy was even more surprised than Mara. He gazed up into the rocks as a pale yellow light flooded the canyon. Were they still here? How many were there?

"Stay put," he told Mara, and he crept away, darting from rock to rock. His intent was to climb to a higher point where he'd have an overview. But suddenly he felt exposed. They could be anywhere in the rocks, taking aim at him right now.

Indy dashed ahead to a rock wall and pressed against it. Safe from one side, but exposed on the other. He didn't like the creepy feeling of an invisible enemy, watching, waiting. He didn't know if they were behind him, above him, in front of him, or to one side or the other. He could still hear Smitty's angry voice echoing in the canyon, growing more distant. But all extraneous thoughts were suddenly wiped from his mind as he saw a snake just inches from his foot. He didn't dare move, but then he realized it was dead and headless.

His momentary relief was replaced by astonishment as his dream once more came back to him—the dream that was like no other dream. The eagle had dropped its snake down a rock face. Was it the

same one? He recalled that the rock had been hollow, and he'd seen into it through a crack, and that
was where he'd spied the symbols. He looked up,
searching for a crack, but he could see only a few
feet above him, and he didn't want to step away from
the boulder for a better view. But if someone had
carved the symbols, there must be a way inside.

Indy had started moving to his right along the
rock when he saw a pile of dirt. He bent down and
ran his hand through the debris. It hadn't been here
long enough to settle.

He moved forward and glanced around the corner
of the massive boulder. He saw that it was actually
two rocks, the outer one lying at an angle against the
other one with a crevice between them. He crept
toward it, wary that Walcott might still be inside.
Again, he touched his holster and wished that he had
his Webley. He cautiously peered into the shadowy
hollow. A beam of sunlight penetrated a crack in the
outer wall. He saw a series of holes on the floor,
and the handle of a shovel sticking out of one of
them.

Indy eased forward, carefully stepping between
the holes. They'd been digging here for the staff, and
by the looks of it, they hadn't had an easy time of it.
Then he saw them. It was hard to believe, but there
they were, the three circular symbols. He moved
closer. The beam of light formed two horizontal sun
daggers on the wall. Both pointed inward, cutting
through the spirals on either side and touching the
outer ring of the concentric circles.

As he stared in fascination, he realized that the
points of the daggers were moving. They now penetrated the second outermost ring. The daggers crept

toward each other, closing the gap, then moved toward the center of the circles in a cosmic duel. Indy counted time in rings, instead of minutes. The Anasazis priests had been astronomers. How else could he explain what he was seeing at the very onset of the solstice?

Then the tips of the two daggers touched and merged. The light seemed to explode in front of him. Indy covered his eyes against the sudden brightness, and heard a ringing, like the sound of bells or chimes. He couldn't tell whether the sound was coming from inside or outside of him.

When he dared to look again, the beam of light penetrated a triangular-shaped hole, illuminating inner walls that he hadn't noticed. How could he have missed seeing it before? It hadn't been there, couldn't have been. He squinted. The triangular tunnel appeared to open into an immense cavern. Mesmerized, he crawled through the tunnel, and into the cavern.

As soon as he was inside, he saw a block of stone. On top of it was a silver, double-headed eagle. Indy moved toward it, blinking his eyes. He had trouble focusing. He felt oddly light-headed; the bells and chimes were ringing loudly. He touched the silver heads, took them in both of his hands. There was a crack in the rock, and a staff of spiraled ivory was fixed to the eagle heads.

He lifted the staff and ran his fingers over the shaft, feeling its cool, smooth, ivory surface. He saw the Greek words on the handle, which identified it as an alicorn owned by an emperor. On the lower part of the shaft another Greek inscription jumped out at him.

"Άγιος Θεὸς "Άγιος Θεὸς ἰσχυρὸς "Άγιος
ἀθάνατος.

He recognized it as New Testament Greek taken
from a service in the Byzantine liturgy called the
Trisagion. It read: *Holy God, Holy Mighty One, Holy
Immortal One.* The final words of the phrase, *Have
Mercy on Us,* were missing from the staff. Rightly so,
he thought considering the history of the staff.

Indy raised his head. The air around him was like
the wavy surface of a lake with the sun shining on it.
Translucent images, mirages, and rainbows shim-
mered around him. He felt incredibly exalted as he
raised the staff over his head. He couldn't help
thinking of his father's continuing quest for the Holy
Grail.

Then he heard a voice like a thought, but it was so
strongly impressed upon him that he knew it was not
his own. It was as if the thought was radiated directly by the double-headed eagle.

*Only he may possess me in whom there is no guile;
in whom all passion has been transmuted into com-
passion, all natural ignorance into divine wisdom, all
selfishness into selflessness; for I am a sacred emblem
of all greatness, all perfection, and all truth. I am the
symbol of the gatekeeper, for with one face I behold
the radiant countenance of my Creator and with the
other, the expanse of the universe which He has fashioned. I clutch the alicorn, the flaming spirit-fire with
which the miracle of my existence was wrought. I am
the symbol of the Initiator who through the ages carries Ganymedes upon his back into the presence of
the gods.*

The light dimmed around him, and Indy looked
back at the triangular entryway. It was pulsing open

and shut, open and shut, and with each pulse, the opening grew smaller and tighter, constricting like the pupil of an eye. He knew he had to leave and quickly, or he would be trapped here for eternity. But it would be so easy to stay. A part of him urged him to flee quickly; another part of him asked, why? What would be better than moving further and further into the warm embrace of the underworld?

That was where he was, the underworld. He didn't belong here. Couldn't stay here. He rushed toward the entryway, threw himself down, and crawled on his hands and knees. But the opening was already tight; it was about to close. He flattened out, wriggling forward as fast as he could, fearing that at any moment he'd be caught, frozen in rock at the gate to the underworld.

His head, then a hand, slipped out of the narrowing tunnel, and he pulled himself through. He dropped onto the floor of the outer rock corridor. The chimes had stopped. Sunlight no longer beamed through the crack. Gloom swallowed the passageway. He straddled one of the holes in the floor as he sat up, and rubbed his face.

Indy looked up at the wall. The sacred Anasazi symbols were there, just as he'd first seen them. But there was no sign of a triangular opening. His feeling of wonder shifted and transformed into suspicion. It must have been some sort of illusion, another trick by Aguila, he told himself. He saw what the old Indian wanted him to see. Aguila must have mesmerized him and imbedded the thought in his mind after he'd drunk the tea. *When you find these symbols, this is what you will see.*

His gaze dropped to the object in his hands, a magnificent silver and ivory staff, the unicorn's horn.

It must have been disguised somehow. That was the only logical explanation. In spite of his certainty that he was the victim of an illusion, he could't help being astonished by the staff. It was both myth and reality, a relic and a legacy from the ancient past.

# 17

## TWISTS OF THE HORN

"Nice going, Indy. Where'd you find it?" Shannon's lanky figure filled the entrance to the corridor.

"Jack, what happened to you? What are you doing here?"

"Never mind. But I think you better give that thing to me."

"What?" Something was wrong. It didn't sound like Shannon. Then Indy saw the shadow behind his friend, and knew it was Walcott.

"He's got a gun in my back and he'll use it if you don't cooperate, Indy."

Walcott passed Shannon a long, hinged box. There was no doubt about its purpose. "Put it in there, Jones," Walcott ordered. "Now."

Indy wished he could bash the Englishman in the head with the double eagle, but Walcott wasn't taking any chances. Not only was Shannon between them, but Walcott's .38 was cocked. "What are you going to do with it, Walcott? Tell me that."

"I'm taking it to Italy."

Indy laughed. "What are you going to do, sell it to Mussolini?"

"Not a bad guess, but wrong. It happens that one of his opponents is very interested in it. He even thinks it will protect him from Mussolini."

"I don't believe it."

"You know the popes once held unicorn's horns in high regard. This staff, in fact, was taken from St. Mark's in Venice nearly two hundred years ago."

"So what?"

"My benefactor, Signóre Calderone, is a very religious man, as well as a strong adversary of Il Duce. He believes in the power of unicorn's horn."

Walcott was serious. Indy was no fan of Mussolini's, but if he had any say in the matter, Walcott wasn't going to take the staff anywhere.

"Put it gently into the box," the Englishman ordered.

"You better do what he says, Indy."

Reluctantly, Indy slid the staff into the box and Shannon carefully slid it under Walcott's good arm. "Try anything and you're dead, Shannon," Walcott warned.

"If this Calderone finds out about what's happened to the owners of this staff over the last two hundred years, he may not think he's gotten such a good deal," Indy said, stalling for time.

"Smitty said something about a curse. I don't believe in such rot, and I don't think you do, either. But I appreciate your concern for my benefactor." Walcott's laughter was low and throaty and darkly menacing. "But neither of you is going to be around to tell him anything." He raised his .38 and aimed it at Shannon's head, and the sound of a gunshot exploded in the corridor.

"No!" Indy yelled.

Shannon's body jolted, and he tumbled into one of the holes he'd dug. Indy figured he wouldn't even hear the next blast; he'd be dead.

But Walcott didn't fire right away. There was an odd expression on his face, and suddenly he dropped to his knees. He tottered a moment, fired in the air, and fell forward, dropping next to the box. His back was soaked in blood, and behind him stood Mara, holding Indy's Webley.

Indy was astonished, and relieved. He looked from Mara to Shannon, who was seated in one of the holes and rubbing his neck. "Are you okay, Jack?"

"Just surprised I'm alive. I thought that bullet had my name on it."

"I saw Walcott climbing down the canyon toward this rock," Mara began. "I guess he didn't know I was here. I followed him and Jack, and . . ."

Indy stepped over Walcott's body and embraced her. "Everything is going to be okay. It's all over."

"I had to do it," she said. "I had to stop him. I couldn't let him . . ."

He stroked her head. "I know. It's okay. Let's get out of here."

Mara pulled back from him. "Do you have it?"

Indy picked up the box and handed it to her as they moved out of the crevice. "It's all yours. I hope you've got a good place for it."

"Oh, I do." She walked over to a boulder, set down the box, and opened it. "It's beautiful," she said in a hushed voice. "Just beautiful."

"Where did you find it, anyhow?" Shannon asked, still rubbing his neck. "I was digging all night, and

you walk in here and you've got it in five minutes.
What did you do, pull it out of your hat?"

"Five minutes? It seemed like an eternity to me."
Indy adjusted his fedora, and glanced uneasily toward Rosie's body, which lay just a few yards away.
"Maybe I did pull it out of my hat. That's as good an
explanation as any."

"I've decided I'm going to donate it to one of the
Vatican museums," Mara said. "It'll be the best place
for it."

"The Vatican?" Shannon exclaimed. "That's pretty
close to Italy, isn't it?"

"Real close," Indy said. "Mara, did you know that
Walcott—"

Smitty suddenly stepped out from behind a boulder, his .45 in his hand. "She ain't taking it to no
Vatican. She's gonna take it to—"

"You betrayed me!" Mara shouted. "You were
working with Walcott."

"And for the same fellow as you, Mara. Walcott
found out you were dealing with Calderone, so he
made his own deal with him."            •

"You're lying." Mara closed the cover on the box
and reached for the Webley.

"Nope. 'Fraid not, girl." Smitty's hand tightened
on the .45. "You're no better than Walcott. You just
want the money from Calderone, and you were going to cut me out. You never even said a word to me,
and after I spent the last of my money on your
schooling year after year." He turned to Indy. "This
Calderone was her boyfriend, and now she thinks
he's some kind of business partner."

"Stop it!" she yelled. She pointed the Webley at
Smitty. "Put it down, Dad. I'm not kidding. You
shoot me and I'll shoot you right back."

Smitty was wavering. His eyes were darting around. He didn't like the turn of events. "Okay." He set the .45 on the ground. "What are ya gonna do now, shoot your daddy?"

"Kick the gun over here."

Smitty did as she said.

"Mara," Indy barked. "Give me the gun."

She spun around, aiming it at Indy. "Stay where you are!"

"Mara . . ." Indy held out a hand.

"Hey, take it easy with that gun," Shannon said.

Mara glanced over her shoulder and saw Smitty dash behind a boulder. She fired once as he bolted to another rock. Then she spun around and pointed the gun at Indy and Shannon again. She took a step backwards and let out a short, harsh laugh tinged with irony. "That's just like him. He gets in a fix and takes off like a rabbit."

"The gun, Mara."

"I'm sorry, Indy. Sorry that I have to do this."

"What are you talking about?"

"You don't understand."

"You can say that again." Indy was about to grab for the Webley, but the look of desperation on Mara's face told him that it would be a big mistake. She didn't trust him or Shannon any more than she did Smitty.

"Don't move or I'll shoot," she said.

"We're not against you," Indy said. "We didn't know about Smitty, and we weren't with Walcott."

"Definitely not," Shannon put in.

"It doesn't matter. Turn around and walk slowly over to that wall. Then put your hands up on it.

"I can't believe this," Shannon said. "Some vacation."

"Just go along with her," Indy snapped.

"Remind me never to go hunting unicorns with you," Shannon muttered.

"Just stay calm, Jack. Stay calm." Indy placed his hands on the rock wall. Maybe Mara's mind had cracked when she'd realized her father was with Walcott. She was dangerous with that gun in her hand; there was no sense agitating her. He glanced over his shoulder at her.

"Okay, Indy, get out the key to your car."

"Mara—"

"The key, Indy. Now!"

The sharpness of her tone was forced, Indy thought. She didn't really want to hurt them. But he knew she would shoot in desperation if they defied her. He reached into his pocket and found the key.

"Okay, throw it over here."

He half turned and tossed it to her. It landed at her feet.

She scooped it up and dropped it into a pocket of her khaki slacks. "I don't like doing this. But I have no choice."

"What are you going to do, Mara?" Shannon asked.

She didn't answer. A bad sign.

"You know, Dad was right. I am taking the staff to Calderone."

"Have a nice trip," Shannon said. "We're not stopping you."

"Walcott must have found out what I was doing and figured he would beat me to it," Mara continued. "He probably thought that Diego would just forget about me and give him a fortune for the staff."

Indy knew that Mara had spent nearly two years in Italy after she'd left the Sorbonne, but he had no idea she'd taken a gondola ride with the anti-Fascist underground. She'd never written to him about politics, but then she hadn't written about a unicorn's horn, either, or her friendship with an Indian named Aguila. "If Calderone puts politics first, he probably would do just that."

"I don't believe it. Diego is an honorable man. He values art and his country's cultural traditions. He's a strong supporter of the Church, and he's not a Communist, either."

"Let me guess: He's a Sicilian and he's in the mob," Shannon said. "They hate Mussolini from what I hear."

Mara ignored Shannon.

The more she talked, the more Indy realized how little he really knew her. "Mara, think about what you're doing," Indy said, making another attempt to bring her to her senses. "We're not against you."

"I told you I don't want to do this, but I have to. I can't trust you any more than my own father."

Indy stole a glance over his shoulder and saw that she was standing several feet away, too far for him to lunge for her, but close enough for her to blow the back of their heads off.

"Don't look at me!" she barked. It would be over in an instant if her aim was accurate. He heard a click as she cocked the Webley.

She had to do it, Mara thought. She wished she could just walk away, but she couldn't. Not now. They wouldn't let her; they knew too much. Besides, Diego might renege on their deal if he found out that she hadn't kept her promise of secrecy. She'd been nervous and she'd talked, so now she had to kill them. What else could she do? But maybe she was just overreacting. Maybe they wouldn't try to stop her or say anything to anyone about the staff. She was all confused.

"I really think we ought to talk about this, Mara," Indy said.

"No reason to get nasty," Shannon said. "If you want to take it to your friend, it's all right with me. We're not stopping you."

"Shut up." She couldn't think. No, it was too late. She wasn't going to break her promise to Diego. She tightened her grip on the heavy Webley. She held it with both hands, and aimed it at the back of Indy's head. *Pull the trigger. Now. Do it.*

But her finger wouldn't move. She couldn't bring herself to shoot him. She took the gun by the barrel and slammed it against his head. He groaned and toppled over. Shannon turned and she struck him on the forehead. His knees buckled and he fell back against the rock.

Mara hurried away, the encased staff under her arm. She didn't know whether she'd hit them hard enough to kill them or not. The faster she got away from here the better. She'd drive to Santa Fe, then take a train to Miami, where she'd board an ocean liner to Italy. Once in Rome, she'd be safe.

She'd covered perhaps a mile when the trail along the canyon floor curved around a rock outcropping. As she moved around it, she spotted her father lying next to a pool of water, which had formed at the bottom of a hollow. At first she thought he was asleep. She set down the box next to the trail and climbed down to the pool. She approached him warily, keeping the gun pointed at him. She waited for him to move, but as she stepped closer she saw that his lips were blue. She knelt down beside him. Felt for a pulse. There was none.

She felt a twinge of anguish as childhood memories flashed through her head. She saw her father singing to her as she sat in his lap, and remembered him pushing her on a swing and her calling for him to push higher, higher. But then other memories, painful memories, flooded through her. He had hurt her and her mother over and over, and he'd deceived her right to the last day of his life. No, she knew she couldn't feel any sorrow for him. He was dead; she was glad.

She stood up, looked around, trying to figure out what had happened to him. If he'd been bitten by a rattler, he probably wouldn't have died so quickly. Besides, he'd been bitten before, and survived. He'd built up an immunity to the venom. Maybe the shock of Rosie's death and Walcott's deception and her own actions had combined to cause a heart attack. It seemed the most likely explanation, she thought.

Then she noticed a wooden sign partially covered by shrubbery. She walked over to it, and moved a branch aside. She saw a skull and crossbones, and the words: DANGER! POISON WATER. She stared into the crystal-clear pool. Not a single bug swam in the waters. No sign of life at all, a sure sign of danger, one her father had known. Had he drunk intentionally from the pool, knowing it was poison, or had he thoughtlessly taken a swallow? She would never know.

She turned away from the pool and her father's body, and walked on. She barely noticed the shadow of an eagle as it crossed her path, and headed down the canyon in the direction from which she had come. Dying of poison, it seemed, had been the legacy of the unicorn's horn since the time unicorns had fallen out of history and turned to myth. But now, thanks to Aguila, it was time for the unicorn's horn to return to history, and to make history.

# 18

## ROMAN SOIREE

*Rome—A month later*

It had taken forever, it seemed, but she was finally
here. As Mara stepped down the gangway of the
cruise ship, she put all of the complications and
scheduling problems she'd encountered out of her
head. She would take a train to the center of Rome
and call on Diego. He'd be expecting her. The telegram she'd sent him from the ship had been brief
and to the point, clear to anyone who understood her
mission, yet deceptive to anyone who didn't: *Arriving with staff July 26.*

She'd been introduced to him at a party not long
after beginning her studies in Rome. He was a serious type, an intellectual who had studied the religious history of Italy and was knowledgeable about
religious artifacts. As a way of making conversation,
she asked him if he'd ever heard of the alicorn that

had been kept in St. Mark's Cathedral in Venice. He
not only knew what she was talking about, but cor-
rected her, saying that there had been two such artifacts.

She'd remarked that she only knew about the one
that had been in her family for generations. She was
about to tell him about her family's terrible history
and how many of its members had blamed the
alicorn, but it wasn't the appropriate time. Besides,
Diego seemed so impressed that she didn't want to
disappoint him. The fact was he'd been enthralled
with her from the moment he heard about the
alicorn.

She soon found out he was wealthy, and she liked
being in his company. But she didn't really love him,
and besides, she knew from things he said that he
would never marry her. When he continued to ask
about the alicorn, she offered it to him. At first, she
hadn't mentioned money. She didn't want to offend
him. But when she realized that he considered it to
be a relic of power and he was more interested in
the alicorn than her, everything changed.

By the time she finished her studies, they were no
longer lovers, but business partners. She returned to
New Mexico to search for the missing alicorn. If she
found it, Diego would pay her one hundred thousand dollars in cash.

As she stepped onto the dock, a man in a dark coat
and hat approached her. "Mara Rogers?" he asked in
a thick accent.

"Yes?"

The man's eyes darted for an instant to the long,
slender box she carried under her arm. "Please come
with me." Suddenly, she was surrounded by several

identically dressed men who took her luggage and rushed through the crowd.

"What's going on? Who are you?" She clutched the box tightly to her chest.

An elegant Pierce-Arrow whispered to the curb and stopped. One of the men opened the rear door, motioning for her to enter. "Who are you and what do you want?" she asked, striving for a confidence she didn't feel.

"Get in, Mara," said a man's voice from inside.

She stooped and slid inside, where Diego's dark eyes gleamed.

"I didn't know it was you. I was getting worried." She was relieved, but at the same time on guard. He leaned over, hugged her, and bussed her on the cheek. She returned the greeting, but didn't linger in his arms. They were business partners now, not lovers. She had to keep that in mind.

"Everything's going to be just fine. Just fine." Diego was dressed as impeccably as ever, and he smelled of expensive cologne. His mole twitched as he smiled. "Relax, and tell me about your adventure. I want to hear all about it."

But she wasn't ready to relax. Not yet. "Do you know a man named Roland Walcott?"

"Who?"

"Answer me. Do you know him?"

"I've never heard of him. But please tell me about him."

She met his gaze, and searched for a sign of deceit. "I hope you're telling me the truth. Because if you're not . . ."

"Mara, why are you upset? What did this man do to you?"

She eased back into her seat. It was over with

Walcott. It didn't matter anymore. "Nothing. Absolutely nothing." She ran her hands over the polished teakwood box on her lap, and noticed Calderone's shiny black cane with its silver head resting against the door. "I've got something that will make you want to throw away that cane, Diego. Wait till you see it."

Marcus Brody stared out the window of the airplane that circled above Rome. "It should be a very interesting symposium, Indy. I'm glad that you were able to join me, after all."

"I'm sure it will be," Indy answered, but his thoughts were elsewhere.

The summer was only half over, and it had been a disappointing one. But then again, he was lucky he was still alive. Aguila had found Indy and Shannon at the rock that day, and had tended to them. He'd left them with a canteen of bitter tea, and told them to stay where they were. A few hours later, the authorities had arrived and escorted Indy and Shannon out of the canyon. They were taken to a hospital in Blanding, and released the next day. The doctor who had examined them had commented that they were in remarkably good condition, considering their injuries. But when they told him about Aguila's tea, he just laughed and said that he wished he could heal his patients with tea. Upon their release from the hospital, Shannon had called an end to his so-called vacation and returned to Los Angeles, and Indy had headed for the East Coast.

When he'd arrived in New York, Indy didn't even feel like telling Brody much about what had happened. But Brody pressed him for details and Indy simply gave him Mara's journal. After that the story slowly came out. The cold facts were that his love affair with Mara had never materialized—that she had used him for her own purposes, and left him for dead.

Brody sensed the pall of depression that had fallen over his young friend, and persuaded Indy to accompany him to the symposium as a way of forgetting about the unfortunate events in the Southwest. Indy had reluctantly agreed. Maybe Brody was right. The trip would do him good. But in the back of his mind a thought lingered: Mara herself might be in Rome. But he had no intentions of doing anything about it, and the possibility that he would see her was so slim it wasn't even worth thinking about how he would react.

The trimotor plane touched down on the runway, and Brody seemed to relax for the first time since they'd taken off from London on the second leg of their flight. "There's something I've been wanting to tell you. But I've been waiting until we arrived."

"What is it?" Indy asked, warily.

"Well, I think you should know that the guest list for the soiree tomorrow evening includes Diego Calderone."

"What? You told me there were not going to be any political figures involved. No Fascists, no Communists, no—"

"Shh . . . not so loud," Brody murmured, glancing around. "You've got to understand that the Calderone family is a great supporter of the arts. He simply couldn't be overlooked, any more than the premier's cultural affairs attaché. They'll both be in attendance."

"Ah, Marcus. Why didn't you say something about this earlier?"

"I didn't want you spending your whole trip fuming about it, and wondering what you were going to do about it if Mara showed up."

"Mara! Do you think she will?"

"I don't know," the museum director mused. "But it would certainly be interesting if Calderone brought her along, and the staff."

Brody's response made Indy suspicious. "Marcus, did you have anything to do with Calderone's invitation?"

"Me? Well, there is something more to this matter. I just couldn't stand seeing you moping around, and trying to act as if you'd forgotten about the staff and Mara."

"All right. Let's hear it. What did you do?"

"It's not only what I did, but what we're going to do." The door of the trimotor opened and the passengers prepared to disembark. By the time Indy and Brody stepped down onto the runway a few minutes later, Indy had a whole new outlook on his visit to Rome.

It was still light outside as Indy crossed the Piazza della Republica on his way to the soiree for the opening of the Symposium on the Future of Roman Antiquities. He paused at the fountain in the center of the piazza, where voluptuous bronze women were wrestling with marine monsters amid the sparkle of the bubbling fountain. They didn't look worried; they were smiling. He'd have to take their cue, he thought, and ambled on.

Indy walked alongside an ancient Roman wall, the facade of the church of Santa Maria degli Angeli, which bordered the piazza. Since it was still early, he decided to go inside. He already knew what he'd see; he'd been here several times in his travels. But he still found the church an architectural curiosity, since it had been built on the site of an ancient public bath.

As he stepped inside, he looked up at the row of mammoth, red granite columns that were more than five feet in diameter and nearly fifty feet high. They were intact from the original building, the Baths of Diocletian, a colossal structure built about 300 A.D., and the greatest of the ancient baths. In the mid-sixteenth century, Michelangelo converted the central chamber into a church. To Indy, no other building in the city displayed the grandeur of ancient Rome so well.

Indy walked slowly forward, passing one column after another. He stopped as he saw a lone figure standing near the next column. She was a tall woman with short blond hair. Mara! What was she doing here? He couldn't let her see him, not now. He took a step backwards, hoping to disappear into the shadows, but his foot scraped against the stone floor and the woman turned.

She was every bit as attractive as Mara, but the resemblance ended there. Indy was relieved. "Quite a remarkable building," he said, smiling politely.

"*Non capisco*," she answered, shaking her head. She didn't understand. She turned and walked away, her heels clicking against the stone floor.

"Me neither," he said to himself. "They should have left it as a bath."

Outside, Indy followed a path through an expansive garden as he headed to the building behind the church. It was the Museo Nazionale Romano, which occupied the rest of the site of the ancient baths. In the sixteenth century, the building had become a

Carthusian monastery before it was adapted into a museum. In recent decades, the building had deteriorated, but during the past year, when it had become known that the international symposium would be held here, a restoration project had been undertaken at what was considered breakneck speed. Brody had talked at length about all the preparations, and Indy couldn't help feeling like an insider, privy to all the gossip.

He took his wire-framed glasses out of his pocket and placed them low on his nose. Then he bent over slightly and walked with a limp as he approached the door, completing his disguise as an old man. With an unsteady hand, he raised his invitation for the guardian of the entrance. Inscribed on it was the name Dr. Felix Schultz. The man nodded and signaled him to enter the hall. Schultz was a professor of classical antiquities in Munich. He was also an ardent supporter of the Nazis, and because of some Nazi activities he had backed out of his plans to take part in the symposium. That, of course, had worked out just fine for Brody and his plan, which had become Indy's plan.

One of the marks of renovation was immediately apparent. Several mirrors with baroque frames had been added, which not only covered crumbling parts of the walls, but made the hall seem larger and brighter. Indy saw the image of a wrinkled old man with white hair, glasses, and a slight hunch, who was wearing a tuxedo, and realized it was himself. His disguise had aged him forty years. As he gazed in the mirror, Indy also noticed at least half a dozen men dressed in black who looked like security guards. He wondered if they were here to protect the museum's relics or were advance men for Calderone.

Indy turned away from the mirror. Tables were covered with food that was laid out in layers and arranged in ornate designs too splendid to eat. Beautiful women in gowns and handsome men in tuxedos moved about. Many of the wealthy and well-known members of the florid Roman social set had been invited to complement the international delegates in attendance. Photographers darted among them, snapping pictures. The attractive people seemed to relish the attention; like the food, they were on display, a part of the decor. Mixed among them and barely noticed were others, mostly older and less attractive, the symposium's attendees.

Indy was tempted to fill a plate with food, but he held off. He hobbled over to the stairs leading to the mezzanine, and slowly climbed them. He found Brody nervously flitting about in a gallery overlooking the main hall. "I've been waiting for you. My God, Indy, I thought you got lost. Where have you been?" Brody didn't wait for Indy to respond. He spoke rapidly in a hushed tone. "He's accepted the invitation, and he's bringing Mara. It's official."

Their plan seemed so unlikely to succeed that Indy wasn't sure whether he was excited or disappointed. "Good, but will he bring the staff? That's the question."

"I know, I know. But if he has any intentions of showing it in public, this would be the perfect place to bring it."

"What makes you so sure?"

"It's a formal occasion and one that deals with antiquities. The staff is not only ancient, but something of a ceremonial adornment. Besides, he always carries a cane with him, so the staff won't seem out of place."

"Yeah, but he might not bring it for just those reasons. He might think something's up. Maybe Mara will warn him."

"Don't be so skeptical, Indy. She has no idea you're here, or that you even know anything about this symposium." Brody adjusted Indy's bow tie. "You look great. But I do think you should stay up here out of sight until the moment of truth. We don't want to give Mara any extra time to see through your disguise."

"I knew I should've gotten something to eat while I was down there."

"Here's your walking stick, old man." Brody handed Indy a staff that was covered by a black leather case. "See the zipper? It's a little tight, but it fits."

Indy tested the zipper. Under the covering lay a fair copy of the staff in Calderone's possession. The double-headed eagle was coated in silver and the spiral shaft was the exact dimension of the original. The main difference was that the shaft was made of milky-colored glass, instead of ivory, and to an expert it would be obvious that the inscriptions had been recently etched. The imitation had been made by two Roman artisans, one who'd molded the silver-coated crest, the other who had fashioned the shaft.

Brody had planned the whole thing from New York. He'd used artisans in Rome who had restored works of art for him in the past. They had closely followed his specifications, which he'd taken directly from Mara's journal. The staff had been waiting for them upon their arrival, and they'd picked it up before they reached the hotel. Indy had etched the inscriptions himself, and the leather case had also been his idea. It had been made at a shop near the hotel, but much to Brody's consternation it had only been completed within the hour. He'd picked it up on his way to the reception.

"It goes well with my black tuxedo, sort of an Old World touch, don't you think?" Indy said.

They heard voices on the mezzanine, and two couples entered the gallery. Indy kept his back to the doorway as he examined a fresco from Empress Livia's villa at Prima Porta. It depicted an orchard filled with birds and a garden in full bloom. The colors were remarkably well preserved, he thought. Mara would no doubt know about the paintings here. Mara, who had been unable to shoot him, but who had no problem deceiving him and abandoning him and Shannon to an unknown fate. But he couldn't let his anger toward her interfere with their plans. He had to stay calm, and ready.

As the couples moved out of the gallery, Brody wiped his brow and silently signaled his relief to Indy. "Not to worry," he whispered, and he moved out of the gallery, leaving Indy to muster his determination.

Indy didn't have to wait long. He heard a buzzing in the hall below and moved cautiously toward the railing. Everyone had turned toward the door, and an aisle opened as if the crowd had been parted by invisible hands. Calderone had arrived.

Indy glanced to his right, then his left. On either side of him, not ten feet away, were men dressed in black. They were definitely Calderone's guards, and their eyes were on him, marking him as a possible threat. One of them had fixed his gaze on Indy's walking stick. A bad sign. He should've figured that Calderone's guards would cover the mezzanine.

He walked toward the stairs, taking short, tentative steps, leaning on his stick. He saw the zipper on
the case was still open and part of a silver eagle head
was peeking out. He nodded to the guard, and asked
for the location of the bathroom. He spoke to him in
Italian, feigning a German accent.

Indy hobbled on, but when he reached the door to
the bathroom, he paused and glanced back. The
guard wasn't paying him any heed. He jerked up the
zipper, then slowly descended the staircase. As he
joined the crowd, a man at the podium announced
the arrival of Calderone, and beckoned him to come
forward.

*Swell, we're going to get a speech,* Indy thought to
himself. Even Brody hadn't expected that. Indy
peered in the direction of the approaching mass of
bodies, looking for Mara, but all he could see were
the black-shirted guards. How in the world was he
going to get through all of them? Maybe Calderone
didn't even have the staff with him. Besides, was it
really worth the risk? Did he actually care that Mara
had sold the staff to Calderone? Maybe this was
where it belonged.

The handsome Sicilian mounted the podium to
the cheers of a few supporters and the polite ap-
plause of everyone else. Then Indy saw it. The sight
of the spiraled ivory and the silver double eagle in
Calderone's grip transfixed and disturbed him. But
then he realized Calderone was talking, and the
speech started to infect him. The words grew in
strength and power and drew him forward.

Italy would soon flourish with a new leader who
would bring the north and south together as one.
When Fascism was destroyed, the flower of a new
order would quickly blossom even before the snow

was gone. The country would again spiral toward a cultural apex. Italy was bold, valiant, courageous, fearless, and so would be the new leadership. Strength . . . unity . . . power. A new order . . . new order . . . Calderone's new order.

Indy listened in fascination to the hypnotic talk. He saw how Calderone clutched the staff. He sensed the man's power and felt it growing as he watched. He wondered if the others were affected as he was, and with considerable effort, he turned his attention away from the Sicilian, and struggled to block out the words. The crowd was nothing less than captivated. They followed Calderone's every word, and they weren't doing so because they feared him. They believed him, they understood him, many for the first time. His words were a powerful drug and no one wanted it taken away.

Indy spotted Brody in the crowd, and saw that there were tears in the older man's eyes as he gazed at Calderone. Tears of joy, not sorrow. Brody was enthralled, and literally hanging on every word. Not only did Brody openly despise politics, but he spoke very little Italian. The words literally transcended language.

Indy had to jolt Brody out of the orator's spell. If they were to succeed, he needed Brody's help. He worked his way through the crowd, trying not to draw attention to himself. He was virtually the only one moving, but no one seemed to pay him any heed, so strong was the attraction to the Sicilian's words.

Indy had nearly reached Brody when he saw Mara a few feet away. She wore a pale blue gown that left her shoulders bare. She held both hands to her mouth in a gesture that revealed a vulnerable side.

She was as transfixed by Calderone as Brody and the rest of them.

Indy moved over to Brody, and took him by the arm. "Snap out of it, Marcus," he hissed. "You told me he was as dangerous as Mussolini."

For a moment, Brody didn't seem to recognize him. Then Calderone finished his speech, and raised both fists above his head. The crowd cheered madly. Brody looked startled and confused. He started to clap, then rubbed his face. "My God, Indy. I don't know what happened to me."

"I don't either. But I'm going after the staff."

Brody nodded. "Are you sure . . ."

Calderone surged from the podium and into the crowd, shaking hands, smiling, chatting. "Now's the chance," Indy said. "Keep Mara busy. That's her." She stood near Calderone's side.

Indy moved forward and hailed one of Calderone's aides. He introduced himself as Dr. Schultz. The man looked annoyed, then said it was nice to meet him, and tried to move on. But Indy kept shaking his hand, then took the man's arm.

"Listen to me. I am an expert on ancient staffs. I would like permission to take a closer look at the one Signore Calderone is carrying this evening."

"I'm afraid that won't be possible. Not tonight. Maybe next week. Now excuse me."

"That's too bad. I'm going to be leaving tomorrow, very early, for Munich. I was hoping to take a look. I understand a man in America is making staffs from ivory that are imitations of certain ancient staffs. I was curious to see if this was an original or one of the new copies."

The man, who had taken a couple of steps, quickly

retraced them. "Wait. Don't go anywhere." He held up his hands as if to hold the old German in place.

As Indy waited, he saw Mara looking directly at him. There was a puzzled expression on her face as if she couldn't quite place where she'd seen the old man. Indy stepped to one side so that her view of him was blocked.

The Sicilian seemed to stiffen as his aide whispered in his ear. Calderone's gaze roved over the crowd and settled on Indy for a moment. Then he made a terse remark to the man, and Indy wondered if he was saying he'd expected something of the sort would happen.

Calderone waded through the crowd in Indy's direction. Indy glanced at Brody and saw that he had occupied Mara in conversation. She was trying to look over Brody's shoulder toward Indy, but Brody was motioning with his hands and obscuring her view.

Calderone stopped at Indy's side. "What do you know about this staff?"

"Let me see it. I can authenticate it for you." In this crowd it would be easy to make the switch. Even though Indy still had to remove the other one from the zippered case, he would need just a few seconds with no one watching him.

"Come to my villa."

"Why not here?"

"No," Calderone said firmly.

Indy knew he'd better take advantage of the offer, even though it wasn't what they'd planned. "Yes, yes. I suppose." He sounded slightly annoyed and his German accent was thick. "Away from all of these people. It will be better."

238                                    ROB MacGREGOR

"I'm leaving soon," Calderone explained. "There will be a car waiting outside in ten minutes."

As Calderone moved away, Indy stroked the leather-covered crest of the fake staff. He'd still make the switch tonight.

# 19

## THE SWITCH

"You're actually going through with it?" Brody looked astonished.

"It's the only way, Marcus. Gotta go."

"What if you don't turn up tonight?"

"Then it didn't work. Wish me luck."

"But Indy . . ."

A sleek, black Pierce-Arrow was waiting outside. "Over here, Professor Schultz," one of Calderone's men called to him.

Indy hobbled over to the second car, leaning on his staff as he walked. The guard held the rear door open for him, and Indy slid onto the back seat. He found himself sitting next to Mara. Swell, he thought. Real swell.

Calderone was on the other side of Mara, and he introduced her as the car pulled away. She extended a hand and Indy shook it. He was grateful that it was dark in the car, because Mara peered at him curiously.

"You work for Signore Calderone?" Indy asked in a heavy Germanic accent.

"We are business partners," Mara responded.

"Oh, what's your business?" he asked.

"None of yours," she answered brusquely in English.

"Mara!" Calderone snapped. "I'm sorry, Heir Schultz. She's upset. A personal matter. She buys art for me."

"I'm sorry," Mara said. "So you are an expert in ancient staffs?"

"That is true, young lady, and the alicorn is a specialty."

"I'm sure you will find Signore Calderone's staff very interesting, as well as genuine."

Indy cleared his throat. "We will see." He turned his gaze toward the window, ending the conversation and making it more difficult for Mara to study his features.

They passed a park and he realized he had no idea what direction they were going. They could be headed toward the Colosseum or approaching the Spanish Steps for all he knew. Then he spotted a landmark he recalled from his first visit to Rome. It was Porta Pia, one of the main city gates. *Designed by Michelangelo,* he thought. *His last major architectural project.* His father had made him memorize such details every time they visited a historic city. Now years later, he recalled the fact as if he'd learned it yesterday.

A few blocks later, the Pierce-Arrow slowed. A high iron fence bordered the roadway and halfway down the block several black-garbed men appeared near a gate. One of them signaled the car to enter, and they followed a narrow, winding road lined by trees. When they reached a three-story villa, the automobile pulled up to the front door.

"You live here?" Indy asked.

"I live in many places," Calderone said. "I move around. For me, it's not safe to stay in one place for long."

A guard opened the car door and Indy climbed out. As Mara stepped out after him, he turned his back to her and pretended to study the villa. Calderone escorted her to the door and two of his men accompanied Indy as if he might not be able to make it on his own. They entered a large foyer with marble floors and the largest chandelier Indy had ever seen. A broad staircase curved toward the second floor, and at the bottom of the stairs stood two more black-clad guards.

"I can't wait around here all night," Indy grumbled to Calderone, trying his best to avoid looking at Mara. "I'm usually in bed by ten with my glass of warm milk."

"Don't worry," the Sicilian answered. "We'll handle this matter right away, and I'll have a car waiting to take you to your hotel as soon as we're done."

Indy glanced at Mara and caught an odd look in her eyes. She knew, he thought. Swell. He braced himself, ready to take flight or defend himself. But when she didn't say anything, he decided he'd misread the look. She was just miffed that Calderone had brought him here.

When they reached the staircase, Indy motioned Mara to go first. He intentionally took his time climbing the steps, and leaned heavily on his black staff. At the top of the stairs, they followed a corridor until Calderone gestured toward a door, then opened it for the aged scholar.

"Please make yourself comfortable. Can I get you anything? A glass of warm milk, perhaps?"

"No, thank you. I want to stay awake."

As Indy walked into the library, he overheard a quick exchange between Mara and Calderone. She wanted to be present when the staff was examined, but he told her to go to her room. If she was needed, he'd send for her. "You can't order me around. I don't work for you," she snapped, and the conversation abruptly ended.

So all was not well in the Calderone household, Indy thought with smug satisfaction.

He padded across the thick carpeting toward a long, mahogany table in the center of the room. The library smelled of old books, and several thousand volumes were shelved around the room. He spotted another door, walked over, and opened it. It was a bathroom, a mere cubicle with a toilet and a sink and a window high on the wall. He turned away, walked past rows of bookshelves, and settled into one of several overstuffed chairs which surrounded the table. He found the zipper on the leather covering of his walking stick and pulled it down several inches. Then he laid the fake staff across his knees.

A couple of minutes later, Calderone stepped into the library carrying the staff. He took a seat across from Indy. "Mara has retired for the evening, but she's looking forward to hearing your analysis."

Indy took the staff in his hands, and squinted at the relic. He adjusted his glasses, muttered under his breath, and held it close to his face. Calderone waited. Then Indy set the staff on the table, looked up, and shook his head. "It's far too dark here. I need light, Signore Calderone. Much more light. Can you get me a table lamp? That's what I need."

The Sicilian hesitated, then nodded. "I'll be right back."

The moment Calderone headed for the door Indy pulled the fake staff out of the leather case. All he had to do now was make the switch. But Calderone merely stuck his head out the doorway and ordered someone to get a lamp. Then he returned to the table.

"A glass of water, too," Indy said.

Calderone frowned.

"Please. My throat is dry."

Calderone spun on his heel, and strode to the door. This time he left the room.

Indy laid the fake staff on the table, and quickly fitted the real one into the case. But he had trouble fitting the leather top over the double-headed eagle. The door swung open and Calderone stepped inside with a guard. For a terrible moment, Indy thought he'd been caught. But Calderone turned to the guard, and told him to put the lamp on the table. "Your water is coming, Professor."

The lamp was set in place under Calderone's watchful eye; Indy continued to fumble under the table to close the leather top over the staff. Just as the guard turned on the light, a woman dressed in a white uniform entered the room. She carried a silver tray with a pitcher of water and a glass. She poured the water, and set it in front of Indy. He thanked the woman and took a sip from the glass, stalling for time. He leaned forward and studied the fake staff. "Yes, yes, *ja*, sure. That is it."

"What?" Calderone asked.

It was time for a decision. Indy could call the staff a fake, and easily prove it. But if he did so, he would draw attention to the staff and Calderone might realize that it wasn't the same one. "This is either a very good copy or the original of one of the two alicorns which were taken at the fall of Constantinople in 1204 and then resided for centuries in St. Mark's before disappearing."

"I knew that much. Which is it?" Calderone sounded exasperated.

"Well, now . . ." Indy moved his legs and the partially encased staff rolled to the floor. He bent over, but Calderone was quicker. The toe of his shoe rolled the staff toward him. He picked it up and saw the silver double eagle head protruding from the leather case.

"What is this?" he demanded.

"It's my staff."

"But it looks like—"

"Like trouble," Indy said, and he flipped over the table, knocking Calderone onto his back. He reached for the relic, but Calderone snatched it away from him and leaped to his feet. He swung the staff, but Indy ducked and drove a punch into Calderone's stomach, then another to his face, and he crumpled to the floor.

"I hereby authenticate this staff," Indy said as he scooped it up. "Now I've gotta run." He started for the door, but it swung open before he reached for it and a massive black-shirted guard blocked his path. The guard took one look at Calderone, who was on his hands and knees, and yelled for help.

Indy knew he was in for trouble now. He sprinted toward the bathroom, and reached it just steps in front of the guard, who was no doubt surprised by the old man's sudden agility and speed. He threw the steel bar through the catch, locking himself inside. The guard slammed into it. The door rattled and groaned, but the lock held.

There was no way to go but up. Indy scrambled up onto the sink, stretching his arms as far they would go. His fingers were just below the window sill. The narrow, rectangular window was the kind that swung out from the frame. It was propped open only a couple of inches, but it was his only hope.

The door shuddered in its frame. Although it was made of heavy wood, the lock was weak and Indy knew it wouldn't hold much longer. He reached up with the leather-covered staff, and pushed the window up until the glass was nearly horizontal with the floor. Carefully, he laid the staff on the sill, then leaped and grabbed the window frame with both hands. He pulled himself up and swung a leg through the window, and felt a narrow ledge. Hopefully, the door would hold long enough for him to get out and find a way to the ground.

The guards bombarded the door, but somehow the lock held. Indy sucked in his stomach and pushed, but the opening was too small for him to squeeze through. He shoved his back against the window, which was held to the wall by strips of ancient copper. The metal stretched, but not enough. He pushed again, certain the window was about to shatter. Somehow it held together, but one of the copper strips snapped.

Then the door burst open and the guards rushed into the bathroom. They bumped into each other as they looked around. "Up there! Get the old man!" one of them shouted.

Indy slammed his back into the window and the other strip of copper tore loose. The window fell into the bathroom just as the guards looked up. Glass

rained over their heads, and Indy rolled out onto the
ledge. He reached back for the staff, but inadvertently pushed it off the sill. He looked down just in
time to see Calderone reach up and grab it.

"Shoot him," Calderone shouted as the guards
brushed broken glass off their heads and wrestled
with the window frame.

Indy didn't want to leave the staff behind, but
then he saw the guns. He dropped straight down,
and caught the ledge with his hands. Bullets ripped
through the windowsill, showering wood splinters
over him. He looked down. He was at least thirty
feet above the ground. He'd be lucky not to break a
leg.

He pulled himself up and climbed onto the ledge
just as a head poked through the window. He kicked
the guard in the jaw, sending him tumbling down on
top of the others. He sidled away from the window,
his back to the wall. He felt like a tightrope walker,
performing for an invisible audience.

Indy opened the jacket of his tuxedo, and jerked
the bow tie to one side. He had no time to think
about what to do next, because suddenly he was
faced with another obstacle. The wall made a ninety-degree turn, jutting out a dozen feet, and the ledge
on the inside corner had crumbled away. Ten feet of
open space separated him from the point where the
ledge continued, but a flagpole protruded from the
wall about halfway across the gap.

He glanced back. A guard had crawled onto the
ledge. He had no choice. He leaped, heart pounding, his breath stalled in his throat. He caught the
flagpole with his fingertips, swung forward, back,
forward again, and let go. He landed on the balls of

his feet, tottered on the ledge, caught his balance. His breath rushed out of him.

"Nothing to it," he called to the guard. But the man pulled a gun and Indy literally raced to the corner. The guard fired before he was able to get around it. The bullet grazed Indy's neck and made a direct hit on his bow tie, which blew apart. He whipped around the corner, touched his neck, and felt blood. "Just a razor burn." Then he heard a long yell that began just around the corner and ended when he heard a thump below. "Guess he didn't make it."

But Indy didn't feel much safer. The guards would be pouring out of the villa at any moment to take target practice, and he would be the target. He had to get down, and fast. Below him, a canvas canopy covered a walkway leading into a garden. He leaped onto the canopy just as several guards rushed out the door. The canopy collapsed, and the men were knocked to the ground.

Indy bounded to his feet and raced across a courtyard. When he reached the side of the house, a guard with a rifle stepped out, and looked him over.

"Who are you?"

Indy had to think fast. Just beyond the guard the driver of a delivery truck started his engine. "There's trouble inside. They need help. Quick! A man with a gun. I was almost killed. Please. Go help!"

Indy knew he had only seconds before the others would catch up to him. Shouts from the courtyard made up the man's mind, and he charged past Indy. The truck was pulling away as Indy bolted after it. He leaped onto the rear fender, and climbed into the back of the truck, which was stacked with cases of wine.

He pulled a tarp over himself as the driver slowed at the gate. If they searched the back of the truck, it was all over. But no one had alerted the guards at the gate. The truck drove away. Just as Indy thought he'd escaped, he heard more shouts. He lifted his head and saw black-clad men pouring into the street. They fired, and bullets pinged off the back of the truck.

Indy ducked down and the driver continued on, apparently unaware that he was being fired upon. *Faster, get moving.* After a few blocks the truck slowed and the driver called out to someone on the street. Indy raised up to see the man engaged in a casual conversation. He slipped out the back of the truck, crossed the street, and hurried down to the corner. He looked back once and saw the truck surrounded by Calderone's men.

Indy walked swiftly, but not so fast as to draw attention. He followed a zigzag route with no destination in mind. He didn't know where he would go. Certainly not the hotel where he and Brody shared a suite. It was where most of the symposium attendees were staying and Calderone would certainly be looking for him there.

Indy had made no plans for this sort of outcome. He'd figured either he would succeed making the switch of the staffs or he'd get caught in the act. Now he wasn't sure what to do or where to go. He had no other clothing, no money, no ticket out of the country. The only thing he had with him was Mara's family journal, tucked in the inside pocket of his jacket. They had intended it to be his safety valve in case everything else went wrong. If Calderone was as superstitious as Indy thought, he'd be shocked by the journal. He'd think he was in possession of a cursed staff, rather than a relic of power. But what good was the journal to Indy now? He'd be shot on sight before he'd have a chance to give it to Calderone.

He came to Via di Sant'Agnese, St. Agnes Street. He knew there was a church by the same name nearby. Maybe he could stay there tonight. He tried to orient himself, then realized the church was right behind him. More memorized history came to mind. Saint Agnes was supposedly martyred right here fifteen hundred years ago, and the church was built above her tomb. Indy moved around the side of the church and found a door leading down to the ancient catacombs. A sanctuary, he thought.

He turned the handle and found it unlocked. Maybe the custodian was down there. He descended the steps, taking care to go as silently as possible. He didn't like the idea of sleeping in a catacomb, but he needed a place to stay for the night. Tomorrow, he'd try to get out of Rome.

A single candle was burning at the tomb, but no one was there. The place was deserted; he was safe for the moment. But he hardly felt relieved. He'd failed to get the staff, and his future didn't look very promising. Maybe he should've just rejected Brody's plan and forgotten about Mara. But it was no time to reconsider what he'd already done.

He heard the sound of voices outside, moved back against the wall, and listened. "Okay, you tell me when you are leaving, Signorina, then I will lock the door for the night," a man said.

The footsteps grew louder. A woman approached the tomb. Mara. Nice timing.

She must have fled the villa after she'd argued with Calderone. She'd changed out of her gown and wore a simple dress and a shawl. She took a candle from her purse, lit it, and placed it on the stand in front of the tomb. What was she doing, praying to the saint? Indy couldn't watch any longer. He stepped forward. "Well, it's not exactly the sewers of Paris, but—"

She spun around, raising a hand to her chest; her eyes were wide with fright. "Indy?"

"Good guess."

"I knew it was you the minute you stepped into the villa. When you were sitting next to me in the car, I thought there was something familiar about the old man. I'm so glad you're here."

"Sure you are. Let's cut the pleasantries, Mara. You're not my favorite person at the moment."

"Indy, it's not what it seems. Believe me, I'm glad I found you . . . or you found me. I have to get out of Rome and away from Diego. He's a madman. I feel like a captive. Can you help me?"

"I didn't know you wanted to leave." She slid her hand into her purse, and he figured she wasn't reaching for another candle. He caught her wrist. In her grip was his .455 Webley. "Thanks. I was wondering what happened to it."

"I was just going to give it to you."

Indy grinned. "Sure you were. Right in the heart, no doubt."

"You were after the staff, weren't you?"

"Brilliant deduction."

"You've got to get it away from Diego. I'll help you."

"Still playing sides, I see. One against the other."

"You've got to understand. I didn't really believe that the staff would have any sort of effect. I mean not like it does. I just thought it was a relic, you know, and I was going to make a lot of money."

"Yeah, at my expense."

"I'm sorry I hit you. I've felt bad about it ever since. I was so confused."

"And what are you now?"

"I'm concerned that Diego will misuse the powers of the staff. You saw him tonight. You saw how everyone reacted. You should hear him; he thinks he's some sort of god who's going to save the people. But he's deceitful. You were right about him. He made a deal with Walcott to get the staff. I overheard him mention Walcott to one of his men."

"So people are gullible. It's probably got nothing to do with the staff." Indy knew she was quick-witted and an accomplished liar. But, then again, he could use her help. "But for argument's sake, what do you want to do?"

"Indy, I know you doubt what I'm telling you, and you've got reason, plenty of reasons. I was hoping you were okay. How's Jack?"

"Oh, he's just fine." As if they were chatting over cocktails.

"I'm not hiding anything from you. I should've listened to my heart, instead of letting greed get the better of me. I wanted you, Indy. I wanted things to work out."

"But not as much as you wanted the staff."

Her shawl slipped off her shoulders and slid down, bunching around her feet. She took a step toward him, and ran a finger down the front of his shirt. "I want to help you." She slowly raised her eyes. "I'll do anything you want."

"Good. Get me the staff."

She placed her hands on his waist. "I can do it tomorrow."

He pushed her hands away, and picked up her shawl for her. "Why should I believe you?"

She pulled the shawl over her shoulders. "Because you've got to believe me. It's your only chance."

"Has Calderone paid you?"

"Yes, he has, but I'm going to leave the money when I retrieve the alicorn. I just need you to help me get out of the country safely."

It was the first time Indy had heard Mara use that word for the staff. "And what do you think I should do with it?"

"I think it should go back where you got it from. That was the best place for it."

And a place where she might be able to recover it again, Indy thought.

The door creaked open.

"It's probably the custodian," Mara whispered.

Indy tightened his grip on the Webley and ducked back into the shadows as someone slowly descended the stairs.

Mara stared into the darkness as a figure moved toward her. "Diego!"

Calderone touched her arms. "I knew I would find you here. I'm sorry I got angry with you. I should have listened to you. We almost lost the staff. The professor was a fraud."

"What happened?"

"He tried to switch it with a fake one. Do you have any idea who he is?"

She shook her head. "No."

He put his arms around her, and slid a hand inside her dress. She struggled against him. "Please, Diego. No! Don't do that."

"Why so cold?" Calderone asked innocently. "Can't it be like the old days again for us?"

"That's over. It was your idea, remember? You wanted an Italian wife. A blond American woman wouldn't fit the right image."

"I don't care about images any longer. I care for you. That's all."

Then Indy saw it. Calderone had the staff with him, and it was still in its leather case. He ran the crest along her leg as she struggled to get away.

"Stop it," she demanded. "I mean it, Diego. Let's get out of here."

Indy stepped out into view. "Leave her alone, Calderone." He aimed his Webley at Calderone, who let go of Mara and backed away.

"Mother of God. Who are you?" He glanced at Mara, then back to Indy.

"He was hiding here."

"Why didn't you just tell me?" Calderone was as suspicious about her motives as Indy was.

"Because he would've shot us."

"Give me the staff," Indy ordered.

"You're the old man, but you're not old or a German, are you?"

"The staff, Calderone."

Calderone turned on Mara. "You know him."

"It's not like you think, Diego. I had to take the staff from him."

"Hand it over," Indy demanded.

Calderone raised his chin; his eyes flared. He straightened his back, and clutched the staff to his chest. "Never."

Indy took a couple of steps toward him, cocking the revolver. "Give it to me!"

"Okay. Don't shoot." Calderone held out the staff.

The look on his face had shifted from arrogance to fear in a matter of seconds.

Indy snared the staff. "Turn around!"

"Why? What are you going to do?" Calderone started to turn. Indy cracked the butt of the gun against his head, and he slumped to the floor.

"Oh, thank God, Indy. Take me with you. Please. There's nothing for me here."

Calderone groaned and rolled over. "See how he's doing."

As she bent down, Indy struck her at the base of her skull, and she toppled over. "Sorry, Mara. Real sorry. But as they say, what goes around comes around."

He stuck the Webley in his belt and the staff under his arm. He had started to climb the stairs when a sickening thought occurred to him. He stopped halfway up the stairs, unzipped the leather casing, and turned the staff around in his hand.

"Ah, for crying out loud." He should've known. Calderone was carrying the fake. "Somehow, I knew it wasn't going to be quite that simple."

There was nothing to do now but get out of here. He angrily tossed the fake staff into the catacomb, and the glass shaft shattered against the stone floor.

As Indy stepped outside, an old man blocked his way. He looked frightened as his eyes focused on Indy's revolver. "Signore, I don't want any trouble. I'm just supposed to lock the door."

"Be my guest. Lock it tight."

A man dressed in black stepped out from the hedge and raised a revolver. Several more of Calderone's guards moved into view, their weapons all aimed at Indy. "Don't move!"

# 20

## CAPTIVATING ENCOUNTERS

The shuffling of boots and the rattling of keys alerted Indy. The door of the bottleless wine cellar opened and Indy squinted as a torch lit the darkness. Its flickering light revealed three sullen guards. After a sleepless night in his tattered tuxedo and the remains of his disguise, Indy probably looked as terrible as he felt.

"Does this mean I can go home now?" he asked.

None of them answered. They rushed into the cell, and yanked him out. He was dragged down a hallway and into a larger room with a wooden chair in the center. His hands and feet were buckled into straps, and the guards left.

So the man who was going to save the people from fascism had his very own torture chamber. He probably had several, since he moved around so much. An hour passed in silence. Psychological torture. They'd probably try to get Indy to sign some phony confession saying that he'd attempted to kill Calderone. He could imagine the tactics they'd use. Oddly, the thought of confessing to such a crime made him think about his colleagues in the archaeology department. He could literally hear them talking.

*He was supposed to study petroglyphs in the Southwest this summer. Instead, he went to Rome and tried to kill a man who's working to overthrow Mussolini.*

*I never knew Jones was a Fascist.*

*No one knows why he did it, but there's a rumor that he thought Calderone was harboring a unicorn, of all things.*

*I heard he left the desert babbling something about Anazasi astronomers. He must have gone completely mad.*

*Too bad they executed him. He was a boon for the department.*

Wait a minute. Who said anything about an execution? He wasn't confessing to anything.

Footsteps. Two men appeared. The first was a mass of muscles, with a thick neck. He looked like an unhappy bulldog. Just the kind of guy who you'd expect to show up for a torture session. Then Calderone stepped into the room. A gauze pad was taped to the top of his head.

"Good morning, Professor Jones. As you can see, you've turned out to be a big headache for me, a real big headache, and it's put me in a very foul mood." He circled Indy as he spoke, then stopped in front of him and struck him across the face.

The fact that Calderone knew his name meant that Mara must have been talking. Indy wondered how much she'd told Calderone, and exactly what she'd told him. "What do you want from me?"

"I'll ask the questions," Calderone growled. The

goon stepped in front of Indy and backhanded him twice across the face. He stripped off his own shirt, revealing beefy arms and a length of thick chain around his neck. He unhooked it, and wrapped it around his fist.

"You see, the more you cooperate, the less Alberto will be required to assist the interrogation," Calderone said. "Is that understood?"

"So get on with it," Indy answered.

Alberto started to backhand him again, this time with the chain, but Calderone held up his hand and the goon stepped back.

"Before you tried to escape, I heard you say something to Mara. I was just waking up, but I heard it clearly. You said, 'What goes around comes around.' Why did you say that? Did Mara do something to you?"

"You could say that. She wanted the staff and me out of the way."

"I see. So she double-crossed you. I think I understand now. You two were in it together. You were going to verify it as authentic, then switch it for a fake. Then the two of you would have the money and the staff."

So that was it. He was trying to pin a conspiracy on him and Mara. "Not even close."

Calderone wasn't finished. "But Mara double-crossed you and took the staff on her own. You showed up, and tried to get it back by making the switch yourself."

"Wrong. We never planned anything together."

"But you wanted it for yourself."

When Indy didn't answer, Calderone reached inside his jacket as if he were about to pull a gun. Instead, he held up Mara's journal. One of the men

who'd accosted Indy outside of the catacomb had
taken it from him.

"I read this story. Very interesting."

Indy wondered if he'd questioned Mara about it.
Maybe she'd come up with an explanation that had
satisfied him. But, then again, maybe Indy's insur-
ance policy would still pay off.

Calderone tapped the journal against his palm.
"Let me tell you a story now, Professor. Four years
ago I fell in love with Mara, and I found out about
the alicorn. It interested me, and I said I wanted it.
At first, she didn't want any money, only my love.
But by the time she left Rome, she demanded a fortune for it. I went along with her, but our relationship has never been the same."

Indy had the feeling from what Mara had said in
the catacomb that there was a lot more to it than
Calderone's simplified version. "But you could afford to pay what she wanted, I guess."

"Of course. But the point is I lost trust in her."

"I heard you're not so trustworthy yourself. You
hired Walcott to get the staff when—"

"I had to protect my interests, and keep track of
Mara. I'm not a fool." The goon tensed, but Calderone held him off. He tapped the journal on his palm
again. "But now it seems I wasn't as vigilant as I
should have been. Do you believe this alicorn is dangerous?"

The goon ran a hand along his chain. He looked as
if he were just waiting for a chance to throttle Indy.

"I'm a scientist. I don't believe in superstitions,"
Indy scoffed. He immediately regretted his words.
He'd spoken too quickly. He should've said he be-
lieved it was cursed.

But Calderone surprised him. "Good. I'm going to give you the staff. After you do something for me."

"What?"

"I'm not taking any chances with the staff or with Mara. Do you understand what I'm saying?"

"No."

"What goes around comes around, as you said. Mara knew that the staff was deadly. She was willing to see me die for my money. Now she's going to pay; you're going to kill her."

"Forget it. I'm not doing your dirty work."

The goon took a menacing step forward and snapped the chain. His face now looked like a bulldog ready to attack.

"It's the best I can offer you. You're not exactly in an advantageous situation." Calderone nodded toward the goon. "I can have you eliminated at any time."

And he probably still planned to do just that, Indy thought. Either that, or Calderone was setting him up so he'd take the blame for Mara's murder. "Mara's *your* problem, Calderone, not mine. I'm not killing her."

Alberto cracked the chain across Indy's shoulders. Indy winced, and gritted his teeth as he was lashed a second and a third time.

"I'll give you one more chance, Jones. You should feel fortunate to have an opportunity to get away alive."

"Forget it. I'm not making any deals."

Alberto wrapped the chain around his fist and smashed Indy in the jaw.

"Take him back. Let him think about it," Calderone said.

\* \* \*

When he showed up at Indy's cell, Calderone was in no mood to talk. He snapped his fingers and the goon appeared with a pail of water. He grabbed Indy by the hair and ducked his head into the pail. A minute later, his head was jerked back and he gasped for air.

"Now are you going to do what I say?" Calderone asked.

Indy could only see a blur in front of him. He was gagging from the water he'd swallowed. Bad water. Suddenly, his gut wrenched, and he spewed a stream of filth over the blur that was Calderone.

A chain-covered fist struck him on the temple. The blur vanished as he sank into darkness.

Indy lay on a slimy floor covered by maggots. They were eating his eyeballs and foraging in his mouth and ears. He couldn't move, he was being eaten alive . . . Icy water splashed over his face and he jerked out of one nightmare and into another.

Calderone hovered over him. He was saying something about Mara. Kill her . . . kill her. . . .

Indy lay on mattress springs that felt like barbed wire, and Calderone was standing over him. "Are you going to cooperate, or do you want more?"

Indy managed to sit up. "More what?"

He was groggy, and it took a minute for him to get his wits about him. But it all came back as he saw the goon stretching the chain between his hands. He knew they were going to kill him. "Okay . . . okay. I'll do it. But I want the staff first."

"Ah, now we're getting somewhere." Calderone turned to the guards. "Clean him up, get him some clothes, and feed him. I want him ready in an hour."

\* \* \*

Mara gazed out the window and watched the guards stationed at the gate of the courtyard. Calderone's men were everywhere, even at her door. She was under orders not to leave the room. The only person besides the guard who had said anything to her today was the doctor who had examined her and said she might have suffered a slight concussion.

Concussion or not, everything was confused now. Where was Diego and what had happened to Indy? Last night, after she had recovered enough to talk, she'd found Diego already alert and in charge. She'd told him about Indy, saying that he was an archaeologist who had stumbled onto the trail of the staff and that she'd left him for dead in the desert. But she knew Diego was suspicious.

Maybe Diego had spied on her. A short time after she'd returned to New Mexico, she'd started corresponding with Indy. Had Calderone found out about it? At first, she had just wanted to renew her relationship with Indy, but soon she realized that he might help her find the alicorn. Although she'd kept the details to herself while waiting to see him in person, she'd wanted him to join her as a partner. She'd even planned to share the money equally with him. But then everything had gotten confused. Now, the three of them—herself, Indy, and Diego—had come together in a fateful collision of aspirations.

A knock on the door. She turned from the window as Diego entered the room. "Why have you locked me in here?" she demanded.

"I know what you're up to, Mara. You're trying to undermine everything that I've attained."

"What are you talking about?"

He pointed to the bed. "Sit down."

"Go on, tell me. How am I undermining you? I'm

trying to help you." She reached out to him, but he pushed her firmly down onto the bed.

"You know me, Mara. I'm a religious man. I believe in good and evil and that we are God's children and must follow His wishes. I believe Italy is under the influence of an evil force, who should be removed from power."

She gave him a hurt look. "You don't have to lecture me on your religion or your politics. I'm very familiar with both. What's your point?"

"You were trying to infect me with poison. That staff, that alicorn, is evil."

Mara was baffled. "I don't understand. Just last night, after you spoke, you thought it was wonderful. You said you were unbearably happy. You even whispered that your place in history was going to surpass Charlemagne's and Alexander the Great's."

"Now I know better."

She shook head. "What are you talking about?"

"Your family journal said it all."

So that was it. Indy must have brought the journal with him, and had used it against her. "What happened to my family is in the past. The alicorn has been cleansed and its powers have been renewed. It's not like before."

"You told me about the old sorcerer. He's the devil's man, Mara, and you are his wench."

She leaped up from the bed. "How dare you talk to me like that! And what about you? I know you sent Walcott to steal the staff from me."

"I was right not to trust you. You wanted to sell me evil, not power." Calderone turned his back on her and walked away.

"Diego, that's not true," she called after him, but he'd already slammed the door.

\* \* \*

Two guards entered the cell and jerked Indy to his feet. Although a shower, clean clothes, and food had vastly improved his disposition, he resented the rough treatment. He resented the surly attitudes of the guards, resented that it was time for him to play executioner. But he didn't feel much like an executioner. More like a man heading to his own execution.

Calderone was waiting for him. "If you want the staff, you're going to work for it."

"You said you'd give it to me first." Indy spoke through swollen lips; his left eye was so puffed up from the beating he could barely open it. He had more bruises and cuts than he could count. But he couldn't let his injuries get in his way.

"Sorry, Jones. We do it my way."

The guards hustled him down a hall and up a set of stairs. They passed the kitchen and dining room and crossed the spacious foyer. Several guards stood near the base of the wide staircase and stepped aside as Calderone led Indy and the guards toward the stairs. When they reached Mara's room, where another guard was posted, Calderone handed Indy his Webley. "Okay, go do it!" he hissed.

Indy lifted a hand to knock, but then opened the door. Executioners didn't knock. His good eye darted around the room. "Mara?"

No answer. What was going on? Where was she? Then she emerged from the bathroom. Her short blond hair was ruffled and her eyes were red. She looked as if she'd been through the wringer.

"Indy! What . . . what are you doing here? What happened? Oh, my God, they beat you."

"I escaped and I've got my gun."

She shook her head. "But how . . . ?"

"Don't ask."

He moved to the window. At least a dozen guards milled around a courtyard. He snapped open the cylinder of his Webley. As he expected, it wasn't loaded. Calderone was no fool. Indy was supposed to beat Mara to death with it.

Out of the corner of his eye he saw Mara reach behind her back and into a drawer in the nightstand. "I don't understand," she said. "You knocked me on the head last night, and now you're risking your life to save me?"

"Who said I'm here to rescue you?"

"Then what are you doing here?"

"Looking for a way out." He tried the door and found that it was locked from the outside. "That figures. Too bad we don't have the staff."

"I know where it is."

Indy spun on his heels. "You do?"

"In the next room."

"Yeah?" Indy peered out the window again. There was no ledge, and the window to the adjacent room was a good dozen feet away.

"Why don't we go through the side door?" Mara suggested.

"What side door?"

She pointed to a chiffonier. "It's behind there."

Indy wedged himself between the tall bureau and the wall and shoved the bureau to one side. He turned the doorknob. Locked.

He took a closer look. "Give me that knife you took out of the drawer," he said with his back to her. "I can pry it open."

"Do you trust me now?" she asked, handing him the knife.

"Not a bit, Mara. It just happens that I trust your buddy, Diego, even less."

She didn't reply, so he went on. "He wants me to kill you, then he's going to let me go, and give me the staff, too." He chipped at the doorframe near the lock, and bits of wood dropped to the floor.

"Diego wants you to kill me? I don't believe it."

"I believe that much," he said as he continued working on the frame. "It's the rest of it that I find hard to swallow." He jerked on the doorknob. The wood splintered near the lock. He jerked again; the door popped open. "Here we go."

He walked into the room. It was similar to Mara's, with a bed, a desk, and a dresser and other bedroom furniture. "Okay, I give up. Where is it?"

Mara walked over to a chest at the foot of the bed. She opened it, and there was the long, teakwood case. It seemed too good to be true. Indy unlatched it. The ivory staff lay inside. He lifted it carefully from the case and ran his hands over the spiraled shaft. He held it up to his good eye. Why would Calderone leave it in a place Mara knew about? If he didn't trust her, he would've hidden it somewhere else. But then Indy realized that Calderone probably hadn't wanted to even touch the staff after he had read the journal. He wanted to get rid of it.

He carried the staff over to the door leading to the hall. It was locked, but from the inside. "Let's go."

She touched his back. "Do you really want me to go with you?"

"In spite of your faults, I can't kill you any more than you could kill me."

"I'm glad," she said. "Just a minute." She hurried

into the other room and returned with a suitcase.
"It's the money. We'll split it later, okay?"

"Sure." He reached for the door.

"Do you really think the staff is going to protect
us?" she asked.

Indy held up the shiny, double-eagle head. In
spite of everything he knew about it, he didn't think
the artifact possessed mysterious powers. The only
way it could protect him was if he used it as a
weapon. In a sense, that was exactly what he was
planning to do. If Calderone feared the staff, maybe
the word had gotten around. "We've got nothing to
lose."

He heard voices coming from the foyer. There
were two guards in the hallway outside of Mara's
room, but both were looking down the stairs. One of
them turned just as Indy struck him on the head
with his Webley. He aimed his revolver at the head
of the other guard and the man held up his hands.
He shook his head and whispered, "Please. Don't
shoot."

Indy pulled the trigger. "Bang!"

The man collapsed as if he'd been shot. Indy exchanged a puzzled glance with Mara. "That part was
easy."

As they approached the top of the stairs, Indy
could hardly believe what he saw in the center of the
foyer. Marcus Brody was arguing with Calderone,
and they were surrounded by a cluster of guards.

"I told you, Mr. Brody, there is no Professor
Schultz here. I don't know anything about him."

"But he came here last night to examine a staff. I
was supposed to take him to the airport this morning."

"The man who came here was not Professor

Schultz. He was a fraud. Are you interested in the real Schultz, or the fraud?"

"I'm okay, Marcus."

Everyone looked up as Indy descended the staircase, tapping the staff on each step as he went.

"Indy, I mean Professor . . . I mean . . . You look horrible. What did they do to you?"

"What is this?" Calderone barked. "What do you think you're doing?" The guards suddenly tensed, and raised their weapons.

Indy kept walking. He held up the staff in front of him; the silver double eagle looked ready to fly. He hoped that the word had gotten around about the evil stick. Several guards moved forward, and Indy's confidence waivered. No one was buying the power of the staff. He raised the staff high over his head, but this time it was simply to defend himself. He was about to take a desperate swing when Mara stepped forward.

"You coward," she screeched at Calderone. "Kill and run. That's all you can do. You will never defeat Il Duce. You're even afraid of a unicorn's horn."

"I've heard enough from you," he said coldly. "Kill her," he ordered. The guards had frozen; no one followed the order. "You bastards," he shouted, and he grabbed a revolver from a guard. Mara charged him and they struggled for the weapon. It fired. They staggered face to face in a deadly embrace, then Calderone let go. Mara collapsed. Indy caught her, but she was already gone, shot in the heart. He looked up and into the barrel of Calderone's gun. The moment froze in the anticipation of death.

A voice boomed from the door. "Diego! You've got

to leave. Immediately!" Indy recognized the aide he'd cajoled at the symposium. "The premier has ordered you arrested. His men are on their way. I have a car ready."

Calderone hesitated. He looked up at the staff, which Indy clutched in his hand. His expression shifted from confusion to fear and revulsion. He dropped the gun and sprinted to the door. Suddenly, the black-clad guards were rushing about and the foyer was a scene of chaos.

"Do you have a car here, Marcus?"

Brody was pale, but managed to speak. "Not to worry. I've got a taxi waiting outside the gate."

"Good. Let's get out of here."

Calderone's Pierce-Arrow was already pulling away when Indy and Brody stepped outside. They hurried to the gate, and climbed inside the taxicab. As they pulled away, Brody let out a sigh. "Now that was close. I was sure Calderone was going to . . . Look at all the soldiers on the street. Oh, no! Look out!"

The Pierce-Arrow had spun around and was heading right at them amid a barage of gunfire. The taxi driver veered the car to the left and down a side street. Indy looked back just as the Pierce-Arrow slammed into another car and exploded into flames.

"I guess Calderone's not going to make it out of town after all."

Brody was slumped in the seat, dabbing at his forehead with a handkerchief, a man on the verge of heart failure. "I can't believe we're still alive. I say we head directly to the airport."

"I'll second that." Not only were they alive, but they had the staff. Indy was about to say as much when he noticed a suitcase on the floorboards. "Marcus, what's that?"

"I thought it was yours. I just grabbed it as we left. What is it?"

"Oh, that. I believe it's a posthumous donation to the museum . . . from Mara and Calderone."

# EPILOGUE

## *Hovenweep—September 21*

The dawn before the autumnal equinox was cool and clear, and the first beams of sunlight illuminated the high ridges of the canyon as Indy waited patiently in front of the rock. He figured it would be only a few minutes before the sunlight worked its way down the canyon and onto the face of the massive rock where he'd found the unicorn's horn. He heard footsteps behind him and Aguila sat down next to him. "Not much longer."

Indy nodded. Aguila had been elusive when Indy was here three months ago, but upon his return he'd found the wiry old Navajo at his hogan. Aguila said he'd been waiting for Indy. "Tell me what you believe about this place."

Aguila was quiet a moment. "This is a point where the earth aligns with the cosmos, where you can pass through the curtain separating this world and the underworld."

"But I thought the route to the underworld was through *sipapus* in the kivas."

Aguila laughed. "You take that hole in the ground too seriously."

"You mean I take it too literally?"

"You would never fit through any *sipapu* I've seen."

Now Indy laughed. "I suppose not. Is this the only place where the underworld can be entered?"

"There are many such places if you know where to look, and how to look."

"So it's okay to close this entrance?"

"It is your choice. But after the deaths here, it is best."

The staff lay at Indy's feet. It was wrapped in white cloth like a burial shroud and encased in a copper box, which Brody had given him. "The world is not ready to believe in unicorns again, Aguila. That's what it comes down to."

Indy had thought long and hard about what to do with the staff before he had set out again for the Southwest. He had offered it to Brody to display in his museum, but the curator's hesitation to accept the relic had said it all. To possess what some believed was the last unicorn's horn was more of a burden than an honor.

"You've made the right decision. If it remained, the one who already has claimed our symbol for the four winds might capture it and misuse its power."

There was only one person who Aguila could be talking about. Hitler had turned the ancient swastika into an emblem of hate. Somehow, Aguila's comment didn't surprise him. While Indy doubted that the staff was made from a unicorn's horn or that it possessed any special power, he was well aware of the power of belief. That power could attract the likes of Hitler.

Aguila gracefully rose to his feet. "It is time."

Indy carried the box over to the crevice. The holes in the floor of the cavity were still there, a reminder of Walcott's futile attempt to locate the staff on the eve of the solstice. He stopped in front of the three circular petroglyphs, and as he stared, the light beaming through the hole in the wall behind him coalesced into the shape of two daggers. Slowly, they moved across the circles toward each other.

Indy leaned the box carefully against the wall. The top of it just touched the lowest point of the central circle. He recalled his last experience here as the two light daggers had touched. The world, it seemed, had literally exploded in a swirling rainbow of color and sound. Chimes rang in a complex harmony that was unbearably beautiful and had seemed an intricate part of the light itself. He'd been drawn inward as if the underworld were a temptress and its allure overpowering.

The two beams inched closer together. It would be just a matter of seconds now before they touched. Was Indy really standing at an entry point to the fabled underworld? And if he actually entered it, what would he see this time? He had a brief image of himself being swept into the swirling void like a ship caught in a giant whirlpool, pulled down into the fathomless underworld, deeper and deeper, never to return.

"Indy, come quickly," Aguila said. "We have to do it now. We can't wait."

Indy took one more look. The light daggers were

separated by a fraction of an inch. He turned away, and as he did, he thought the light had grown brighter and that he'd heard the first note of a chimeral chime. No, it was merely his imagination, he told himself. Nevertheless, he didn't look back.

As he stepped outside of the crevice, Aguila leaned down and struck a match on a rock, then touched the short fuse on a stick of dynamite near the entrance of the crevice. "Run!"

They both dashed away, and had gone barely a dozen yards when a blast hurled rocks through the air and knocked Indy from his feet. He buried his face in the dirt and covered his head. The smell of gunpowder and dust wafted over him as an eerie silence followed the explosion.

"You okay?" he asked as he stood up and brushed the dirt from his clothes. But Aguila was already walking toward the rock. Indy joined him and inspected the damage.

He peered up at the front of the rock face and saw that the opening through which the sunlight had beamed would never shine again onto the three circular petroglyphs at the solstice or equinox. He walked to the side and saw that the crevice had vanished. The outer rock had shifted, sliding forward so that even a rabbit would have a difficult time finding a way inside. The door to the underworld had been sealed, with the last unicorn's horn inside it.

Forever. Or so he hoped.

## ABOUT THE AUTHOR

ROB MACGREGOR wrote *Indiana Jones And The Last Crusade*, a novel based on the movie script. He is also the author of *The Crystal Skull*, a novel of adventure and intrigue, and *The Rainbow Oracle* (with Tony Grosso), a book of color divination. His travel articles have appeared in the *Miami Herald, Los Angeles Times, Boston Globe, Newsday* and elsewhere. He is also a contributor to *OMNI* Magazine's "Anti-Matter" section. Besides his work as a writer, he has organized adventure tours to South America for travel writers, and led the first group of U.K. journalists to the Lost City in the Sierra Nevada of Santa Marta Mountains in Colombia in 1987. He lives in Boynton Beach, Florida, where he is at work on his next novel.

Here is a preview of the next
Indiana Jones adventure

**INDIANA JONES AND
THE INTERIOR WORLD**
by Rob MacGregor

on sale in November from
Bantam Falcon Books

# 1
# RONGO-RONGO TABLETS

*Spring 1929*
*Easter Island*

The handpick flashed in the waning light and stabbed the earth again and again. Finally, the soil was loosened, and Indy scooped it out with his trowel. Then he went to work with the handpick once more. Over and over the same process repeated itself, as though it had nothing to do with him. This was the fifth house in the long-abandoned ceremonial village of Orango, and the fifth time, it seemed, that he was coming up empty-handed. Tomorrow, he'd return and replace the dirt, and cover the floor with the same stones in the exact arrangement he'd found them, and move on to the next house.

The stone houses were situated precariously on the rim of Rano Kau. Most were still in good condition even though seventy-five years had elapsed since the islanders had last climbed the volcano to praise the gods Makemake and Haua.

He raised the handpick, struck again. He hit something solid. He dropped the pick, and carefully scraped the dirt aside with the trowel. A long, rounded wooden surface was emerging. At last. It looked like the edge of a rongo-rongo tablet, the object of his search.

Although Easter Island was best known for its moais, the massive, solemn heads carved from stone, Indy's interest here was the wooden tablets, which were inscribed with a mysterious script. He'd been studying the tablets for weeks, but had gotten nowhere in his attempts to decipher the glyphs, which resembled stylized plants and animals. Supposedly, the islanders had forgotten how to read rongo-rongo, and with only a few tablets in existence Indy had found that the task of deciphering the system was nearly impossible. So for the past couple of weeks he'd been digging in Orango, hoping to uncover tablets that might provide the key to comprehending the script.

He set the trowel aside, picked up a brush with stiff bristles, and continued removing dirt. He'd been concentrating on the script so intensely that every night in his dreams the tiny creatures danced across his vision in sets of parallel lines. They motioned to him with their fins and fronds, arms and legs, stems and bills. They were telling him the key. Over and over again. It was so obvious. But only while he was asleep. Once he awoke, the images vanished and nothing was obvious.

He paused a moment and glanced over his shoulder toward the setting sun. He should stop now, and continue the work tomorrow. The sun would sink into the lapis waters in a matter of minutes, and he didn't like the idea of riding his horse down the slope of the volcano in the inky darkness. But it was no time to be practical, not after so many days of frustration. He needed to discover something for his own piece of mind. He couldn't go back to the States having accomplished nothing. Not that he hadn't been warned. No one had cracked the unique rongo-rongo script, and it had been studied by linguists for decades.

He set the brush aside and began working with his fingers. He rubbed the dirt from the wood and leaned close. It was in good condition and wasn't about to crumble. Then he touched metal, and felt an acute sense of disappointment. It wasn't a tablet. But maybe it was a spear from the days of Captain Cook. He quickly worked his way along the metal. To his surprise it didn't taper to a point; it grew wider. He scraped furiously at the dirt, then abruptly stopped.

"Oh no!"

He grabbed the wooden handle and jerked it free. *Ah, for crying out loud.* The only thing worse than finding nothing was digging up a blasted shovel.

He threw it to the ground in disgust. Another

day of disappointment. He brushed the dirt off his hands, then gathered his tools in his pack. He slung it over his shoulder, and headed toward the far end of the village where his horse was tethered.

"Time to go, fella." He patted the horse's rear and was about to mount the steed when he glimpsed something moving in the rocks above his head. "Wait right here, Champ."

He climbed a narrow crevice between two boulders. Cautiously, he raised his head and looked around, then smiled as several terns darted out from a rocky recess. "What are you guys doing up here?"

Birds were special, even sacred in Orango, or at least they had been at one time. In fact, the rocks on which he stood were inscribed with drawings of creatures that were half-men, half-birds with long beaks, each of them clutching an egg. The petroglyphs had been carved by the followers of the birdman cult, which had thrived for several centuries on the island. Supposedly, the cult had died in 1862 when the island's king and many of his priests were kidnapped and taken to Peru as slaves, thus ending the populace's knowledge of its ancient past.

He peered over the rocks and down into the lake, which filled the crater of the dead volcano. A steam-like fog was forming over the water, and the round depression reminded him of a huge witch's cauldron, or the home of a god. He raised his gaze and looked out over the island. It was hilly and roughly triangular shaped with a volcano at each corner. Much of the land consisted of rough lava fields, which looked nearly black now in the dying light. In contrast, the slopes of the volcanos were gentle and grassy, and still bathed in sunlight.

He climbed back down the rocks and walked over to the horse. The south face of Rano Kau dropped sharply and beyond the cliffs were three tiny islands. The largest, Motu Nui, was the nesting grounds for thousands of sea birds, and along with Orango, had been the focal point of the birdman cult. He'd asked if any remnants of the cult still remained, figuring they might know something about the rongo-rongo script. But so far he'd only gotten blank stares and a few laughs from the islanders.

"Let's go, boy." He swung his leg over the horse's back. But he never reached the saddle. A figure dashed from the rocks, grabbed his pack and jerked him to the ground.

A knife glinted in a ray of sunlight, and Indy rolled over just as the blade stabbed the dirt next to his throat. The man pulled it loose and stabbed again. This time, Indy grabbed his forearm, and they twisted and turned like dancers, edging closer and closer to the cliff.

Indy glimpsed the man's face and saw fear. He was just a kid, sixteen or so. He was slighter than Indy and no match for his strength. The knife dropped to the ground, and the kid tottered near the brink. A slight shove and he'd fall to his death, but Indy pulled him away. He grasped his shoulders and lifted him up so his toes just touched the ground.

"All right, what's this about? Who are you?"

The kid shook his head, and gasped for breath. His eyes darted back and forth as if he were looking for a way to escape. Indy lowered him to the ground and loosened his grip. A mistake. With a powerful thrust, the kid kneed Indy between the legs, slipped out of Indy's grasp, and raced over to the archaeologist's horse.

"Oh no you don't!" Indy was doubled over in pain, but he managed to reach into his pack and jerk out his whip. He'd brought it along for diversion. It was good luck, part of his gear, and a weapon in a pinch.

He snapped it toward the kid just as the horse and rider galloped off. The whip fell harmlessly to the ground amid a cloud of dust. "I must be getting rusty."

As he reeled in the whip, he spotted the knife. He picked it up and turned it over in his hands. "Well, well. What do you know?"

The handle was wooden, and carved on it was a half-man, half-bird figure grasping an egg. Maybe the birdman cult was still alive, after all.

# 2
## FALLEN MOAI

"Indy, where have you been? You almost missed supper."

"Evening, Marcus." Indy ambled across the restaurant and sat at the table where Marcus Brody and a few of the others on the expedition were eating. "I got delayed on the volcano."

A kid approached Indy, and for a moment he thought it was the same one who'd attacked him. He held a wooden figure up in front of Indy. It had a human face with a large, hooked nose, sharp cheekbones and hollow cheeks. Its earlobes were long and complemented by a goatee. Its ribs and spine protruded and its hands and penis hung down to its knees.

"You want to buy, mister?"

Indy looked past the hand-carved demon, known

as a moai kavakava, and saw it wasn't the same kid. "No thanks. I've already got one."

"Just go on. Let us eat in peace," said an archaeologist named Howard Maxwell. "Obnoxious kids."

"They can be that way," Indy commented.

"So any luck up there, Jones?" asked Maxwell, a chunky, pug-nosed man with slicked-down hair that was always neatly parted in the middle. "We're leaving next week, you know."

"You don't have to tell him that, Howard," Brody said. "You can be as annoying as those young salesmen."

"It's all right, Marcus," Indy said. Brody was an Englishman who had lived in the States for years and was an old family friend and virtually a substitute father for Indy. "In fact, I did find something this afternoon."

"Oh, what is it?" Brody asked, his curiosity piqued.

A waitress brought Indy a glass of Chilean wine, and he took a sip. "A shovel. It was buried three feet under one of the floors."

Brody looked perplexed. "Well, I guess that means someone else has already been digging."

The others laughed. "The kiss of death," Maxwell crowed, making no attempt to hide his glee. He was a few years Indy's senior, and Indy sensed that the man resented him from the first day when Brody had introduced him as one of the best young archaeologists in the field and classroom.

Indy decided not to say a word about what had happened to him at Orango. He'd probably tell Brody about the incident later. Not only did he want to avoid sounding boastful or over dramatic, but he also wanted to see if any of the islanders who were helping them acted any differently toward him.

After he'd recovered enough to walk, he'd started down the road, convinced that he would have to hike back to Hanga Roa, where the expedition was headquartered. It wasn't far away as the crow flies, but the road down the volcano twisted and turned and seemed to go on forever. Then, half a mile from Orango he found his horse. From the footprints he was able to tell that the kid who had attacked him had switched horses, riding off on his own steed.

"I wonder if the shovel came from the east or the west," one of the others said.

"Oh, brother," Brody said. "Here we go again."

There was an on-going discussion among the expedition members about whether the people who settled the island had come from the west, Polynesia, or the east, South America. Most were certain the islanders arrived from other Polynesian islands. But Maxwell contended that the enormous moais that dotted the island's coastal area were built by the same South American Indians who had constructed massive stone cities on the mainland.

"Jones, what do you think?" Maxwell asked. "We have yet to hear your ideas on this matter."

Indy shrugged. "You guys are limiting the possibilities. I've heard theories that the original inhabitants were Egyptians, Greek Hindustanis, and even red-haired caucasians from North Africa. They've even been called survivors of a lost continent."

"Good points, Indy," Brody said.

"Don't confuse the matter, Jones," Maxwell blurted. "Get serious."

"Okay, I think you're both right. Look at the legends. They talk of two groups arriving on the island, the Long Ears and the Short Ears. King Hotu Matua and his followers came from the east, and Chief Tu-ko-ihu and his people arrived from the west."

Maxwell waved a hand at Indy. "You can't count on those old stories. They get all twisted around. You've got to look at the facts."

"Where're your facts, Maxwell? Tell me that," demanded a Frenchman named Beaudroux.

"I've told you over and over. There are Peruvian Indians who elongate their ears. They were the same Long Ears, who carved the moais."

Beaudroux, a tall, slender man, peered down his long nose at Maxwell. "But do they live near the sea? No. Do they make ocean-going vessels? Of course not."

"The Indians who lived two thousand years ago probably had an entirely different perception than you do of an ocean-going vessel," Maxwell countered.

And so it went on and on. Indy's dinner, a lamb stew, arrived as the discussion continued.

In spite of his difficulties with the tablets, Indy was glad that he was working on his own, rather than excavating ahus, the stone platforms on which with the moais had been erected. That was the task which occupied the others, except for Brody, who was constantly involved in mediations with the island's mayor to make sure that everything went smoothly and to assure the islanders that their intent was to obtain knowledge, not artifacts. But Brody had been bewildered to find that the islanders wanted to sell him artifacts, most of which were replicas of recent origin, like the moai kavakava the kid was selling.

"Maybe Indy's right," Brody said when the comments started to turn caustic. "There may be no one simple answer. It's like the name of the island. Some call it Easter Island, others call it Isla Pascual. The islanders call it Rapa Nui, and even Te Pito o te Henua, the Navel of the World."

"We also call it, Mata Ki Te Rangi, which means Eyes that Look to the Sky."

They all looked up to see an attractive, dark-eyed woman. "That's a lovely name," Brody said. "Davina, I don't think you've met Indy yet. He's working up on Orango."

Indy shook her hand. Davina had distinctive Polynesian features with deeply tanned skin and long, braided hair. She could have been thirty or forty. He couldn't tell. Her dark eyes met his for a moment. Her hand was cool, and her grip was firm.

"Davina is studying for a graduate degree at the University of Santiago. She's the curator of the local museum."

"Right," Indy said. "The one who's been away."

"I just returned from the mainland yesterday."

"Well, please sit down and join us," Brody said, pulling out a chair.

"No, thank you. I just wanted to say that the mayor has found several men who will help you raise the moai."

"Do they know how to do it?" Brody asked.

She nodded and smiled. "They have a method."

The mayor had allowed Brody to bring the team of archaeologists here to excavate as long as they re-erected at least one of the many fallen moais. Brody had quickly agreed, without thinking how they were going to raise a twenty-ton block of stone with no modern equipment. When no one came up with an answer, Brody had put off the task. When the mayor had finally inquired about what was taking them so long, Brody had confessed his problem and asked the mayor for suggestions.

"Well, that's a relief. When can they begin?"

"First thing in the morning," she said.

"We'll be ready."

"Good." She glanced at Indy again. "Nice to meet you, Professor Jones."

"It's Indy. And speaking of names, why did they call the island Eyes that Look to the Sky?"

"Because of the moais. They once had large eyes that gazed out to the heavens." She turned and walked off.

"Indy, you will join us tomorrow, won't you?" Brody asked. "I'm sure we can use your help."

"Be glad to." But Indy's thoughts were still on Davina. She had been wearing a necklace, a silver pendant shaped like a creature that was half-man, half-bird, and grasping an egg.

# INDIANA
# JONES

Bold adventurer, swashbuckling explorer, Indy unravels the mysteries of the past at a time when dreams could still come true. Now, in an all-new series by Rob MacGregor, officially licensed from Lucasfilm, we will learn what shaped Indiana Jones into the hero he is today!

❑ **INDIANA JONES AND THE PERIL AT DELPHI** 28931-4 $3.95/$4.95 in Canada
Indy descends into the bottomless pit of the serpent god of the Order of Pythia. Will Indy find the source of Pythia's powers—or be sacrificed at their altar?

❑ **INDIANA JONES AND THE DANCE OF THE GIANTS** 29035-5 $4.50/$5.50 in Canada
Indy takes off on an action-packed chase from the peril-filled caves of Scotland to the savage dance of the giants at Stonehenge—where Merlin's secret will finally be revealed.

❑ **INDIANA JONES AND THE SEVEN VEILS** 29334-6 $4.99/$5.99 in Canada
With his trusty bullwhip in hand, Indy sets out for the wilds of the Amazon to track a lost city and a mythical red-headed race who may be the descendants of ancient Celtic Druids.

❑ **INDIANA JONES AND THE GENESIS DELUGE** 29502-0 $4.99/$5.99 in Canada
Indy sets out for Istanbul and Mount Ararat, fabled location of Noah's Ark, when various forces try to bar him from finding a certain 950 year-old boat-builder...

---

Available at your local bookstore or use this page to order.

Send to: **Bantam Books, Dept. FL 7**
**2451 S. Wolf Road**
**Des Plaines, IL 60018**

Please send me the items I have checked above. I am enclosing
$_____ (please add $2.50 to cover postage and handling). Send check or money order, no cash or C.O.D.'s, please.

Mr./Ms._____

Address_____

City/State_____Zip_____

Please allow four to six weeks for delivery.
Prices and availability subject to change without notice.     FL 7 3/92

# THE LEGENDARY MAN OF BRONZE—IN A THRILLING NEW ADVENTURE SERIES!

## DOC SAVAGE